Like Minds

Acknowledgments
"Wings" won an Honourable Mention from, and was published in, *Other Voices*.

Author/Cover photo by Paul B. Friesen
Design and in-house editing by Joe Blades
Printed and bound in Canada by Sentinel Printing, Yarmouth NS

The Publisher acknowledges support
from the Canada Council for the Arts
-Emerging Publisher Program and
from the New Brunswick Department
of Economic Development, Tourism
and Culture-Arts Development Branch.

THE CANADA COUNCIL | LE CONSEIL DES ARTS
FOR THE ARTS | DU CANADA
SINCE 1957 | DEPUIS 1957

Canadian Cataloguing in Publication Data
Friesen, Shannon, 1958-

    Like minds.

    (New muse award ; 1998)
    ISBN 0-921411-81-2

1. Women — Fiction I. Title. II. Series.

PS8561.R4972L5   1998   C813'.54   C98-950187-6
PR9199.3.F7716L5 1998

Broken Jaw Press
MARITIMES ARTS PROJECTS PRODUCTIONS
Box 596 Stn A
Fredericton NB E3B 5A6   ph/fax 506 454-5127
Canada   jblades@nbnet.nb.ca

Like Minds

Shannon Friesen

Fredericton • Canada

To my sister Linda,
for finding humour with me in everything

Table of Contents

Like Minds

Janine always feels better when she leaves her support group. Not because she is any closer to conquering her problems but because she meets people in much worse shape.

The newest member, Ben, begins his first session by racing into the meeting room breathless and more than fashionably late. An attractive man in his mid thirties, no one on the outside would assume he has any quirks. Janine watches him, waiting for a head-bobbing tick to shadow his handsome face, for nostril poking or rhythmic eye movements to give him away. Nothing. Not one sweet thing. Except she knows it has to be something for him to be here, and this something probably made him late tonight.

As hard as she tries, she can't concentrate on the others who shift in plastic seats waiting for their turns to speak, the ones who complain of being unable to enter a room without looking at each corner of the ceiling. The ones who can't pass a parking meter without touching it, a quick brush of the fingers enough to quell their insatiable craving. And the ones speaking in hushed voices about needing to stir their coffee in an identical manner: three stirs to the left, three to the right, just so. If a kindly stranger fixes it for them, the coffee is undrinkable.

Most of them look as normal as Ben, except for Mrs. Paterson who has the face of a crazy, clutching her purse to her droopy breasts and constantly glancing over her shoulder even though her chair is pushed flush against the cinder block wall. She wears the perpetual mask of a hunted animal. Janine smiles when another woman, seeing her watch Mrs. Paterson, leans over and whispers in her ear: "I bet she has rearview mirrors on her toilet seat."

Janine has a hard time sitting still tonight, the result of a new member with a fresh set of variables, and the result of him being so appealing. But first she has to sit through another of David's inane problems, inane because they never involve real or everyday situations. She reminds herself that David's problem's are real to him but, come on, what *are* the chances of winning the 6/49 that he can't chuck his lottery ticket for weeks after the draw, even rooting through his garbage can for a final inspection "just in case."

What is his problem? He's so damn good looking... maybe that's it, yes... look at him, he's too perfect.

"Janine? Do you have anything you'd like to share with the group? about last week?"

She jerks her head towards the counsellor, a guilty blush seeping up from her neckline, even though she's positive her internal monologue is safe. "Um, I had a pretty good week, no major problems except for the usual laundry." The room is quiet, fourteen sets of eyes (plus Mrs. Paterson's, off in their own netherworld) waiting for her explanation. Janine has earned a baccalaureate of respect by being one of the original members. It's not that former members have necessarily gotten better, drifting out as soundless as they drifted in. And maybe it's not by their own volition; more likely little Jimmy demanded Mom's car-pooling skills for his soccer season, or little Jimmy's Dad needed his own support group.

But Janine knows she'll attend her Wednesday evening sessions for as long as they're offered, with a need to surround herself with others like her. The solace of like minds. "I know I said it was getting better but I had a slight relapse. I'm feeling stronger about the detergent thing, but I still can't leave the dryer without returning two or three times to make sure I've pushed the button. That means starting up the stairs and then having to go back."

"Can't you hear it running?" Ben says, his first words of the evening. Janine is mildly flattered that he should choose to speak while it's her turn. Others don't like this intrusion but Janine receives it as a sign of interest. And possibly the fact she hasn't had sex for close to a year makes his voice deep-fried delicious. Belgium waffles dusted with icing sugar and sticky jugs of maple syrup skitter across her mind, an oddly sensual connection that makes her lick her lips.

Counsellor Rita answers before she can. Now that annoys her. "Janine lives in a building with a communal laundry area — oh, sorry, you can tell him. "

"Gee, thanks. "Janine sees Rita stiffen and uncross her legs, aware that she has done it again, spoken on another's behalf. But then it's cheap counselling, thinks Janine, what does she expect, Deepak Chopra? and takes a breath. "Usually several washers or dryers are running when I do my load so I can't tell. Should I mention the other part?" she says in Rita's direction. Rita reads this as forgiveness and nods with enthusiasm. "The other part I have trouble with is the dirty clothes/clean clothes issue. When I take my dirty stuff downstairs in one garbage bag, I have to bring it up in a clean one and the problem is in the bags, like if I run out or forget to bring a second one with me. I live on the top floor of an old three-story that doesn't have elevators."

Ben leans into the circle with both elbows resting on his knees, his chin supported by interlocking fingers. "What about folding everything in the laundry room and then carrying it in your arms?" His voice isn't accusatory, not a bit curt like the string of short-term men who breeze through her life.

Instead it's soothing, very sexy. *Whoa there, girl, you haven't heard his story yet. He might be like the stockbroker who never came back after admitting he fingerpainted with his own feces. Boy, was he in the wrong support group.*

"I can't, what if I drop something? Then I'd have to wash it all over again."

Ben massages the back of his neck, stretching his lips across his teeth in an attempt to think of a solution. "What about sending it out to a laundry service? I used to —"

"Oh no, no, no! Strange people handling my personal things? I don't think so." Janine rubs her upper arms as if she is cold when in fact the thought of foreign fingers on her panties and bras, akin to pin worms or pubic crabs, makes her skin ripple.

Janine notices a delightful pink creeping across his face. The colour deepens when he realizes she's watching. His embarrassment makes him more attractive, despite his peculiarities. *How bad can they be?*

Rita jumps back in, destroying the moment like a bad

smell. "Ben, your suggestions are rational but we're not here to look for substitute solutions. We try to uncover the reasons behind the behaviour. In other words, why is doing the laundry so stressful for Janine? Why is it such a focal point of her day?" Ben returns to his silent state and Rita snaps back on her intrigued therapist expression. "While we're on the subject, what did you mean when you said you were stronger about 'the detergent thing'?"

Janine feels too distracted to dwell on her problems when Ben's story is what she craves. "Nothing major, I decided to buy detergent without bleach, that's all. "A lie — there is no way she can wear dull whites — but she has to try and reconnect with Ben. "Maybe Ben would like to go next, since it's his first night," Janine says, hopeful.

Ben looks stricken. "No, thanks, I'm not in a rush," he says and pats the sides of his closely-shorn head.

Curses. By the end of the two-hour session Ben still hasn't offered any information and Janine is forced to wait an entire week before seeing his handsome face again.

*

Ben more than makes up for his silence during the second session. He is late again and this time agitated. At the first pause he speaks: "Rita, could I say something now?"

"Of course, feel free."

He sighs and carefully touches the top of his short hair, as if shaping it. "It's about the reason I've been late. I've got a... a grooming problem." Pause. Janine sits so still she hardly breathes. She does a quick check of the room, sending warning glares at anyone who might interrupt, even those shifting in their seats.

"Would you like to tell us about it?" Rita asks with a low-pitched voice, her eyebrows crinkling and lips pursing, equally excited with the anticipation of a brand-new set of foibles.

"I'll try. All of you seem able to express yourselves but I know it'll sound weird when I verbalize my... situation."

"That's because we've had more practice, this is your first time," Rita says, eager to recruit him into the ranks.

"Okay, here goes." He takes a breath. "I'm late for pretty much every appointment because I can't leave my place without re-washing and re-styling my hair."

Christ, thinks Janine, *his hair isn't more than an inch long, how much styling can it need? But I can live with that.*

"Maybe that in itself doesn't sound complicated but after I wash and condition it, I use a gel and then blow it dry. On a bad day, I repeat the whole process three or four times."

Janine wants to suggest starting his routine earlier but Ben is a mind-reader as well as a poster boy for the cover of *GQ*. "The more time I allow myself to get ready, the more anxious I get and the longer it takes. I've even tried the opposite where I don't leave myself any time. But then I'm *really* late."

"How has this been an issue for you in your life, besides the obvious inability to keep a schedule?" Rita asks.

"It's pretty tough to build a lasting relationship when women think you're mental." Ben laughs, breaking the tension, which starts the rest of the room chuckling. But he's on a roll and keeps talking. "If it were just my hair, I could live with it, but there's more."

Now Janine is the one who leans into the circle, his story the most intriguing in recent years, except for the cute man in 1995 who was late for other reasons. The poor guy swore he hit pedestrians while driving his car, actually seeing imaginary bodies fly up from the bumper. It was his continual circling around the block to double check for casualties that made him unable to function. *Get ready, here it comes, it was too good to be true.*

"It's like I can't do any grooming within the normal parameters. Take my teeth, for instance." He flashes his even smile in the direction of the counsellor. "It's great to floss, right? but once a day, not *every* time I eat something or brush them. I've done it so much I've damaged my gums and need oral surgery." Rita begins to say something but he holds up his palm to prevent her from speaking. His fingers are long, smooth. "And it's not that I haven't tried, even when I'm doing it and telling myself to stop but I lose myself in the mirror. I'm a prisoner, I'm addicted."

"Yes, it's very much like an addiction, where you feel totally overpowered," says Rita.

"Hang on, can I finish? I want to do this before I lose my nerve. It sounds even more ridiculous when I hear it out loud but here goes: I can't go shirtless, like to the beach or the pool? I can't go unless I have my back waxed, and I'm not even hairy."

Janine hasn't taken her eyes off him. *I'll wax your back for you, baby... Oh my God, did I say that out loud?*

"Say what? You said 'Oh my God, did I say that out loud?'" the woman next to her whispers. "What were you wanting to say?"

"Nothing, nothing, sorry." Janine is horrified, having been good for months and with little medication. She wills herself to breath deep and relax, counting backwards from ten and trying hard to concentrate on Ben's story.

"... wasn't surprised when my wife left. The more I fussed over my own body, the less she took care of hers, I guess a sort of protest. She eventually stopped bathing and washing her hair, and she sure as hell wouldn't touch my back. I can't really blame her, here I go and marry someone totally normal, as if that'll help me. Instead, it only emphasized how strange I was, am. Hey," and he lets out a big puff of air, "that wasn't so bad after all, saying it in public." He loosens his straight back and slumps into his chair.

"You're among friends, Ben, none of us would be here unless we felt it necessary. Admitting you have obsessive behaviour is the first step to recovery."

Yeah, right, thinks Janine, praying she's only thinking it. She's okay, nobody is looking at her, the signal that she's speaking her thoughts out loud. It would be less jarring if her outbursts were pleasant but they usually involve sex or anger. Time for another visit to Dr. Bradford.

Ben is silent for the rest of the evening but at least is no longer disturbed like at the beginning. When the session ends and the group streams through the heavy front doors of the school, Janine feels compelled to say something. She times it so they reach the lot together where their cars happen to be parked side by side. The overhead branches drip from an earlier shower. She leans over his hood.

"It doesn't make a difference when people you trust say you're being nutty, does it. Like your wife. I bet she said you looked fine and told you to stop fussing but it didn't help, did it."

"Yeah, not a bit. I'm out of control, like someone else is pulling my strings." He bends to unlock his door. She never realized how tall he is until they stand facing each other. *Hormones be still, be still.*

"What be still?"

"Nothing, my stomach is growling, that's all." Janine has become good at improvising. She takes her time in finding her keys, first digging in her purse and then in her jacket pocket. "Do you think you'll keep coming to these sessions?"

"I don't know. Why do you?" he asks, making no further move to get in his car.

"I guess because it makes me feel better knowing I'm not alone, that others I walk past every day have their own story, and it can be a pretty weird one." She waits a few seconds, picking a wet leaf out of her hair. "And because I no longer feel alienated. Until these meetings I never met anyone like me, I mean really full-blown like me."

"Do you want to go for a drink?"

Janine suppresses a grin. *Would I? Are you kidding?*

"Why would I be kidding? I feel like a beer."

Damn, again out loud. "I didn't mean were you joking. I meant I'd... yes, love to. There's a good bar a few blocks from where I live, O'Toole's."

"Sounds good, I'll follow you," he says.

Her hands sweat with excitement on the steering wheel. Every few seconds she checks her mirror to make sure he's there. Aloud, and this time by choice, she lists each of his anal retentive traits. Still, he ends up looking pretty good. "At least he's clean, really clean. At least he's not a pee drinker or a scab picker, that's where I draw the line. So I have to buy an extra dental floss, what the hay, and so I don't make too many early dinner reservations. I have a feeling there's more but... what the hell, he's gorgeous!"

They don't end up at O'Toole's, they never make it beyond the front lobby, the bar already too noisy and crowded. Janine isn't about to let this opportunity pass her by and suggests they have a drink at her place. On the weekend she bought twelve Corona and three fresh limes for this very possibility but honestly believed she would drink them herself, two at a sitting in the company of *ER* and *Chicago Hope.*

While Janine gets the drinks and pours a bag of chips into a bowl, Ben wanders through her livingroom. He examines the people in her picture frames and flips through her CD collection. Before sitting on her leather sofa, Ben wipes the spot with the back of his hand, unaware of Janine standing behind him with two frosty bottles.

"What's wrong? Is something spilled on the couch?"

"Do you have a cat? There's orange fur all over the seat. I don't want it sticking to me."

"It's not fur, it's just fluff from an old mohair blanket. And you're wearing jeans, it's not going to stick to denim." Janine feels her eyes roll involuntarily, surprising herself, she of all people. "And I don't have any pets, I'm allergic to fur." It's at this moment she remembers seeing a beach towel draped across the driver's side of his car.

"That's good," he says and takes the beer from her. "Not good that you're allergic but that you don't have any animals. They shed so much."

After three beers each, they end up cross-legged on the rug in front of the stereo, pretending to choose the next music. In the middle of her defence over a Christmas tape by Burl Ives, Ben leans over and gently kisses her. For Janine who's suffered a dry spell, the kiss travels straight from his lips to her inner thighs. She relaxes and responds to his mouth until her eyes pop open with the realization that she hasn't flossed in over a week. And her with that food-trapping tooth in the back.

"What's wrong, am I moving too fast?" he says, brushing away the strand of hair falling over Janine's eye.

"No, I had to come up for air, that's all. It was really nice." She raises her hand to touch his sandy-coloured hair but his fingers wrap around her wrist and stop her mid-air.

"What —"

"Sorry but it's one other little thing I can't handle, anyone touching my hair. "The mood is broken for a moment when he sets her arm back in her lap.

"You never mentioned it tonight, why didn't you mention it?"

"It's only a two-hour meeting." His smile is infectious

and Janine giggles. His teeth are even and white, like Chiclets.

"Did you let your wife touch it?"

"Nope."

"Never?"

"Never. Unless she did it when I was sleeping. Then I wouldn't know."

Janine feels her one eyebrow raise again and quickly turns toward the row of alphabetized CDs. Somewhere during the sorting of Steely Dan and Sting, Ben leans over and slides his finger slowly down the side of her cheek, a gesture she finds endearing. Janine has never been an advocate of casual sex, at least not with all the recent risks, but between the ear nibbling and the neck kissing and the arm stroking, she already imagines herself naked and entwined in Ben's long legs. As he slips her top up and over her head, she's grateful for changing into new thong panties before going to the meeting.

Besides, her box of condoms have sat so long in the bathroom cabinet that they're ready to expire. *Can't have that, now.*

"I can't? Don't you like me doing this?" he says with a concerned look.

"No, I love it, I must have been thinking out loud again. That happens to me sometimes." She decides to stop thinking altogether and tips into his arms.

She hears him pulling on his jeans and opens her eyes to a dark room. Her bedside clock radio reads 2:48. "You can stay if you want," she whispers, dragging the covers tighter around her shoulders. Except for his ticklish ribs, she didn't discover any other areas off-limits.

"No, I have to go, I didn't bring my toothbrush." He sits on the side of her double bed to button his shirt. Janine is relieved since she prefers sleeping alone, and decides not to mention the new toothbrush under her sink.

"Did you want to get together this weekend? Go to a movie or something?" Since soon he'll be out the door, she has nothing to lose. She knows hardly anything about him except that he's divorced, presently unattached, and sells to corporate customers for Loomis Couriers.

"Sounds good. I'm doing my laundry Saturday morning, do you want to bring yours over? I have my own private washer and dryer." He says the last sentence in a singsong voice, comprehending the weight of her privy information. She could like a man like this, a man who accepts her for what she is. And isn't.

"It's a date, but Ben?"

"Uh huh?" he says while leaning over to kiss her lips. She kisses back, careful not to move her hands in the vicinity of his head.

"I'm not quite ready for the back waxing thing. You'll have to give me some time on that one," and she pats his hip.

"No big deal, we've got plenty of other things to keep us busy." Again a touch to her cheek. For a moment his hand cups her chin, making her tremble. A good kind of tremble, an equal wave of vulnerability and confidence. "I'll call you soon."

She doesn't get up, hearing the door click when he lets himself out, but rubs her face into the pillow to capture the last of his smell, the fresh scent of citrus. Grapefruit.

As she drifts into sleep she fantasizes about the two of them laughing and talking in his laundry room. She has to invent the picture because she hasn't been there but she's certain the room will be spotless. She lets him pour in a few drops of bleach which he does with the skill of a sous chef, exactly the right amount. It's like they have done this forever. She even lets him put her clothes in the dryer. Two of her renegade panties break free from the damp ball and fall to the gleaming tiled floor. He scoops them with his perfect square fingernails before she can and with his eyes, nothing more, asks if she wants them re-washed. "No, not necessary," her eyes answer back and he smiles "that's my girl" while turning the dryer setting to low heat.

Homeless

Sophie almost leaves him when she turns thirty-five. It isn't fear of being alone or duty that keeps her with Peter, but the dreaded act of splitting up their personal belongings. The sorting, the arguing over what belongs to whom, and finally the packing with tissue and tea towels. Worse, it's the image of half their things pushed against the walls of a new apartment. It isn't about the value of a few pine bookcases or bed linens as much as what each represents: union.

She gets ready, ready to tell him that he's skating dangerously close to the edge of the pond (she likes that metaphor) or that it's over for good but then loses her bravado. A bead of sweat breaks away from her breastbone and rolls down her stomach. She hides in the bathroom until the desire for violence or flight, or both, subsides.

Sophie has had the same mental conversation for at least two years, reviewing the lines until they're scored in her blood vessels. The script is memorized, percolating at the back of her teeth and prepared for the moment, providing Peter stays in the room long enough for her to unfurl her list. His specialty is exiting stage left when any form of emotional atmosphere grips him by the neck.

"This isn't about being right," she'll start. "It's about being happy." Naturally he'll refuse eye contact. The more composed she stays, the more victimized he'll grow, looking downcast and biting the skin off a rough thumb, or digging at the tattooed grime under his mechanic fingernails.

If, instead, she grows weepy and passionate, he'll flash the ceiling a look of disgust and with a quick wave of his hand, will dismiss her like a silly schoolgirl. Or worse, he'll slip on his leavin' loafers and disappear for several hours, ignoring Sophie on his return and spending the night wrapped in a musty sleeping bag on the sofa.

Her final eureka whacked her in the stomach last fall while window shopping with a friend. They walked past a streetperson sitting on the pavement next to a scrawny dog. He wrapped an arm around the mutt and the dog grinned with pleasure. His stick-tail thumped on cardboard the man had spread across damp concrete like a beach blanket.

Sophie's friend Emma looked back and said, "That dog's probably thinking, 'hey, I can do this homeless gig on my own, what do I need *this* bum for?'"

Sophie stopped and bent over, her face near enough the ground to sniff the earthy smell of worms and wet cigarette butts. Her friend joined in the laughter, until realizing that Sophie wasn't laughing.

"Soph, what's wrong? Are you in pain?" Sophie shook her head. "Are you worried about the dog? He's okay, the guy obviously loves him... hey, should I go back and give him money for dog food?"

"If you want to," Sophie said with a nose-clogged choke as she lifted her head and straightened her back, surprised at herself. "That's really kind." She watched Emma walk away, digging into her pocket. She knelt to pat the dog and his tail thumped harder. Emma spoke to the man before handing him money and he nodded, a yellow-toothed promise.

"What happened to you?"

"I don't know, I guess seeing that homeless pair." What really made her cry was the thought that she can be miserable on her own, who needs Peter?

Sophie had been branded as a Pollyanna. After she became skilful at it, this confidence was expected, even demanded.

"You're a real upbeat gal, aren't you," her Aunt Joan would say with every visit, pinching Sophie's cheeks until she wanted to scream and slap. "And a dead ringer for Princess Grace."Her birthday happened to fall on the same day Grace Kelly died in her car wreck, only interesting to Aunt Joan and 900-number psychics.

Sophie believes she's a positive person. If she lost her job, a new one opened up; if she had to move, a nicer apartment materialized. And if she had romance troubles, a more interesting prospect landed in her lap. Peter came on the heels of a lousy relationship with a separated man. The guy wasn't living with his wife but he was so heavy with baggage that Sophie told him, the day it was over, he might as well be.

If she did feel down, someone, even a complete stranger would restore her faith with an unexpected kind deed. Or while carrying groceries home she'd pass a young mother with a child unfocused and slumped in a wheelchair. First she'd experience a shiver of emancipation, then a freeing of her spirit, and finally a sense of upgrading in the knowledge that others were in much worse shape. *Who the hell am I to complain, I've got it easy*, she'd think.

But at thirty-five, the optimistic streak dried and left dusty tracks in its place. She could pass any twisted victim of genetics or motorcycle accident and hardly notice, not even a two on the Richter scale of thank-Christ-it's-not-me.

Peter. She realized downtown with Emma that Peter was to blame. Single-handedly, and without mess or smell, he had dipped the last thimbleful of life from her well.

"Why do we always have to talk when I get home? I'm tired and wanna relax. Jesus, you work in a bookstore, how much news can you have? What do you want from me?" he says while dropping heavily into his recliner, reaching for the *TV Guide* with one hand and the remote with the other.

"What do I *want* from you, Peter? I wouldn't mind five minutes of conversation with my husband, maybe a tad more attention. And while you're at it, how about throwing in some —" No point. She doesn't think Peter listens as he roams from channel to channel. He hunts for the same mind-numbing tabloid TV every night.

Sophie turns on her heel to pull out a knife from the cutlery drawer and loudly tosses it onto his TV tray. She picks up the collapsible table and sets it next to him. An expressionless "thanks" is the extent of his acknowledgment. Sophie walks back to the table with a rivulet of sweat trickling down her ribs, even though it isn't warm in the apartment. She adjusts the dimmer switch for the light over the table and sits down. Her feet don't seem to touch the floor, that same levitating sensation she gets in job interviews for positions she knows she won't get or won't take. She opens her book and looks across at the empty place mat. He hasn't eaten dinner with her since buying the wide-screen TV with money — she ungrits her teeth — that could have been used for a trip to Paris, for a honeymoon they never had.

"Didn't you put any meat in here?" Peter says.

"I did." She doesn't ask what's wrong with his supper; she's made it the same way for years. Maybe she did scrimp on the ground beef but was afraid she'd be short at the cashier.

Sophie chews her lasagna slowly and methodically. Pretending to read, she stares over her book at Peter. *Did he always have that mean look?* She watches his eyes stare dully at *Entertainment Tonight*, or maybe it's *American Journal*. Even the way his jawbone shifts when he crushes each mouthful has an ugliness. She blinks and re-reads the same page of her novel until the meal is finished.

In bed that night, she feels a pang of pleasure (gratitude? relief?) when he slides his rough hand from her knee towards her thigh. Peter repeats his stroking routine for about two minutes and then searches in the dark for Sophie's hand, planning to lead her up that well-worn path.

"Honey?" she asks, hiding her arm under the covers.

"What." It isn't in the form of a question.

"Why don't you turn this way... no, on your side and face me."

"I'm too tired. Why don't you just sit on me. You always like that."

She has nothing left in her reserve for further negotiation. Worse, he'll get angry if she mentions her weariness at being on top, of having to do all the work. So she straddles his hips without great desire and without apology for the sharp bristles on her legs. While slowly rocking against him she scrunches her eyes to prevent the tears from escaping. Peter stays still, not touching Sophie but squeezing his own inner thighs or gripping the edge of a pillow.

There was a time, although the memory is so old it could belong to someone else, when he never got enough of her, waking her in the night with his kisses. They'd hurry to meet at his apartment during lunch breaks where they'd hug until her backbone ached. She always carried some small mark from their lovemaking — a purple smudge on her neck, a bruise on her thigh, a kneeburn from the rough pile of his carpet. She liked the way his cologne transferred onto her skin, small bursts of scent to remind her, to sustain her through the long afternoon until she could be back in his arms. It was passion in it's simplest and ripest form. Wet, willowy, light as lint as heavy as black holes. It is this passion, somewhere between contentment and obsession, she longs for but can no longer evoke from Peter.

The moonlight isn't bright enough to illuminate his features and she's glad. For brief seconds he becomes anyone else, without the thickening jowl and slack chest muscles, a depressing downward shift. The day he came home with a contraption to better pluck his nose hairs, she could have been watching her father in the bathroom mirror, not her once-adventurous lover. Sophie feels the stirrings of a pathetic smile at the same moment Peter's leg muscles tense two-three-four and relax.

Sophie can live with that. Peter *does* work six low-paid days a week and he is tired, and pretty unhappy to boot. But what she can't live with lately (although she admits it's a minor point) is picking up the hardened balls of tissue carelessly abandoned next to his side of the bed. He insists they're from his nose but Sophie never hears him blow it, unless he's legitimately sick. One morning, angry for everything he had and hadn't done in their marriage, Sophie made the bed. With rage banging in her temples, she pulled up the duvet and beat the pillows into submission, tossing them like sandbags against the headboard. That's when she found the Kleenex balls. She scooped them with one hand but quickly threw them to the floor after a touch of the hard surfaces. It was the act of leaving his messy remains for her to find that disgusted her, more than the image of him furtively rubbing while she slept inches away. Who did he fantasize about when he did it?

"IF YOU'RE GONNA JERK OFF," she yelled in the direction of the bathroom, even if he couldn't hear over the running water,"IS IT TOO MUCH TO ASK THAT YOU THROW OUT YOUR OWN CUM-BALLS?"She kicked the three tumbleweeds under the bed. The thought of him preferring his own hand
(*cum-ball-weeds*)
to her body made her snicker into her housecoat sleeve, her mind quickly tamping down a word
(*loser*)
that serpentined its way to the surface.

Sophie never talks to anyone about how she feels. No one knows how she dreams of running away, of packing her one suitcase and looking back to see four keys on the kitchen counter before hearing a final click of the apartment door. She is too proud to admit that she could fail at a project as weighty as marriage. She never failed at anything in her life.

When she married Peter twelve years earlier, she experienced pure optimism, surprising even herself. Peter had plans, Peter had abilities, and most important, Sophie believe in him. Because she'd tasted true joy, she assumed it would always be there. Encased like a wiener, this wrapping of protection would magically protect her from future miseries. While most people search their entire lives seeking happiness, by her mid-twenties she'd already been there, read the book and seen the movie. Or so she figured. All of this thinking helped her ignore the silverfish darting through their cramped apartments, and overlook the steady stream of rust-bucket cars she dragged home only to lose money.

By age thirty-five she realized that her talisman of protection was an Etch-a-Sketch mirage, a fabrication invented to keep fear at arm's length. For some reason this knowledge hit her like a claw hammer when she saw the skinny dog with the bum, the dog so damned appreciative for any scrap of affection thrown his way. She was the one who felt homeless. Peter's decade of lost jobs and letdowns have taken their toll on Sophie as much as on him. Perhaps more, since his anger filtered down to her, a crumb tray to catch his daily dregs of frustration. She watched his high spirits slowly drain over the years, his sense of humour along with it in sympathy. A pilot light in her brain flicked on the day she saw the dog. *I can be homeless on my own. Why should I stay with a man who makes me feel bad?*

She'll tell him as soon as he finishes dinner; only someone heartless could drop a bombshell on a hungry man. Sophie goes though the routine with mechanical movements. She purposely dishes a small serving for herself. The few bites of chicken pot pie form a fistful of dough in her nervous stomach. She scrapes the remaining food into the garbage pail under the sink when Peter calls out.

"Come here for a minute. Come sit with me but get my knapsack first."

Sophie leaves her dirty dishes and licks her lips, a *do it — do it* mantra pulsing through her head. She stands in front of him, blocking the TV screen, and hands him the knapsack.

"Turn down the volume, Peter, I have to talk to you." The words slip from her mouth like they have on a hundred occasions in her mind, except this time she hears them aloud, oddly high-pitched and breathless, unfamiliar. Peter punches the mute button and pats the armrest for her to join him. He doesn't move until she sits. Reaching into the biggest zippered compartment, he pulls out a plastic bag.

"Here." He sets it on her knee.

"What is it?"

"Open it, it's for you... see?" Sophie doesn't react but turns it over and over. "It's a reading light. You clip it on the rail of the headboard and the beam hits your book." He stretches around Sophie's back to plug in the cord. Demonstrating with the *TV Guide*, Peter looks into her face."See? Now you can read in bed with me while I'm sleeping. You don't have to fall asleep on the couch with your books anymore." She doesn't realize she's doing it but while Peter speaks, Sophie lightly rubs his denim-covered forearm.

"I don't like waking up and not having you next to me." Peter adjusts the beam over the TV listings, showing how easy it is to read the small print. "I saw them in a flier from Canadian Tire and went over on my lunch break." He speaks with a gentleness she hasn't noticed for a long time. It's the best he can do.

Sophie looks at him while he waits for a reaction, peering into her eyes. He squints with the concentration of a child.

"Why are you crying? It's just a cheap lamp. Why would you cry over a cheap lamp?"

"I don't know." Sophie puts the lamp on the coffee table, the yellow beam aimed straight at Peter's angular face, and leans against his shoulder. "But it's a good gift." The cologne he sprayed on that morning has faded, but it's still there.

Just Lucky, I Guess

Lucky for Shirley that her brother lives nearby, the organized one, not the recluse who lives in an old fishing boat somewhere on Lake Ontario. Trent took care of all the grisly details while Shirley played with the condensation on her bottomless vodka tonics. It's still sinking in, the news. If Trent hadn't been around, the body would have sat at the airport until it rotted. At least rotted more than it already had.

"Shirley... sis? you're going to have to make some decisions about —"

"There's nothing to decide. He didn't want a funeral, he wanted to be cremated. Simple. Hey, if you're coming back later, could you pick me up some bread? And another bottle of tonic? Diet, if you think of it." The lip of her glass is an oily smudge after using the same one for days. Shirley circles the rim with a finger, the nail ragged and framed by hangnails. She makes a mental note to set up an appointment for a manicure, maybe even a facial, for the first time in her life. She has walked past the picture window of Lookin' Good Boutique for years, where women are served coffee in glass mugs, their hands lovingly buffed and stroked by girls in white smocks. But she's never had the courage to treat herself. William would have a bird (would have had), the thought of his hard-earned dollars wasted on frivolities, on Shirley's frivolities.

Funny, she thinks, she can remind herself to make an appointment for a "Morning in Glory" beauty treatment but can't seem to get poor William seen to. But then poor William already got himself seen to, by a small man wielding a large knife in the Philippines. She supposes she should be more curious, more outraged that only last month he kissed her forehead good-bye, packing twelve new pair of boxer shorts still crisp in their cellophane wrap, and now he gets himself killed. The report that the knife belonged to a pimp and that he died in his own puddle in the backroom of a strip joint should make her feel wronged. But it doesn't, it leaves her numb. And free.

Flies out in boxers, flies home in a box. She stifles a giggle into an unwashed hand smelling of Ritz crackers, surprised at her sick humour. Trent says nothing but shuffles uncomfortably in front of her, and then starts repositioning flower arrangements on top of the TV cabinet.

"There's nothing left to do, if you've been good enough to let them know about the cremation. Did you tell them I want him in an urn?" She sets down her drink, adding a fresh ring to the growing mosaic on the coffee table, a glass and brass relic from a bargain furniture depot.

"Of course I told them, something simple, like you said... that's it? Won't his family have a say in all this?"

Trent is doing his best. At that moment Shirley loves her brother almost more than she can stand. An ache travels upwards from the base of her neck to her forehead.

"I talked to his dad, who he never had much to do with, and he promised to let the rest of the family know. Didn't seem all that interested, just thanked me for calling, like I phoned to say he'd won ten free dance lessons." Her brother stands with shoulders hunched and both hands in his pockets the same way since he was a kid, the same way in all of her photo albums. "But I've had some nice calls from his side... I'm okay, really." She smiles up at him from the couch, curving her eyebrows to show she can deal with it. "I got used to him being away on business, I'll just think of this as one long trip." It's more the look of compassion on Trent's face than any twinge of liquored self-pity. But something flicks a switch that starts her crying. It feels good, even if the guilt of letting herself fall apart and upset Trent over-rides the pleasure.

She started by disliking William and then grew to hating him for the better part of their marriage. She never got around to leaving him, since he conveniently left her for as much as six months of the year. First marriages for both, she was forty-two when they got together. And resigned to the fact that he was all she could get, her expectations were moderate to low from the start. It made the disappointments easier to handle. And who stopped her from getting a manicure before they met? Nobody. It's a free country, she thinks, and takes small sips of her drink.

When he was away, when she could spend contented evenings working on crossword puzzles without interruption or flipping through home decorating magazines, she fantasized about his death: his plane goes down in a ball of flames over a remote jungle somewhere in Malaysia. The man delivering the news happens to look like MacGyver and since it's *her* fantasy, her legs are freshly shaved and she's lounging in a slimming teddy when the doorbell rings, not her usual jogging pants that cover patches of cellulite. Since it's still her fantasy, it would be rude if she didn't invite him inside for a polite drink of bourbon before ending in a sweaty tangle, to help her through the night. And the mourning.

That was her common fantasy, except she felt greedy about dragging in all those innocent passengers and flight crew. Another fantasy, more frequent in the last year, is while paddling down a piranha-infested river, he falls into the murk. Feeling philanthropic, she excuses his guide and fellow workers from this tragedy. If the flesh-eating fish don't finish him off, the fever he develops finally does.

Yup, I sure won't miss him, that's a fact. Even his last action brings shame, at least with her brother. William can't manage to go down proudly with the plane or the plague but more likely arguing over money. Shirley realized she no longer liked him the day she could comfortably imagine him sleeping with other women. Relief, if anything, is the prevailing emotion. At least he stopped bothering her in the bedroom department, always wanting her to tell him how good he was, how big he was, begging her to say his name over and over like some Greek god. Shirley had his script memorized: "Say my name, tell me you like it, cradle the balls." Never *my* balls, but *the* balls, like they were a separate entity. Soon his dear wee jewels would be ash.

But the other emotion besides relief is embarrassment, since her brother sat next to her watching a video when she received the news. Now she can't forget that he was in a brothel, and she can't distort it into fantasy when someone else knows the truth.

Years ago Shirley watched a gritty documentary about the working girls and boys of Thailand, the ones reared early into lives of sexual service for cut-rate travellers. The image that haunts her is an interview inside a smoky club. A balding man in his fifties drapes a fleshy arm over the shoulder of a long-haired girl anywhere in her teens. She stands next to him, tiny in a string bikini and white high-heeled pumps. The music blares and the sweaty man explains to the camera in halting English why he's doing these people a favour by bringing in his tourist dollars, and that "it's good fun, they love it." Throughout his short interview, the girl-child smiles brightly into the camera, a close-up, while tears fill her eyes and roll down her cheeks across quivering lips. The shiny man ends his monologue by pulling the girl against him and shoving his tongue in her mouth. Shirley can't shake that memory; sometimes William's face replaces the European's.

She doesn't hear Trent leave, having let herself fall asleep curled under an afghan. With the level of pounding in her skull, she decides to retire the vodka. The TV is on but the volume is muted with a slim-phase Oprah doing the Macarena alongside an aisle of audience members. Shirley finds the remote under several days worth of unread newspapers and turns it off. She only likes the more provocative shows, the ones where mothers steal their daughter's boyfriends. Or where girls of thirteen go on national television to proclaim they should be allowed to have sex. "Send her to Bangkok," Shirley says to the TV, "She can have all she wants." Sitting next to these heavily made-up girls are weepy mothers, either over or underweight, always with that haggard trailer park-living look.

But who am I to feel superior, Shirley thinks, gazing around their (no, her) mortgaged livingroom. The furniture is cheap and not her choice. But William reminded her — continually — that he made the big bucks so *he* had final say in the major purchases. She could have put up more of a struggle to get her pick occasionally, but it was easier to let him win. When they married he convinced her to get rid of her own pretty things, that they would buy new pieces together. She made the mistake of assuming his taste would be better and his purse strings looser.

He wouldn't even let her call him Willy or Bill, his own wife, in case it made him sound ordinary. *Who does he think he is? I mean was, Zeus?* She has already vowed never to say his name again. From now on he's a Willy. She wanders into the kitchen and looks at the calendar tacked to the cork board, triple-checking that he'll be *en route* to the crematorium today. Until she has that urn, has it in her hands, she can't believe it's over. What if she awakens to find him standing there smirking, like the dream sequence on *Dallas* where JR wasn't dead?

He always liked the dry heat, she thinks, and an awful titter like a wounded sparrow rises from the bottom of her windpipe.

Pinned next to the calendar is a check for $500 in Trent's meticulous printing. Shirley takes it down and holds it against her chest like a precious gem, knowing how scarce money has been after losing his business. She'll be fine, she keeps telling herself. If she's lucky, there might be a few thousand leftover after she sells the place and then she can rent a little apartment. And good thing she doesn't have many bills because Willy amassed a grand total of two thousand, four hundred and eighty dollars in their savings account. It isn't much but for a man who resignedly attended Gambler's Anonymous — one more darling trait she was introduced to after marriage — it's better than nothing. But then I stayed with him, she tells herself, it's my own fault for not being more assertive.

She puts the check back on the cork board and starts to make a smoked turkey and tomato sandwich with the two remaining crusts. When the phone rings she almost doesn't answer, but on the fifth ring lifts the receiver, hoping it's the funeral director with news of her little package.

"Mrs. Winkler? It's Garry Tate from the office. I'm calling to give my condolences... did I get you at bad time?"

"No, it's fine, and thanks for the nice plant you sent, it's real pretty." She can't think of anything to say and hears the man clear his throat a couple of times.

"Besides telling you how sorry I am, I wanted to let you know that I sent William's insurance claim by courier to Maritime Life this morning."

Shirley almost drops the phone. "He had life insurance? He had a policy?"

"Well, yeah, we all do, just a standard part of our benefits package. You didn't know? I guess this is good news then. Someone from Maritime Life will be calling to get a copy of the, um, death certificate and whatever else they'll need to process the claim. I don't really know what they'll want since no one has ever passed away on us before." He speaks quickly, trying to get through his managerial duty as fast as he can. She imagines sweat ringing the armpits of his short-sleeve shirt. "It's not great but I guess it'll be a bonus since you weren't expecting it. I don't mean bonus like it's supposed to be a good thing but —"

"No, don't apologize, it's a bonus all right. Thanks for calling, Garry. Bye." Shirley starts to hang up but hears his voice.

"... much it's for. Wouldn't you like to know?"

Shirley is too rattled to think. "Sure, how much?"

"One hundred and twenty-five thousand."

"Wow, that *is* a nice bonus, isn't it. Thanks again for letting me know." She hangs up before he can ruin the moment with more strained conversation.

"Jackpot!" she yells in the middle of her kitchen.

Wearing the same leggings and thick socks that she had on when she first received the news of Willy, she scans the room with its avocado appliances and lowers her voice to a reverent whisper. "First he dies and now I get money for it!" She drops to her knees and clasps her hands together in prayer, a motion she hasn't caught herself doing for years. "Please, dear Lord, don't let me wake from this dream!"

She laughs when she looks up at the counter to see a meaty bluebottle cleaning its legs on her turkey and tomato. She whisks the sandwich along with the Corelle plate into the trash can under the sink. She is ravenous for something special, and she licks her lips imagining the taste of prawns sauteed in garlic and olive oil. And grilled swordfish with those tiny roast potatoes — no, saffron rice — and a side of mushrooms. She grabs her purse from the telephone table and heads to the door, determined to celebrate her new freedom with an expensive seafood dinner. The vision that hurries by the front hall mirror is shocking but she doesn't care: clothing slept in, hair unwashed, face slick with excitement. Grinning into the oval mirror, she dabs at her eyebrow with an exaggerated gesture before yanking her car keys off the hook.

"It's a higher price when you book as a single. See? Have a peek at the rate sheet," the travel agent says and pushes the brochure towards her.

Shirley doesn't bother to look at the figures, she's not even listening. Her mind is already made up: Willy is about to make amends for the stingy weekend he tried to pass off as a honeymoon. He could give everything to Lady Luck time after time but as for Shirley, she got three rainy nights in a Seattle motel room with lumpy pillows and noisy air conditioning.

Again she smiles, forcing out those poor-me thoughts.

She could never explain it, even to her friends from the deli, how he smothered her power like a heavy blanket. The rumour mill would do her in, the gossip mongers behind the counter with thick fingers greased by animal fat. All those sets of sad eyes sneaking quick glances like she was a kicked mongrel.

When alone, her thoughts were packed with strength but when Willy started on a noisy rampage, her spunk shrivelled. She became a mute little girl, accepting what Daddy dished out, even if it meant no new appliances, chosen and promised the year before, and no trip to Honolulu, after Shirley scoured the travel agencies for seat sales and left pamphlets on the table for him to find.

No poor me anymore. "The Ilikai, it means what? where the water meets the sand? Ooo, that's pretty, book it." *Sounds good, eh Willy? You're finally taking me.* She pats the side of her bag like the head of a good dog and reaches in for her credit card. "Remember, the next available flight, please."

Now that she's transferred a cupful of his ashes to a container the size of a big saltshaker, he goes everywhere with Shirley. She knows it's bordering on ghoulish, that's why she hasn't told anybody, especially Trent. Something she found interesting, sending a shiver up her neck when she broke the seal on his urn, was the texture of his ashes. She expected to find them light and feathery, the gray paper of a wasp's nest, or the fine powder left from a campfire. Instead, with a trembling hand, she discovered hard bits of bone, appallingly chunky; maybe they didn't leave him in the furnace long enough. She had to hold her lips together to keep that bird-like snigger from escaping. Shirley still has boundaries, regardless of how the goal posts have widened over the past few weeks.

Her kitchen funnel had been too large so she rolled the thin cardboard from her pantyhose into a cone. She almost resealed the mini-urn with Krazy Glue but decided against it. She taped the lid and with little ceremony, tossed him in her shoulder bag.

Even inside the never-ending terminal, the moist Hawaiian air makes Shirley euphoric. She knows she made the right decision. Before boarding the charter bus, all passengers are presented with a lei, kissed, and photographed next to young Hawaiians in grass skirts. The group buzzes with chatter but Shirley chooses the sights, watching walls of hibiscus and bougainvillea flash past her bus window, a patchwork of reds and oranges set against rolling green mountains.

The Ilikai is lovelier than the picture, with its open-air lobby and tiled courtyard ringed by curving fish ponds. On the beach like the name promised, her room overlooks the ocean. The sand below is a beige carpet of multicolored towels and striped umbrellas.

Shirley can't be bothered to unpack, too anxious to dip her ankles in the warm Pacific. She reaches into her beach bag and pulls out Willy's mini-urn.

"We made it, Willy," she says softly, her words carried away on a fragrant breeze. She unwinds the tape and sprinkles a few flakes first into the ocean, and then onto the beach. "Where the water meets the sand. I knew if I waited long enough..." She hears, surprising herself, a loving tone in her voice. And she feels something else ripple up with it: nerve. Over the past few weeks between apartment hunting, dealing with real estate agents, labelling furniture for a yard sale, and tossing out bag after bag of Willy's junk, Shirley is exhilarated with her quick decisions, each one leaving her braver for the next. She has already mailed gracious thank you notes to anyone who sent her flowers or cards of sympathy. To think Willy *really* wanted a lavish funeral with a dignified marble headstone on his grave where, of course, she would be expected to tend his flowers on a regular basis. (This from a man whose most prized possession was a ceramic ashtray in the shape of a reclining naked woman.) Beans to that! The only burial he'd get is on top of a blackjack table, or stuffed into a slot machine. Even better, under the stage of a stripclub where he apparently felt quite at home.

*

By her second Mai Tai, Shirley decides to return every year on the anniversary of Willy's death. While relaxing in the outdoor bar, she also decides to fly to Maui the next day. That morning while pretending to read the *Honolulu Advertiser* in the lobby, she eavesdropped on two women. One spent a week in Maui and described the highlight of her stay: a helicopter tour that included flying over George Harrison's tropical home. Now Shirley wants to fly over a Beatle's home.

As the sun starts to set, a man lights the gas torches in the Ilikai's courtyard. She watches Japanese tourists gather for a group shot, flash bulbs bursting against the dark sky. Shirley's head is strangely light, loose and bouncy on her shoulders. She is close to reaching a state which must be nirvana, based on all the articles, until a man in need of a shower and a breath mint joins her on the next bar stool.

Although she is clearly not conversational, the man persists. She refuses to move to another seat; she has given in and bent over for too many years. He isn't even flattering, with his slurring come-on and eyes that won't focus. When the guy, Hal, leans over and envelopes her with sour breath to suggest they get naked on his lanai, Shirley has enough. Ignoring him, she reaches for her wallet to pay the bill and her wrist brushes against the jar. Reassured, she strokes it like an amulet of courage. Hal puts his clammy hand on her bare shoulder and stands up, listing into the bar. The bartender arrives at the same moment and sets a platter of nachos next to his glass.

"Be right back, buddy. Bring me another rye and 7 while you're at it. Now don't you disappear on me, sugar, I'm off to the can."

Yeah, right, you creep. Shirley pops the lid on the jar and with a graceful hand movement, dumps a pile of ashes into Hal's salsa. *Here Willy, you two should have a lot in common.* With a generous tip to the bartender, she slides off her stool and heads toward the elevator. Before the corner she looks back like Lot's wife and watches Hal return, scooping a tortilla into his salsa. Except Shirley doesn't turn into salt. Instead, she shakes with laughter in the elevator, happy tears streaming down her sun-kissed face.

Hey Willy, I lied. You weren't good, you weren't even big. I've seen more meat on a pastrami sandwich. She continues to laugh from her balcony with the Friday night fireworks lighting up an ultramarine sky.

Shirley sits on the couch in her new apartment, legs tucked under her like a teenager. Coiled on Willy's favourite afghan next to her is a striped cat, an adopted one from the animal shelter. She asked for anything next in line for euthanasia and was presented with an old but beautiful creature.

Trent sits on the hearthstone of Shirley's fireplace, enjoying the heat on his back. "I forgot you liked cats. He looks like a big striped raccoon. How'd you find such a nice one?"

"Just lucky, I guess." Shirley tickles the cat's chin and his face grows long and pointed with pleasure.

"Are you really calling him Jack?"

"Darn right, it's strong and it's simple. You could be

a Jack, couldn't you?" She strokes his soft fur until he yawns and stretches into an arch before settling into his blanket.

Trent peers hard into her face, so hard he scowls, his concerned gaze again. "What a pretty blouse, such a nice green. Did you get it in Hawaii?"

"I did, in Maui. It's the same colour as my eyes." She opens them wide. "See?"

He keeps staring at her until his forehead relaxes and he lets out a big sigh, relief perhaps. "So it is." He glances down to the generous check from Shirley and smiles at something, pretending to admire her new pine coffee table, rubbing the smooth patina. Maybe he is remembering how Willy hated cats.

Shirley also smiles when she looks up at the mantel. That morning she finally framed her picture, the one taken at the Honolulu airport. In it, a Hawaiian boy has his arm around her waist squeezing her shoulder bag between them, the one carrying Willy. By the expression on her face, anyone can see she's ready to embark on paradise. It's her turn.

The Brief Pitch

At thirty-four, Jackie has come to terms with relationships on a scale as big as the Grand Canyon. Her realization: it isn't a given that you'll go through life with a man by your side, it's a privilege. Never married, no closer to the altar than bridesmaid spitting distance, the image of herself taking the aisle walk is growing opaque. During her early twenties the could practically hear the rustle of satin and smell the lily of the valley woven through her bouquet with sweet peas.

"You can't have sweet peas in a bouquet, who's ever had sweet peas?" her younger sister said.

"Of course I can. They were good enough for Christie Brinkley's fourth wedding, why not mine?" She thought she had it figured out but she's let her plans vaporize.

Dream all you like about the perfect groom but if he's a no-show, flipping through *Bride's* is as near as you get.

And if her last string of boyfriends is indicative of what's out there, she'll be driving buyers from Squamish to Chilliwack for the rest of her life.

The last man she slept with, almost a year ago, started out with potential but had too many layers to contend with, weird layers she really didn't want to peel back. After a couple of unremarkable nights in bed, Luke wanted Jackie to be his Mommy and pretend she was having sex with him as if he was nine. On top of that, he was such a lame lover that without kick-starting him and placing his hands on her favourite spots, she wouldn't get any attention. After a month Jackie decided she wasn't lonely enough to settle for a cold fish with an Oedipal complex. Ten or fifteen good years with him maybe, maybe then she could deal with his wacky sex games, or sit by any number of Prozac-buffered mid-life crises but not after four weeks. She wanted some simple cherishing; he wanted diapering.

When she told Luke to take his fetishes and hit the road, she purged herself by telling people in her office about him and having a good laugh. "He didn't even deserve to be that creepy with the lousy money he made."

Then there's her subconscious, still teasing with dreams starring Ray Liotta as the tuxedoed groom (when he was younger, not bloated and pasty like now) or Richard Gere (in earlier movies like *Breathless* or *Looking for Mr. Goodbar*). Jackie ages but the men of her dreams conveniently stay locked on twenty-five.

And children, what about motherhood? Romance has been so desert-dry that Jackie toyed with the idea of sperm donors until she got to know Paula, a single mother in her office who purposely got pregnant by a married man. After watching Paula struggle with a baby while juggling her career and what was left of a spotty social life, it was enough reality check to cancel her doctor's appointment.

"I don't even like kids," she says to herself, relieved she found the snooze button on her biological clock in time. "What was I thinking?" and she returns to worrying about career plans and how she's going to sell enough houses to buy RRSPs when interest rates are unstable, and whether her new shade of auburn hair suits her.

By now Jackie has some things figured out, like when a man in a bar says, "so what's your story, pretty lady?"

"Who, little ol' me?" she says in her best Tennessee drawl. "I've got a darling boy named Johnnie Wayne. He's in counselling right now for his iddy biddy arson tendencies. But I hope to get him back real soon, before his father gets out of jail and comes lookin' for us... so what are you doing for the next ten years, handsome?" If that doesn't scare the lycra rug right off the feller's head, she progresses to mention her fresh-baked yeast infection when he insists on buying her a drink she doesn't want. The whoosh of air he makes as he steps back creates enough of a draft to ripple her pant leg.

"My black hole technique," she tells Paula over a carafe of red wine. "Works every time. The gaping hole he leaves is like magic. Presto! the geeky man disappears. You should try it."

"Are you kidding?" says Paula. "I've been on my own so long that even *he* was starting to look do-able!" They laugh together but in a competitive way, never breaking eye contact, sister sharks in a fixed sea of men to catch and homes to sell.

But she only uses the black hole routine on annoying non-prospects — the category where she files nose-pickers, public urinators, and men with hopelessly bad teeth — never on nice guys. Jackie isn't civil to men in bars because she can't imagine meeting any nice ones. Paula tells her she's being close-minded and that she might be missing perfectly good opportunities.

"Then why haven't *you* met any knights in shining armour?" says Jackie. "You're here enough."

The liquor has malaligned Paula's left eye, just enough of a drift to be distracting. She shrugs her shoulders. "Since Rachel was born, I've lowered my expectations, you should too."

"Hah!" she says and dismisses Paula with a wave of her hand. "If I go any lower, I'll be passing my dead Uncle Harry on the way down. Let's order more wine."

Jackie is convinced the meeting will be while she's cycling the Seawall, or at Sav-On struggling to put heavy groceries into her trunk, when a robust guy hops out of his Land Rover and saunters over to help (here we go again, says Paula), a Kurt Russell type with week-old stubble, like he's come down from the mountains for supplies. No, she says, nix Russell, he's a hunter in real life and even in my fantasies I couldn't be swept away by any man who kills animals for sport. Paula sighs and says "whatever," knowing this conversation goes nowhere.

At least Jackie loves her West End condo, choosing to live alone for the past seven years, except for a series of weekenders with men like Diaper Boy, and a man who sniffed her armpits to arouse himself. And except for a diabetic cat who came with the place. The previous owners were ready to put him down rather than subject him to a Hawaiian quarantine. By promising to take good care of Max, she whittled another $1500 off the price. How do they know I won't dump Max and his insulin down some back lane, she thinks during the first shaky injection.

She never expected to love an animal this much but since she doesn't have a partner, Max has become the vessel to pour in her affection. When he developed glaucoma and had an eye removed, the vet offered to put in an artificial one. Through streaming tears when she told the vet it wasn't necessary, the vision of Sammy Davis Jr. made her laugh into her clump of soddened tissues.

With his sewn-up right socket he is the picture of asymmetry. Daily, she stares at Max, calmed by the way he can be content with one eye, no balls, and a shot pancreas, his off-balance body a hindrance only to those who feel sorry for him.

That's how she feels lately, off-balance, as if there should be two of something when she's limping around on one. It takes so much energy to keep an open mind, when pessimism is more vaguely comforting.

"Lucky Max," she says to the fourteen pound bag of purring fur. "I'm the disabled one here." She tries to plant a hard kiss on his long-haired belly but never makes contact with anything firm, kissing gelatin. The beep of her pager makes them both sit up with hopeful expressions. But Max quickly returns to his normal state of enthusiastic disinterest, making two full rotations before settling into his blanket.

The message is to phone a man she doesn't know, a Mike Thorogood.

"Try to look a little more excited, you, I'm the one who pays for your catnip." At the last word he raises his head and slips on his one-eyed eager face, a teddy bear missing a button.

"Hello, Mike? It's Jackie Conners returning your page."

Pause, as if he doesn't recognize the name he called moments earlier. Or is surprised she called at all.

"Thanks, thanks for getting back to me so fast. You gave me one of your cards last week... at the Bean Machine?"

Bean Machine. Which Bean Machine? "Right. So

what can I do for you, are you phoning about one of my listings, or are you thinking of selling your property?"

"No, I was wondering, Jackie, if there was something I can do for you."

Oh Christ, he's gonna pitch me. "How's that?"

"I know you're a realtor, Jackie, and most likely a great one, but I assume you wouldn't turn down extra cash."

"I'm pretty busy with my listings and don't have much spare time." *He's saying my name too often, like he's got a quota. But must be civil, never know who he has for relatives in need of an agent.*

"What if I told you, Jackie —"

Here it comes, here comes the pitch.

"By the way, Jackie, how much money would you say you'd like to make, total annual income?"

"I'm used to $100,000, as much as $150,000 and I don't like to work too hard for it, either." *If that doesn't frighten him off nothing will.*

"Okay, that sounds great. Now what if I told you that in only a few hours a week, Jackie, you could make thousands of extra dollars."

What, didn't this guy hear me? Hel-lo! "Look Mike, I'm sure you've got a good proposition —"

"It's not a proposition, Jackie, it's an investment, an investment in your future."

He's speeding up, he knows he's losing me. "All right, investment then, but I'm not looking —"

"Wait, please, don't say no yet, I'm begging you, Jackie, hear me out."

"Mike, I really have to go, I've got a showing in a few minutes."

"Please, before you write me off come hear what I have to say. I'm holding a seminar tomorrow night at the Pan Pacific with ten other people. It's at seven sharp and I want to show you what I can offer."

"I'll tell you right now, if there's any up front investment I'm not interested."

"No, Jackie, I promise you there isn't."

A funny thought hit her. "Mike, is this Amway? Are you trying to get me into Amway?"

"No!" he says with such force that he sounds hurt. "So will you come? It'll be worth your time, I promise you."

Too many promises. "I won't guarantee it, but I'll try. You said the Pan, will you have a conference room booked?"

"I will, but first we'll meet in the lobby. See you tomorrow, Jackie."

"Wait!" she says but knows he's gone. "I don't remember what you look like... I won't go, he sounds like a goof," she says in Max's direction, who is busy sleeping, and hangs up the phone. *But then, what if he's the one in a million who does have something? Real estate is boring, you see one three bedroom two bathroom split level with patio doors off the family room leading to a fenced back yard in affordable Surrey close to all amenities, you've seen them all*, and she clicks on the TV.

She tells herself she won't go, wild horses can't drag her, but at 6:55 she's nodding hello to the doorman and entering the Pan's busy lobby.

Since she doesn't know if she'll remember Mike's face, she picks a seat in the lobby where he can spot her. For thirty minutes she watches crowds breeze in and out, little slices of conversation catching on her like dandelion fluff. A teenager with junkie-thin arms tries to quiet a fussing baby; young men in good suits and bleached teeth discuss the success of recent mergers; waves of foreign babble fill the room for several minutes and then pull away like an undertow. Jackie doesn't mind waiting, enjoying the soup of humanity that swirls around her as if she's invisible.

Two men in their late fifties stand next to her, speaking quietly but loud enough for Jackie to listen. She hears better by watching their moving mouths in the mirror across the room.

"What are you complaining about, Hans, at least she's getting married in a couple of days."

"I know," says the other man, "but he's such a dolt. She could have done better. My kids have been nothing but trouble."

"But Hans, think how lucky you are. You have three children to carry on your name, three Gunnersons to give you a little piece of immortality."

"Aach," he says and shakes his head from side to side. "I should have masturbated more often."

A hand taps Jackie's shoulder and she jerks away, guilty as charged for eavesdropping.

"Sorry, but you didn't hear me call your name."

"That's okay, I was thinking about... Mike?"

"Hey, sorry I'm late. My car wouldn't start and I had to bus it here."

"No problem. But where is everybody?" Jackie scans the room but no one else acknowledges him.

"Now here's the bad news," he starts. *Uh huh*, thinks Jackie. "Everyone but you cancelled so I figured there wasn't much point in bothering with a conference room. How about I buy you a coffee and show you my plan in the restaurant."

"How about you buy me a drink."

Mike signals for the waiter, ordering coffee for himself.

"So I'm the only one who showed up? Those are pretty lousy odds." Jackie knows she's in for a long evening.

"Yeah, talk about disappointing." Roughly, he rolls a

sugar packet between his palms until it breaks open, scattering crystals across the table. With a quick swipe of his sleeve, he sends the sugar flying. Glancing up and aware of Jackie's scrutiny, he keeps his arms under the table until the waiter sets down her wine glass.

"Let's get to it, shall we?" he says, fighting with the lock on his briefcase. After several minutes of battle, the waiter helps by breaking the lock with a butter knife. A shimmer of perspiration forms on Mike's upper lip despite the air-conditioned room. Jackie swallows her drink in three mouthfuls, hoping a buzz will get her through this painful ordeal.

Talking nonstop, with Jackie not interrupting for fear of prolonging the agony, Mike picks heartily at a scab near his ear. A tiny trickle of blood makes its way toward his frayed collar. By the end of Jackie's second drink, she feels a pathetic sense of appreciation. Just when she thought her life was meaningless and going nowhere, here to bail her out from self-pity comes Mr. Thorogood.

"Mike, my friend, you promised me this wasn't Amway."

"It isn't, Jackie, it's Watkins and the two are like night and day."

"I make thousands selling one house. Why would I want to sell ten-dollar items door-to-door? Tell me."

Mike looks stricken, about to cry, and lets his large head sag over a messy writing pad. He has been drawing circles and arrows with cartoon dollar signs to show Jackie how she will make huge bucks, big sacks of dough. To her, it looks more like the scrawls of a madman. Staring into his coffee cup, he tugs methodically at his right eyebrow. After two or three painful moments for Jackie, with an equal pull of fascination and repulsion, a small mess of coppery eyebrows form on the side of his saucer. She watches the skin around his eye turn a blotchy pink. Before

54

deciding how to make her exit now that Mike's motor is
fading, he yells loudly: "BUT IT'S NOT DOOR-TO-
DOOR SELLING," and flails his arms, knocking over the
last of Jackie's wine. "IT'S RECRUITING!"

"Okay, okay, it's recruiting, I believe you," Jackie
whispers, adding up the sets of eyes throughout the room
now locked on their table. "Take it easy. Everyone's
looking at us."

"Listen," he begins again but at a more controlled
volume. "Each time I bring in a new rep, I get an override,
like you would." With a puff of air he disperses his
eyebrows to join the sugar in the carpeting. Jackie is about
to say that eventually *somebody* has to sell a few crappy
bottles of barbecue sauce but stops herself. After another
brief pitch, this one more canned than the last, his volume
level rises again. A pick to his scab, another bright trickle
of blood. As his neck thickens with the intensity of his
speech, the ends of his shirt collar bob up and down like
divining rods.

Jackie feels her lower lip slowly drop open as a
comfortable tunnel vision kicks in. She doesn't fight it and
tunes out his voice to watch him like a muted television.
Foamy spittle hits the shoulder of her blazer but she
doesn't flinch. She is hypnotized by Mike's stalagmite
lower teeth. Several grow sideways, a broken picket fence,
with brown tartar forming a ridge near the gum line. The
tip of his tongue pops in and out of the darkness where a
lower tooth might have been.

Jackie moves a notch up the horizon and stops at his
nose. A luxuriant tuft of asparagus-like hair sprouts not
from inside, but from the surface. Only a blind man could
miss those in a mirror. *But then he's not spending much
time in a mirror, judging from his teeth*, she thinks, her
cheeks aching to laugh, to howl. Each feature she focuses
on magnifies and moves independently. Mike is an

animated mouth, then a furry nose, next, a crusted pimple. Why hadn't she noticed all of this bounty before?

During his ranting, Mike knocks the briefcase off the table, sending a fan of colourful bar graphs flapping to the floor. He leans over and picks up the pile, then shoves a brochure under her nose.

"So? Is this not *the* greatest? What do you think?"

"Sure, it's great. I'm getting tired but I'll think about it, I promise." The spell is broken and Jackie wants to leave. Now. Her head searches the room like a mechanical beacon, desperate to find the waiter and get the bill. Mike pulls a handful of coins and shredded lining from his pocket.

"No, please," she says, suddenly weak with pity. "I can write this off." But her desire to leave overrides any momentary sympathy. She hands the waiter her credit card and moves to the door to wait for the receipt. It's a small price to pay for tonight's production, a raconteur's trophy.

In the lobby, Mike has to trot to keep up with her. He puts a hot hand on her arm. "Say Jackie, I have a big favour to ask."

"You need a lift home, right? Where do you live?" *Anything to shake him.*

"I live in North Van but I'm late for another appointment in the West End."

"Even better, I'm going that way. I parked a couple of blocks from here." The night air blowing off the ocean is heavenly. Jackie inhales a lungful, soon to be rid of another loser in her landscape.

"Why didn't you use the valet parking?" he asks.

Like he uses it for his corporate Watkins deals! "Because when I drove in, the area was plugged with tour buses, that's why."

Mike doesn't say anything else until he's firmly buckled

into the passenger side of Jackie's Taurus. "Jackie? I've another little favour to ask."

"Uh huh," she answers, feeling less and less altruistic.

"I left the notebook I need for my next appointment on the kitchen table. My apartment's just over the Second Narrows and there's not much traffic —"

"Mike, be honest with yourself," and she turns to look into his face after starting the car. "Will it be earth-shattering if you don't have your notebook? I mean really catastrophic?"

He pauses, rubbing his hand back and forth across the dash, thinking hard. "Now that you mention it, absolutely."

"O-kay," she says. *And then it's over.*

Nearly. Simon the waiter trips on a forgotten briefcase and cracks his elbow on the edge of the table, moments before Mike realizes his briefcase is back in the hotel. And mere seconds before Jackie says to "get the hell out of my car and find your own ride home. And don't bother calling me again."

She leans back in her seat after hitting the play button on an old George Jones tape, with an urgency to hear the nasal twang of love gone wrong, of missing his sweet Tammy. She'll stop into the 7-Eleven on her corner to pick up a can of tuna-flavoured Pounce for Max. And to see if the latest *Bride's* is on the shelf yet.

Afterbirth

I only agreed to babysit their children because I couldn't believe such a tumble-down family lived this close to me. My tidy and predictable life was a parallel universe when placed alongside that of Eva and Joe Proskurniak.

My first emotion toward Eva was curiosity. She smoked thin cigars, kept her red hair long and unstyled (a contrast to my blond bobs), and drove herself to university classes in a noisy Volkswagon beetle. None of this was dramatic on the surface unless you compared her with the rest of the mothers on my suburban street, the patron saints of clean sheets and Swiss steak suppers.

It surprised me when Eva whistled from the back of the checkout line in Buy Low Foods, motioning with her head for me to wait. I leaned against the snake of shopping carts outside the store with my armful of bags. Even though she lived around the corner from me, fewer than a dozen homes away, she never offered more than "hi there" and "howya doing" when we crossed paths. We're near in age but our kids are a decade apart. And hers were all bused to a French immersion school which meant the chance of meeting at parent-teacher evenings or school functions was nonexistent.

By the time she pushed out her cart she had a cigar stuck in the side of her mouth. She clamped it between large stained teeth when she smiled, and forced me to put down my bags so she could pump my hand.

"Hey, Karen, you up for a little babysitting this Thursday night? I never planned to ask you but my regular sitter has become more interested in boys. And I'm desperate." She stopped to pull a couple of wooden matches from her pocket. For a moment her head disappeared in a cloud of smoke. "I've got an exam to write for my night course and no one else to ask. Lucky I spotted you."

Now if there's one thing I hate in this world more than cold sores and bridal showers, it's looking after kids. I love my own boy but overall, I don't care for children. I find them noisy and needy and generally annoying.

"Sure, love to, what time?" I heard myself say, when I could have said I'd be busy entertaining a Latvian exchange student, or vacuuming the dust balls from my refrigerator coil, anything. But like I said, I was curious. Plus, the family would make delicious fodder for my son who thrives on stories about the offbeat lives of others.

At the good news, her brown eyes opened wide and she leaned over to give me a hug. The smell of incense and unwashed wool tickled my nose. But this slight aura of uncleanliness added to her earthy appeal. While she rambled in a quiet monotone, about how she expected Joe to be home but he was putting on an exhibit at the museum, I daydreamed about what the inside of her place would look like.

The Proskurniak's home was built on the bank of a dried-up creek bed. Their gloomy ravine-of-a-yard and weary bungalow was known in the neighbourhood as "Halloween House." It did have a spooky quality, with its feeble exterior lights obscured by tree branches and unruly ivy. No manicured lawns and birdbaths here; it didn't look like Mr. P. owned a lawnmower. He was more the intellectual than the handyman, always unkempt and hurrying to the bus with a pipe in one hand and a tattered briefcase flapping against his leg. On several frosty days I offered him a ride but he shook his oversize head and said he "needed his space in the morning."

*

After two knocks on the door, Eva pushed past me.

"Have-fun-won't-be-long," she called out through another spit-shiny cigar.

"Wait, am I late?" I automatically looked at my watch. "I'm sure you said seven."

She stopped long enough at the bottom of the crumbling concrete stairs to give me a quick salute. "You're right on time, I'm the one who's late. Tonya can tell you everything you need to know. Thanks a million. Ciao."

When I turned around, three faces watched me from behind the screenless door. I held a folded sheet of paper with questions like who to call in case of an emergency, where she could be contacted, who had food allergies to what, and all sorts of responsible child-minding questions.

The children, from ages five to ten, each had Eva's huge brown eyes, the whites so white they looked blue tinged. Their heads of bushy dark hair, more like their father, glistened under the hallway light. I'd noticed the two girls riding their bikes for a couple of summers but with them living around the bend, they could have been in another world. Streets are like townships, each having its own personality and separate gang of children.

Tonya was the oldest girl, followed by Katya, and then little Ivan — who clutched a bedraggled piece of blanket to his chest.

My first impression of their home, besides the obvious decay both outside and in, was the faint smell of body oil and dirty socks mingled with stale smoke. After the three looked me over, they returned to their places at the kitchen nook to finish dinner. An extra place was set for me; a kind gesture, I thought, until I saw the menu of head cheese and thickly pre-buttered white bread. No one had touched the sliced tomato wilting in a saucer.

"Here," said Tonya, "Mom said you could use this again," and she pushed toward me a withered tea bag in an egg cup, long since left for dead.

"That's okay, I've already eaten." I wanted to join them, to get to know more about this mysterious family. Katya shoved over so I could sit beside her and I did, ignoring the painful spring digging into my haunch through the torn vinyl seat.

Ivan hadn't touched his glistening lump of room temperature head cheese, which I couldn't have choked down. "Do you want me to look for something else to eat?" I asked.

"No! Mom says he eats that or nothing, right Tonya?" Tonya nodded with a full mouth and I shrugged my shoulders "sorry" to Ivan, who didn't look bothered. He chewed his bread and played with a wooden truck on the table's edge.

Supper ended with a few dusty wafer cookies and a pitcher of red Kool-Aid. The children led me from the kitchen mess into a bedroom mess to show me their toys.

They were outgoing, friendly children and in spite of Mom and Dad's lack of housekeeping skills, they didn't seem to be suffering.

Next, they moved into the livingroom. It was in more disorder than the kitchen and bedroom combined. One wall was dwarfed by a picture of the Last Supper and the rest were draped with abstract wall hangings in reds and yellows. Treasures, everything from mildewed paperbacks to scavenged chunks of driftwood, were piled several feet high in all corners. I cleared a space on one of the two sofas, both heaped with clothing, and watched the girls dance for me in their Ukrainian costumes. Ivan sat cross-legged and played with his truck, still clutching his security rag. Feeling left out of the dance, he kept my attention by waving a tiny cut on his finger. I fussed over it, even though it looked like an old wound.

"I'd better get Ivan a bandage. Are they in the bathroom?" The girls nodded in unison but ignored me, dancing furiously to loud taped music.

At first I decided the kitchen was the worst room, with it's swarms of fruitflies hovering over uncovered food on the counter, all in various stages of decomposition. The black bananas were beyond banana bread, the bowl turning into a bubbling compost. The glassware, even the clean ones in crumb-filled cupboards, felt tacky. I used my own cupped hand to drink from the faucet when the children weren't looking.

But I was wrong. The bathroom was the trophy room. I would have welcomed cigar smoke instead of the sweet scent of overripe melons. Someone, I assume Eva, left a gumbo of bloodstained panties soaking in the sink. I knew that if I couldn't hold it, I'd have to squat over the toilet seat, not about to let my clean cheeks brush against any filth, seen or unseen.

When I knelt down to look under the sink for a box of

bandages, I came eye-level to a shelf lined with tampons and pads. Used tampons and pads. I stayed on my knees and stared for several seconds, trying to reason why anyone would save feminine products meant for landfill. Although each of the half dozen tampons was wrapped in a thin gauze of toilet paper, blood had soaked into a checkerboard of maroon and white. Next to that line-up, eight or nine bulky pads were stacked like jelly rolls into a deliberate pyramid. I closed the cupboard doors. Spurting blood from a major artery couldn't entice me to do any more snooping.

The balance of the evening was uneventful, ending quietly with bedtime stories. Although Ivan stayed in his own cot and furiously sucked a corner of his rag, Tonya and Katya insisted I stretch out between them on their sagging futon. The girls fought to hold my hands while I read. I craned my neck away from their dear but greasy scalps, which they kept grinding into my shoulders. While reading to them, all I could think about was getting home to tell Christian of the riches I'd discovered, the odours, the copious spoils.

Although I love my husband, I've developed a special rapport with my son, probably because he's inherited my freakish fascination for oddities. We're a couple of observers and eavesdroppers, so the stranger the better. The same story that evokes an "well now, is that right" from Jeff sends Christian to the ground with floor-pounding hysteria. Now I don't bother telling Jeff about my quirky encounters but wait for Christian. I already miss him. He'll move out soon with his girlfriend, leaving me to face long winters with Jeff and one tiresome war movie after another.

"Oh Mom, gross. Why would she keep them?" he moaned, fourteen at the time. "Why wouldn't she throw them out?"

"I-don't-know. And they were pretty fresh-looking. Maybe she's waiting to chuck them all at once. But that's not something you want to keep, with small kids poking around," I said while plugging in the kettle. "Tea? Raisin toast? How 'bout some nice bagels and cream ch —"

"Nooo! How can you think of eating, it makes me want to puke! Now when I see her I'll think of her big rotten jam rags!" I was about to say that "jam rags" was a horrible thing to call them, but it was an accurate description.

"And when does she plan to get rid of them, Chinese New Year?" He contorted his face and licked his lips like he was tasting spoiled milk. But he enjoyed every moment. (I hadn't even touched on the culinary delights from their dinner table.) "Go wash, don't touch me. Mother... don't!" He didn't like my fingers untangling his long bangs and slapped away my hand.

I was almost disappointed in my clever son, sure he'd ask if I got paid in blood money to which I would have said, "not a penny, like getting blood from a stone." But he sat mute at the kitchen table, still digesting that one.

Instead of being turned off, I wanted to go back. I felt there was more to discover, or at least Christian convinced me of the possibility.

It was almost a year before she asked me again, this time by phone. She explained in her no-nonsense manner that Joe moved out and because of their rocky patch, she hadn't called me sooner. And that she was back to using her maiden name of Zarrillo.

"Oh Eva, I'm sorry about that." I was sorry. The last time I passed her on the sidewalk she had been seriously pregnant, cheese-coloured but still puffing on a cigar. When she stopped to chat she immediately told me that baby number four was an accident. Some tidbits I prefer not hearing because like Christian, once I know, it will be the thought that lingers in my mind. Each time I see that child I'll think accident instead of cute baby.

"All for the best, we've grown apart. I should tell you, I've had my baby so I'll pay you this time."

"Congratulations," I heard myself say although her unwanted pregnancy combined with a separation couldn't be a party waiting to happen. "And don't even talk about money. It'll be my pleasure."

"I really appreciate it, Karen. My sister-in-law has been a godsend but she's busy tomorrow night. Remember that psych course I was taking?" She didn't pause long enough for me to answer. "We're having a little reunion at the Spaghetti Factory and I could use a break. Besides, Gino will probably sleep the entire evening."

Gino? I wanted to ask if she was going to move and what she was planning to do with herself but ended up asking polite questions about the baby's health and weight.

Nobody heard me knocking over the competing mix of wailing and high-pitched shrieks. After a few minutes I pushed the door open and walked in. That was the moment when my curiosity down-shifted into dread. When she said baby, she meant newborn — Gino was all of six days old. The moment I took off my jacket, Eva presented me with a red-faced bundle.

"It's just his circumcision, it's bleeding a bit tonight," she said while pulling an elastic around her hair. Eva didn't strike me as the type to opt for circumcision. Still swollen, she struggled into her winter coat. I stood in the doorway feeling ill-equipped for the job. Both girls stayed close by, wringing their hands each time Gino inhaled for his next pink-gummed howl.

"Mom, do you really have to leave?" Tonya asked, rubbing Gino's leg. He looked tiny in a green sleeper. "He's really crying hard. Can't you go out another night?"

I agreed. "Eva, it's been over a dozen years since I've had anything to do with babies. Maybe you should —"

"Not to worry, he'd fuss the same for me. There's a bottle ready for him on the kitchen counter. You'll be fine."

She left us, again without instruction and this time abandoning an unhappy baby as she disappeared into the night to drink Jell-O shooters. She was gone before I could give her my gift of Baby Gap overalls and two wee T-shirts. With Gino in one arm, I set it on the hallway table, a cheery gift bag dotted with yellow ducklings that contrasted Gino's pinched face. I felt sick, as green as his hand-me-down sleeper.

"Katya," I said, forcing myself to sound calm, "bring me the bottle and a dishcloth for my shoulder, okay dear?" Finding a clear spot on the sofa, I turned off the bright gooseneck lamp. All I could do was pray for Gino to fall asleep and stay that way until his mother returned. Damn her anyway. And damn my curiosity.

I squeezed a few drops from the bottle onto my wrist but couldn't tell if it was cool enough so squirted more out and without thinking, licked it off.

"Um," said Tonya, who pushed in beside me, "that's from my mom, she expressed it just before you came over." Somehow I knew she was going to say that. Too late. My tongue was coated.

After endless fussing and fighting with the bottle's nipple, the poor thing drank a little and started to settle. I rested him against my shoulder and gently patted his warm back. Something kept tickling my hair, swaying from the breeze of the heat register behind me. When Gino finally drifted off, I looked up and over my shoulder to see what dangled from the low curtain rod.

"Tonnn-ya?" I whispered, "what is this... this hanging

above me?" But I recognized that coiled thing, even in its shrivelled state. It was attached to the rod by a blue ribbon.

"It's Gino's umbilical cord," she whispered casually, as if all families hang their umbilical cords in windows to dry like English lavender. I inched away from it, careful not to wake the baby. I had already tasted Eva's breast milk; I didn't want any more to do with her internal workings.

Still whispering, I said, "Why did your mom keep it?"

"So she can bury it next to Baba. We're going to visit her grave next weekend."

Right. I stood up and took Gino to his parent's, now Eva's, dark bedroom. His arms jerked but he stayed asleep when I lowered him into the bassinet. The dust in their house made me feel grubby, ready for a soapy hand wash. And mouth rinse. This time I came prepared with a wad of paper towels in my purse, as well as a plastic cup.

I refused to open the bathroom cupboard again even though Christian insisted I nose around when he saw me pulling on my boots to leave. "Go for the medicine cabinet, Mom, you can tell tons from what people keep in them!" he called out as I shut the front door on the rest of his advice.

My only plan was to relieve myself without touching anything. But when I lifted the toilet seat with my slippered toe, the bowl was brimming with cloth diapers.

"Tonya? Katya?" I called in a low voice, careful not to wake the baby. I heard feet shuffling back and forth behind the closed door. "Do you have a toilet in the basement? This one's got poopy diapers in it."

"Nope. It's the only one. Mom said to pee on top of them, they're already dirty," said Katya.

I sighed and re-zipped my pants. I could wait.

"Mrs. Gladstone? We're hungry, can you give us something to eat?" she said through the door.

"Sure, but not too loud. I don't want your brother to wake up."

"Okay," and I heard her stocking feet pad away.

Before I could make it to the kitchen, Ivan met me in the hall and pulled my hand into the living room.

"I want to show you something on TV. Come on, it's my mom having Gino." Now this sounded interesting. Somebody, maybe daddy? must have videotaped Eva in the hospital. The two girls were already positioned in front of the screen.

"Back up girls, it's hard on your eyes if you sit so close," I said, *and Mrs. Gladstone can't see any of the juicy stuff with you blocking the picture.*

But it wasn't the sterile walls of the hospital I expected: no stirrups, no beeping monitors, no scrubbed nurses in face masks. Instead, I recognized the benign face of Christ and his disciples along with the cluttered couch, now partly draped in a sheet. Eva reclined, panting, wearing only a man's shirt unbuttoned over her bulging belly. I heard Joe explain to the camera he was massaging her vulva so it would be less likely to tear. Before I could get a good look, my eyes moved to the two girls who sat hugging their knees, hypnotized by the re-enactment.

"Are you sure it's all right with your mom to watch this?" I said over Eva's voice, her outbursts growing louder in the background audio.

"Why not?" Tonya said. "We were there for the whole thing. And now that we've seen it a bunch of times, it's no big deal." As she spoke, the person wielding the camera panned the room. In addition to the parents and a midwife, the other couch and chairs were filled with several women, the three Proskurniak children, and a boy of fifteen or sixteen. Although I recognized pure terror in the faces of the children, the teenage boy looked slightly too interested, the camera catching him reading a comic book while he stole glances of Eva's open thighs.

I didn't know what to say but before I had the chance, Katya informed me that her mom's water was about to break. The midwife helped her stand and the camera zoomed on her legs and the floor. Her water didn't break. It exploded. It looked like someone off stage threw a bucketful against her feet.

Joe sweated profusely and strands of hair started to mat against his forehead. He talked nonstop, either to calm Eva or himself. Stockier than I remembered, he crouched awkwardly at her side like a bullmastiff. Looking ready for some serious labour, he helped her into a squatting position over the edge of the couch.

"How are you kids doing?" I asked. "Are you sure this isn't too upsetting? It's pretty... real."

"We're fine," said Tonya fiercely chewing a thumbnail while her mom pushed, groaning and grunting, crying out, "I'm splitting in two, oh-my-God-oh-my-God, make it stop!"

When the baby's head crowned, the camera did another pan: both girls were covering their eyes although the teenage boy had moved to a closer vantage point. One of the adult women must have left the room with Ivan.

I never did see who was doing the filming but when the baby finally squeezed into Joe's waiting arms amid gasps of excitement from the adults, the camera did a final spot check of the room. Tonya slumped, her eyes with that characteristic roll split seconds before a vomit, and Katya buried her face in the sweater sleeve of a woman who stroked her head and murmured into her ear. Only the teenage boy raced in for a better look, snapping pictures with his own camera while Eva lay spent, her legs spread wide and her big dark nipples exposed. The midwife, after checking on the baby's breathing, handed mother her child, with the too-familiar umbilical cord stretched across her stomach. I heard Joe's voice in the background repeating, "it's a miracle, truly a miracle."

Besides a healthy baby, which was a blessing, the things I focussed on were the creepy wet dreams of the teenage boy, and how the little girls would avoid an erect penis until middle age after seeing those sights.

The present room was silent. "Well, that was amazing, and what a beautiful baby brother you have. Your mom's doing great, too. How about turning off the video and I'll get you something to eat." When I stood up and headed to the kitchen, my knees wobbled. The birth process wasn't foreign to me but this one was from an entirely different perspective. When my own water broke, one bath towel between my legs was enough to staunch the flow. At the hospital, I refused to look in the overhead mirror when Christian made his appearance. And then I didn't invite the entire neighbourhood to watch me bearing down in a pool of my own assorted waters.

But witnessing the gritty details with young children, noticeably affected by their mother's distress, diminished the intended splendour of creation; instead, I thought of my own son watching and it felt pornographic. Just too much of a leap from Nintendo and chemistry sets and tropical fish. I relaxed when I heard the theme song from *Jeopardy* blaring.

My son was wrong — it's not the medicine cabinet that divulges personalities but the refrigerator. It was almost bare except for two mismatched casserole dishes, most likely gifts. I never thought to bring food and felt a twinge of guilt, although I didn't expect to find such a new baby. And who did the circumcision? Did someone come to their home?

The empty fridge was forgivable with all the chaos of a home birth. But I figured Joe might have taken the time to do a major shopping, after his film debut and before his departure. Sadness for this family washed over me as I continued to scan the shelves. There were plenty of evil-looking condiments but little snack-worthy to appease young children.

Katya wandered in and stood behind me. I lifted the plastic wrap from a bowl of grape jelly and poked at it with my finger. The surface had a layer of rubbery purple, soft as moleskin.

"You kids better get eating up this jelly before it goes bad," I said, which started Katya screaming with laughter.

"What... what did I say?"

"That's not jelly," she said with a scream through her fingers, "that's my mom's placenta."

I slammed the door, not bothering to re-cover the bowl or to ask why her mother kept it. What I did ask was if they all liked pizza because I was about to order three large pies, enough for them to eat over the next few days. The mention of pizza brought the other two sliding into the kitchen, taking their minds off baby Gino and mother's dilating cervix.

"Can we get Coke, too?"

"Nooo, I want Sprite, you've got to get Sprite" another whined.

"Shh shh, we'll get plenty of both," I said while three sets of arms hugged and patted my legs.

Although I left instructions to enter quietly, the delivery driver banged on the door. Gino started crying. He also forgot to bring the Sprite at which Katya began weeping along with Gino. With trying to serve pizza from one arm and Gino fussing in the other, I smelled my own body odour wafting through my collar, that nervous smell no amount of deodorant can hide. While the heated pot of water made Gino's milk too hot (they needed a microwave, not a VCR), I heard the children giggling together about a teacher's hairdo in school. They seemed happy, despite their unique home life. What do I know? I've never taken a university course; I don't even like making love with the lights on.

Cradling the baby, I laughed with them, not about their teacher but about how I would explain this to my own son. While Tonya used animated movements to describe Monsieur Gautron's ferret face, my mind raced to conjure up ways to best describe the evening. Christian wouldn't be disappointed.

Soon after my last meeting with them, Eva and her four children packed their driftwood and their Last Supper and moved away. We never found out what happened to Joe but Christian heard from a neighbour that Eva moved the kids back to her hometown of Calgary. Apparently the Mennonite Brethren Church on the adjoining lot made them a good offer soon after Joe took flight. The place was demolished and the creek backfilled to streetlevel.

The spot that once housed Eva's cherished belongings — her innards and her garish tapestries and her home birth memories — is now gone. If she ever returns, she'll find its transformation into parking stalls for churchgoers in Honda Civics and Aerostar Minivans.

Still, whenever I drive by groups of children in knee highs and tweed school uniforms, I search the faces for Eva's girls. I won't find them, I know. They've been gone for years but I'm curious, about what partners they'll eventually choose, about what they'll keep in their own refrigerators. I long to know what sort of freedom they will grow up and seek.

Scissor Man

I'm getting too old for this, she thinks, a band of panic tightening her stomach when she remembers it isn't her bed. In her own bed, she'd be wrapped in a quilt and able to look up at a row of ragged stuffed animals perched along the headboard.

The need to flee helps pull open her eyes. She lifts the spread and rolls out with surgical precision, not the first time she's done this. She never planned to stay, to actually share sleep with the man, but somewhere between two and three must have closed her eyes and dozed. She dreamed of her family, a pretty dream dappled with gold and yellow, but woven with an indefinable evil. The dream where she thrashes in her sleep and awakens on a sweat-soaked pillow, where she can't put a finger on what was terrifying since there aren't any visible axe murderers or shrinking tunnels or black-eyed aliens. She doesn't have time to think about it now.

By the colour of the light slivering through his hotel room blinds, she knows before looking at her watch that it's close to six, her favourite time. No matter how tired or hung over, she always manages to wake herself and enjoy the ephemeral quiet of a new day, a slate wiped clean at some unseen point in the night. Soon the downtown streets will fill with slaves — coifed office workers, shower-fresh financiers, bike couriers with rips in their Kevlar — all scurrying like beetles to be on time for meaningless appointments, dogs fighting over the same bone. She will never be a prisoner, she tells herself, but wonders if she has become one: she pays hydro bills, she gets her teeth cleaned, she bears similar needs and responsibilities. Lately, the only difference is a looser schedule.

The man snarks in his sleep and turns over, dragging the blanket that covered her moments earlier. He twirls into a pale cocoon. She stops pulling at the leg of her tights and watches him, his appearance much different without rose-coloured lounge lighting and the shroud of vodka martinis. In natural light he's a good decade older than she expected. His once-clean hair is now tugged to the edge of the pillow where gray patches of scalp give him a sickbed frailty. His double chin is pleated like the bellows of a concertina and she knows that if she takes a closer look, his nose will carry the spidery tattoos of dedicated drinking. How many people travel on business with their own silver wine glass? She tried getting that thrown in last night, merely for the challenge of it, but he wouldn't budge. Probably can't remember his kids' birthdays but he stroked the stem of that goblet like a lover.

The lump of money in her pocket doesn't make her feel much better but, if she has to confess, relief ranks high on the list. To remember finer details over the shadowy ache in her temples, she presses her eyes. When she smells Aramis cologne on her palms, she quickly drops her arms and searches for her shirt and boots.

I took off my clothes and I danced around for him, that's all, she thinks with an urgency, a need to recall and confirm that what she's done isn't too hideous. Liquor is her conduit. She could never do these things without it. *Did I touch him? I hope I didn't touch him. I remember him kissing me, god-awful sloppy kisses, and running a ragged nail up and down my thigh, but he was pissed. I'm sure he fell asleep before —*

"Dolly May, come back to bed, it's early," he says with a hoarse kindness, a tone reserved for wives and real lovers.

She makes a last minute scan of the beige-on-ocher room and pats for sunglasses inside her shoulder bag. "I have to go, I'm already late. It's been fun," she whispers, praying he'll fall back to sleep before getting an identifiable look at her in the daylight. His name is Cam, no Keith... no, Cameron.

"But how can I reach you again?" she hears as the door clicks locked behind her, muffling his words. She takes the stairs on the chance he'll follow her to the elevator draped in his thin blanket, like the guy at the Georgian Court. Better not risk it.

Why do I know that dream? She holds out a five for a tall Americano at Starbucks. She makes a point of tipping the girl a dollar and will continue tipping people throughout the day, the absolution she'll seek for the three hundred dollars she extracted from a married stranger. He said separated but the wedding band he turned when he wasn't cradling his silver goblet, and the anger management book "for couples" pushed under a *Globe and Mail* said otherwise.

It was Easter, we were all sitting down for dinner. She bounces in the backseat of the cab and makes sure she tips the pony-tailed driver more than he deserves, even forgiving his smoking under a "Thanks For Not Smoking" sticker on the pitted visor. At least he is silent.

The hot bath, as hot as she can stand it, makes her feel outwardly clean. The heat is soothing but her mind fights to erase the tableaux darting across her closed eyes: the man from last night throwing back his head and laughing, exposing a blackened side tooth that made him seem unkempt, vulnerable; her adjusting the hotel room radio to an old Jimi Hendrix tune; him keeping his hand over a spot on his belly to camouflage a hernia bulge; the bloated sneer of lust consuming his face (him thinking he looked sexy when she hated him at that moment, enough to slit his throat and watch his draining blood envelop the plastic-wrapped mattress); the Scissor Man. *That's it! That's the dream,* and she mashes her eyelids together to better capture the picture.

Except it isn't a dream, it happens when she is almost eleven. They are settling into their Easter lunch when the doorbell rings. Her mom follows Dolly to the door where they find a mangy man with an equally tattered bag slung over his shoulder. He looks like a little troll bent under the weight.

"Good day, ladies. Sorry to interrupt your dinner (he has already craned his neck inside with a clear view of the table, of Dad and Jeremy who sit with cutlery poised) but I was wondering if you have any scissors or knives that need sharpening." His hand, a sickly shade of tallow, trembles when he adjusts his canvas bag. Now she'd wonder if he carries a chainsaw and a severed head but back then, she figures he's a hobo forced to drag along his belongings.

"I'm afraid we were just sitting down to dinner so this isn't a very good time —"

"No trouble, good ladies, enjoy your celebration and I'll be off. Some other time." They return to their seats but a guilty hush replaces the lighthearted atmosphere. Before Dolly can take her first mouthful of ham spiked with cloves or glazed yam drenched in butter, her mom is gone, hurrying out the front door. She whistles at the man, loud enough to stop him in his tracks as he makes his way to the next driveway. Not a delicate exhalation through pursed lips from this slender lady in her gingham apron, but a cab-calling blast through her thumb and index finger, a sturdiness straight from the farm.

But not sturdy enough to save me from Dad.

At the last thought, Dolly's stomach roils and contracts. She lurches up from the tub but doesn't make it to the opening, getting more on the toilet than inside. She stays there, kneeling in her own sick and bathwater, resting her head on the seat. When she opens her eyes and looks out through crossed arms, her legs are frog-like, gaunt from too little food and exercise, and too much drinking.

"That's when it started," she mumbles out loud, the sound more gargle than voice. She hates her dad for cheating her out of a childhood — as if little girls are interested in sex — and for damaging her in ways she doesn't know how to repair. She wouldn't date until she turned eighteen and then it couldn't really be called dating, what she did. It was a furious exchange of body fluids, a self-inflicted torture test with no winners. Forget about remembering first and last names; she can't even remember complete faces, only interchangeable pieces like Mr. Potato Head: big nose, hairy back, nice aftershave, nasal voice, scuffed cowboy boots, polished loafers, skinny fingers. After last night she'll add hernia bulge to the roster.

Worse, she hates her mom more for not seeing it. How could she live in the same 1200 square feet and not see it? not hear it? not feel it? It dripped from the walls and pooled against the baseboards, the weight of it measurable in ounces, its duration endless as a magician's trick scarf. At his funeral she wept for herself and for the father she wanted, not the dusted monster in a satin-lined box. The same person caring enough to give Scissor Man warm gloves and several packs of cigarettes after dinner, the same monster capable of haunting his eighty-five-pound daughter on Mother's bowling night.

Convinced she is a victim — she watches *Oprah* — not a horrible person despite her horrible habits, she can't bring herself to confront her mom. It's been too long and what if she honestly didn't suspect anything? She couldn't have, she wouldn't have let it go on. Dolly May can't bear the thought of adding more guilt to her own tally of regrets.

The years of hiding from herself have been wearying, leaving her unable to sustain relationships or amount to any caliber of career beyond dead-end jobs. Her heart has become veneers of tamped down hurts, a substratum of dirt layered from different ages. She feels a membrane, like plastic wrap, starting at the back of her teeth and stretching tight over her head, Ziploc-ed at her feet. She's no longer a person, she's a laminate.

Click-bang, what a hang, your daddy just shot poor me.

A nap revives her and after paying the balance on her rent, Dolly May adjusts her Walkman and heads out for groceries. Never too late, never too late to pull herself together. Instead of taking the short route over concrete sidewalks past cookie cutter stripmalls, she zigzags through back lanes until reaching an empty field. Dragging her runners through dandelions and overgrown vines, she squints at the rough ground, loving the dusty perfume she stirs in the flattened grass. There's nothing in her world but singers singing about being born under a bad sign and if they didn't have real bad luck, they wouldn't have any luck at all. She listens, knowing the words are written for her, and maybe half the screwed up world including her lonely travelling salesman with his self-help book.

She doesn't see the dog and trips, landing on her knees to keep from crushing it.

"Jesus!" She yanks out the earphones and surveys the heel of her hand. "Sorry, I didn't see him, is he okay?" She stops worrying about her scraped hand when she notices the fresh gash on his back, shaved in a rectangle down to the red wound.

A woman built like a box bends over and gives her white terrier a quick inspection. "No damage done. I should have his leash on but this is the only place he can be free, at least as free as his old body lets him." Mannish glasses have slipped to the end of her nose.

"Why did he run into me?" Dolly May stays on her knees and gently strokes the soft fur on his head, thinning like an old man's. She rubs her fingertips across his baby-pink hide.

"He's blind and deaf, he's almost fifteen." She says this quickly as if annoyed by the delay. Over the rim of her glasses she stares across the open field. Dolly May ignores her, concerned for a helpless animal, drawn to him as she is to every stray and limping creature. She's a magnet for birds with broken wings and cats squashed by hit-and-run drivers. Once she almost got slammed when she kamikazied into a busy intersection to rescue a dog. One moment she was on the sidewalk minding her own business, and the next she was walled in by screeching breaks and the harsh stink of melting rubber. Her arms wrapped around the dog's neck as she prepared to die for forty pounds of mange-covered fur.

"He doesn't look old, except for his bald spots. What happened to his back, poor baby." The terrier is enjoying the attention and raises his head, panting rotten hot breath in her face, old breath over old teeth.

"We went camping and left him with friends who have a big Doberman. Everything went fine until the night before we came home. I guess the Doberman got jealous 'cause he bit into McDuff and shook him like a rag doll, so my friend says." Her tone is deadpan.

"Don't you feel awful? I mean, guilty for leaving him there?" She doesn't intend it as an insult but expected more emotion.

"What can I do? Things happen, you go on. He's managed to live this long, haven't you, Mick?" The woman looks at a distant spot in the field, ready to gather her survivor dog and continue on. The dog is oblivious to his injury, contentedly sniffing the air and grinding his hairless bum into the grass to scratch a flea.

"I guess if you don't realize you're hurt," Dolly May says, "life is pretty easy." The women shrugs and starts walking. *But my wounds are invisible. How do I heal something I can't touch?*

A flashback of last night scurries across her mind's eye: the man is stretched across the bed, nuzzling her big toe with his mouth while she sits opposite him, naked except for her panties. The look on his face is pure pleasure, thinking it makes her laugh when all she really wants to do is scream and slug him in his hernia bubble. But it's his dime and she keeps grinning, flirting like she's been waiting all her life for this.

She can drink enough to blackout memory but it doesn't let her off the hook completely, pelting back in bits, tagging her before diving into its deep hole. When

Dolly May allows herself some post-liquor indulgence, she imagines her heart as Swiss-cheesed. She walks quicker now, not noticing the fragrant air or the gentle breeze across her cheek. Instead, she feels the familiar finger of bile tickling the base of her throat. She won't do it, she refuses to let herself fall apart in a public place with baby strollers rolling past on the sidewalk, pushed by young women blazing with auras of motherhood.

"You're a good girl, you'll grow into a lovely woman, you will," Grandma says, her words brushed with a hint of Irish, soothing. Decades later she can still remember her voice and the slippery feel of her polyester housecoats covering withered pancakes-for-breasts. She can see the wrestling match on the TV angled in the corner of her cramped suite, the picture always flipping and Dolly May wondering how she could stand it.

Not doing so great now, Grandma, for a good girl.

"Never too late, darlin', you'll always be my good girl." Waiting for the wave to pass on a bus stop bench, her head tucked close to her knees, Dolly May knows she's making it up. Her grandmother has been dead for a million years and maybe never said anything like that, but the softness of her smiling face is beautiful. She did have Aero bars and big purple plums waiting when Dolly May visited, that she's not making up. Dolly May keeps her eyes closed tight, shutting out the sunlight and the people scuffing their feet along the sidewalk. She doesn't care who sees her. She's not going anywhere until she can wrench free of herself, until she can figure out something.

She waits, she gets hotter and thirstier in the late afternoon sun but no monumental realization appears, no discovery, not even a pint-sized genie. By now she's too tired to brave the after-work crowd in the checkout lines. She can order Greek from the corner restaurant on her street.

She decides not to pick up her usual chicken but will eat there, surrounded by hanging rugs and tapestry pillows. She will slip off her runners and feel the rough floor tiles under her feet. The Greek music will be loud, loud enough to drown out her own thoughts so she can concentrate on other diners — what they eat, what they wear, the body language between men and women. Hell, she can afford to order a half carafe of their house white, providing her stomach doesn't object. It's her turn to be catered to and the servers will be predictably kind.

Hungry, the cool breeze from the overhead air-conditioning vent makes her shiver. While she waits for her meal, she runs her hands up and down her bare arms for warmth. As she starts to chuckle quietly, George deposits a steaming plate under her nose.

"Laughing into your Demestica again, eh? What did I interrupt *you* in the middle of, anyone special?" He stops to look at her and cocks his head to one side, a benevolent gesture.

"Nothing, George. I was just thinking about a silly thing on *Letterman* last night. This smells fabulous."

"It *is* fabulous, it's *always* fabulous." George spreads his arms into an expansive arc. "It's your little bit of heaven direct from the Aegean. One meal and you're hooked."

"Like heroin," she says. George gives her an okay-you're-the-customer shrug and bids her good feasting.

Dolly May returns to her thought, the one before the waiter appeared. She wasn't laughing at a *Letterman* episode (didn't watch TV; chose to perform a wobbly striptease) but at how it was her own ragged fingernail pestering her last night, not her date's.

The souvlaki *is* heavenly, charbroiled with just the right amount of garlic and lemon juice. She berates others for eating flesh but her one secret passion, never consumed unless by herself, is poultry. *How can you eat something that had parents?* she'll say, especially to fleeting friends like Cameron. But here she is tearing through crispy chicken skin, ignoring the juices that roll down her chin.

It happens while she watches the table across the aisle, while she dips her roast potato into the saucer of tzatziki. The memory comes fast because it's quite simple, and harmless. Here the monumental insight her mind searched for since dawn is nothing more than a trigger.

It happens when the man across the aisle pulls out nail clippers from his pocket and snips the dangling price tag from a new pair of sunglasses. It's then she recalls the key that unlocks the Scissor Man: in her blurred state last night she remembers an open manicure kit on the hotel table, the little leather travel-size with scissors, clippers, tweezers, and a metal emery board cum cuticle pusher. One of those practical gifts a wife gives her husband for a Christmas stocking-stuffer. Nothing more, nothing less, just a glimpse of shiny scissors that fluttered in her memory, a piece of thread caught against a spider web.

Dolly May sets down her fork, letting the sensation of relief stroke the length of her spine. She sways her neck from side to side. That's all it is, a reminder that branched to an old incident. A beautiful incident after all, when her family was still normal, and still charitable to people less fortunate. Somehow her mind dragged it through the scum, connecting it with her dad and the painful year she endured. Her salvation was his lathered collapse in the shower from a brain aneurysm. Dolly May will forever think of it as retribution, convinced it was the work of her guilt-free prayers. After all, his death delivered her from murderous fantasies, sometimes suicidal, back into the splendid realm of what to wear to a school dance and whether Alfresco Brick lipstick is a shade too orange against her rosy complexion and how she can make enough babysitting money to afford her own Princess bedroom phone. His death delivered back her free will. It's still waiting for her to notice.

Dolly May deals out such a generous tip for George that she leaves the restaurant before he can find it tucked under her empty baklava plate; he'd put on a performance about accepting it while trying to shove change back into her hand. But Dolly May justifies it as cheap therapy that she wouldn't have found in her airless apartment.

The sky, when the sun finishes setting, will be beautiful, a cloudless blue-black and full of stars. Even after a huge meal she feels weightless. She wants to run and skip and does for half a block until her stomach slows her down with a string of hearty garlic burps.

Tonight she'll stay awake, she'll camp out on her east-facing balcony and wait for the sunrise. Tonight she can stop chasing her memories. For a change, she'll let them find her. Standing at the corner of her street, the pungent smell from a wood-burning fireplace makes her smile and weep into her handful of restaurant napkins.

Wings

It isn't a case of falling out of love with him, but falling
into dislike. While deadheading the delphiniums, she tries
to recall an actual day. It was close to the same time her
fourteen-year-old daughter told her she was "totally not
cool." The signs, sliding into her awareness, were subtle.
No blow-ups and rages (except on Melissa's part, which
isn't shocking at her age. Poor kid is a churning hot pot of
hormones), and no discovery of romantic trysts between
Harold and any of the women at work, despite the ongoing
talk. Even when his horoscope read: *A co-worker initiates
flirtation. This lends spice but you could be asking for
more than you can handle. Passing notes is not advisable,*
Laine still didn't worry. The horoscope that really got her
thinking was her own: *Refuse to be discouraged by your*

partner who knows the price of everything and the value of nothing. The time has come to spread your wings. That was the moment when it happened.

Laine decides to get the spray bottle of diluted dish soap after discovering the aphids are back. Her knees click when she stands. She makes a mental note to turn the compost pile after she drenches the aphids.

Correction. It was the day after that one, when she felt bored and evil, frustrated and unappreciated from top to bottom. With no one taking an interest in her, she stopped painting her toes shades of chilled apricot and sun-kissed coral; she stopped doing waist bends and leg lifts; she eventually stopped shaving her legs and began wearing the same pair of Sears catalogue sweats like military issue. And just what she feared, Harold didn't complain, not a word, not one "Lainey? how come you never wear those nice dresses anymore? You have a good figure, you shouldn't hide it." Instead, he asks if she made peach pie for dessert and how come she didn't remember to pick up his fan belt and can she use more detergent in the wash because the towels haven't had that fresh smell lately. *A far cry from when I was pregnant, she thinks, when he'd hurry home smelling of sawdust to feast on my swollen body.*

She had plenty of chores waiting but she couldn't get moving on that day last month. Instead of bringing in the laundry from the line or finding a simple cookie recipe to batch for Melissa's school bake sale, she read the classifieds from end to end.

She even opened a bottle of Harold's homemade red wine at 1:15 in the afternoon and filled one of her crystal goblets to the brim. She usually saved them for store-bought liquor, to serve Harold's city friends. But the thought of driving to the hotel and running into any of a dozen locals convinced her to put up with the cheap wine heartburn. A buzz is a buzz. If she no longer liked her husband (or if he no longer wanted her; she was bouncing that one back and forth) and if her daughter no longer worshiped the ground she walked on, she might as well take off the rest of the day and get pissed.

Harold does it every weekend. What makes it acceptable for him is that he stares at uniformed men in frenzied states of running, throwing, tackling, kicking, or shooting slapshots. As long as there's a 26" colour screen and some totem of male potency to fight over — a ball or a puck — this endless season of competition washed down with gallons of skunky homebrew isn't merely forgivable, it's a national pastime.

"Why don't they bat around a couple of freeze-dried testicles already," she'd mutter to herself while refilling the popcorn bowl and emptying full ashtrays.

While Harold taps his tube-socked feet on the ripped ottoman surrounded by several buddies from the mill, Laine is expected to wait on their needs and wrap up the afternoon of boisterous hollering with a meat and potato supper.

But her mind won't stay on one subject at a time anymore. She returns from the shed and soaks the leaves of her peppers with sudsy water. "Out, damn aphid," she says loudly to nobody, because it feels good. She moves next to the current bush but decides to give up the battle, impressed with how the ants have claimed every second berry. An all-powerful shared mind keeps them working toward the same goal. She follows the trail of fast-moving insects, winding like thin ribbon under the branches to their rounded hill. From her height, it's impossible to tell who's leading whom. It's more like a continuous loop of organized activity.

It isn't her age, she figures, but the stage she's fallen into. "Forget fame and fortune," she mutters, muttering becoming another characteristic of her present stage. "Just give me some god-damn fun!"

Her stab at freedom started innocently enough, over her pretzels and bitter wine at the kitchen counter, when she created an ad to sell her husband. "It's his own fault!" she said to her reflection in the kettle. "He's the one who wants me to look for another used dryer."

Her ad read: *For sale — one middle-aged husband with his own power tools. Tools hardly used; husband seen better days.* And then, since she wasn't actually paying for the word count, she expanded her categories. *Will trade for one-way ticket to anywhere hot: forty-plus mill worker, non-drinker (except on weekends, statutory holidays, and during the* X Files*),hard worker (for low wages), and great lover (except on weekends, statutory holidays, and during the* X Files*).*

By her second glass of wine she not only muttered but giggled out loud while scribbling onto a pad of paper. *Free to good home: half Ukrainian half Irish. Loves hot borscht, hard liquor, and hand jobs. Housebroken (although still dribbles down the toilet bowl), comes with his own papers (mortgage and truck loan), is good with children, and needs plenty of room to roam. Fifty dollars O.B.O.* Okay, so he is a decent father.

"Wait, wait," she said to herself, as if some part of her might wander towards the stove and start the cookies, the part with the pen in her hand. *Found: balding man with hanging belly and lazy left eye, answers to Harold. Owner must reimburse for vasectomy and two speeding tickets. Call to identify.*

The next ad was her second last. *Lost: all future hopes and dreams, not ready to give up yet.* Laine put down the pen and stared at the blue lines of the paper. A finger of bone-wearying sadness tunnelled into her solar plexus but she dodged it and started to write again: *Independent lady enjoys gardening, slow-dancing, and dining by candlelight. Wants to meet open-minded man for afternoon delight. Send phone # c/o this paper.* She added the word "employed" as well as an age range when she had a flash of buying lunch and new shoes for a pitifully broke university student, or a middle management schmuck recently downsized out of a job. She started to scratch out independent to write in SWF but except for being female, she isn't single and she doesn't care what colour skin this classified man has as long as he shares the same interests. Quite a stretch from Harold who still says "Chink food," "look at that darkie run," and "for a fag, he's not half bad." Laine does her best to coast into the year 2000 with computer courses and AIDS fundraisers while her husband is still plodding into the early '70s. He was once more promising; now, more and more he reminds her of Archie Bunker.

When she met Harold, both in their late teens, she was fearless. Stupid but fearless. Smoking and snorting whatever was offered, speaking her mind like she was the gatekeeper of divine wisdom, and accepting rides home with drunk drivers were all typical weekend activities. Having sex possessed a fierce power over her. She could be angry, sad, or stoned but it held the same urgency. The mood and the partner didn't matter as much as the being wanted.

But that fearless thinking changed the day Melissa clawed her way into the world. Less clawing, with more popping and tearing. (Out of the entire birthing process, Harold was most astonished by the fact it took fourteen tea towels to clean up her water from the kitchen floor. "*How* can a body hold so much liquid?" he kept saying, even in the delivery room. "Good bloody thing you weren't sitting in the new truck!") After the birth, after a glimpse of the baby's translucent skin and delicate blue flutter of blood along her temple that made Laine's throat tighten, she knew she couldn't go back, as much as she told everyone that motherhood wouldn't change her a smidgen. But after, for example, she couldn't enjoy a motorcycle ride with her brother. Visions of an accident followed by a brightly-lit intensive care unit haunted her. Or images of being wheeled over in her spinal halo and deposited in front of the TV for afternoons of Ricki Lake danced through her brain while the wind whipped her face. Maybe more of a breeze than a whipping since Jake never went over sixty clicks, with her clutching his slim waist in a death grip. He stopped inviting her for leisurely rides after admitting it was too tough to manoeuver the winding country roads with her perched ramrod-straight on the back. In one sense it was a relief when he stopped asking but in another, she knew it meant the forfeit of her courage, of the old Laine.

Even though being a host to anything — tapeworms, lice, Super Bowl — makes her shudder, Laine has to give credit to the aphids. The green of their succulent bodies perfectly match the leaves they devour. Their job is witless, without annoying emotions to cloud their existence. The only requirements are a little egg-laying and a good set of mandibles.

"My problem is I think too much. Harold says it and Melissa would say it except she's too busy calling me a retard under her breath." She keeps pinching aphids while she talks to the plants and then gives up, deciding to pay some attention to the compost pile. The sun is moving westward at an alarming rate and she hasn't accomplished a third of what she intended.

With a spade, she assaults the rotting foliage and cantaloupe rinds until perspiration trickles down her neck. And then with no real thought or melodrama, she digs into the side pocket of her sweatpants and pulls out a piece of creased paper. She tosses it into the warm earth and covers it with several shovels of dirt.

Laine hears the squeaking door of Melissa's school bus which starts her thinking about dinner, reminding her that she forgot to go to town for ground beef. "Never mind, I can thaw some meat pies. They like those." She heads toward the backdoor and arrives at the same moment as Melissa and a girlfriend.

"Hi sweetheart, how was school?" She leans over to kiss her daughter's forehead but isn't quick enough. Melissa ducks and escapes her mother while reaching for the door knob. "Oh sorry, kissing isn't very cool, is it? I forgot."

Even angled, she can see the blush moving across Melissa's cheeks, maybe embarrassment because her friend is witness, or maybe regret because she knows her mother would surrender her own life for hers, and here she shuns a simple kiss. *Probably embarrassment*, Laine thinks, still trying to accept that her baby is spreading her wings.

"Mom? Can Jennifer stay for dinner? And Mom?" she asks before Laine has a chance to answer the first request, "can you make me a costume for next week 'cause we're having a Medieval Day party and we're supposed to —"

Laine doesn't hear the rest of the question, she's too busy thinking how sad that Melissa inherited her father's lantern jaw. At least she got her big hazel eyes and straight nose, Laine's best features. She feels her lips pull into a smile.

"... and can you make us some of those little Pillsbury cinnamon buns before dinner? We're starving!"

Laine's head nods even though she's sure there isn't any more pre-made dough in the freezer, except for a roll of wiener wraps. Still smiling, she heads back to the compost pile, continuing to memorize the fresh face of her daughter.

She has to dig for several minutes before she can find

it but then her spade tears through the sheet of embossed paper. He must have answered her ad while at work because he used company stationary. *Braver than me. I wouldn't want a stranger knowing where I work.* Luckily, the moist earth hasn't smeared his phone number. The spade has sheared his signature in half.

She shakes the loose dirt off the paper and wipes it against her leg. Laine carefully re-folds it back into a small square and shoves it deep in her pocket. She feels the fog lifting, the cloud that keeps her sleepwalking through the motions of caring for everyone but herself.

Before she looks for any dough, before she starts on the one millionth dinner for her family, and before she washes off the sweet fragrance of flowers and soil mingled with her own skin, she walks to the calendar on the refrigerator. Crouching, she squints at her schedule to see what day she has free next week to make a quick trip to the city.

Body Parts

When I asked my grandmother to tell us about her grizzliest moment as a nurse, she couldn't come up with one story. She came up with three and would have kept going all night.

"The first one that comes to mind," she said with a thoughtful expression like she's pulling pages from the family album, "was the cyst taken out of a woman, a real nice gal in her forties. After surgery the doctor instructed me to open it up and examine the thing, big as a Spanish onion." She stopped to take a deep drag of her cigarette and pick at a pilled spot on her sweater sleeve. It was all part of the hand ballet combined with story telling she loved to administer, healing for the mind versus the body. To me it was brain candy, a blend of too much and not enough every time she dispensed a dose.

"Grandma, pu-lease, I'm still eating!" Nancy said.

I couldn't stand the suspense but my sister was three years older and played it cool, pretending she wasn't interested. Or that she was above such inappropriate table talk.

"No you're not, you've been pushing around that same forkful of Apple Betty for the last ten minutes. Leave if you're so dang squeamish, it's a free country."

I loved my Grandma, the latticework of creases in old skin matching her pachyderm strength. She spoke her mind in ways I've rarely experienced since. None of this smile in your face but then talk bad behind your back nonsense. I've run across a couple of women strong enough to be comfortable with themselves and their beliefs but nobody has been able to take her place, not even come close.

With Grandma, you knew where you stood. If she said, "you looked beautiful," you believed it, and if your hair was curling-ironed too high she let you know and you went back to the bathroom mirror for adjustments. Even Nancy listened, for all of her protesting.

Voracious, Grandma couldn't get her fill of people's stories, appreciating how she could collect a little treasure from everyone she met. To me, her wisdom was vast considering her insight came from observation more than experience.

Nancy stayed, of course, but did flash the heavens a dual head and eyeball roll, once to the right and then to the left. Her lips shrank to a scowl, already stiff and opinionated at eighteen. A beautiful open face contrasted a closed mind, preparing the way for two failed marriages.

"Keep going, Grandma, don't listen to her. What about

the cyst?" I was afraid Mom would interrupt by calling me to help lift Dad from the tub. Or start the dishes.

"When I cut it open, it was filled with a gray lard —"

"Stop, that's disgusting. Grandma, you're making me barf." Nancy's objection again, not mine.

"Wait, it gets better." She ignored Nancy and looked at me, aware that I enjoyed the sensation of saliva squirting into my cheeks, both repulsed and intrigued by atrocities the body commits on itself. Odd stories still fuel me like a shot of vitamin B. Maybe a little less now.

"Coiled through this gritty-feeling goo was a hank of long black hair (her fingers are suspended in a strumming motion) and buried in this... ready girls?" Her head doesn't move but her eyes glide back and forth between ours, with the right amount of pause. "Two molars, girls, two perfectly white teeth covered with this dirty gray grease." At that, Nancy pushed back her chair with a bang against the antique sideboard. She strode heavily out of the dining room, the cabinet's good china rattling in her wake, and into the living room to turn on the TV.

"What a wimp."

"Never mind her, she doesn't appreciate my old nursing stories. Cripes, she faints at the sight of a squashed mosquito."

Me, on the other hand, to conjure up a good picture I need descriptive colours and textures. Don't tell me someone's skin is pale, tell me it's pale as a dead fish floating belly-up; don't let their hair be a generic drab, but make it a long drink of dirty water drab. Grandma rarely disappointed me.

I wasn't satisfied, not yet. "What did you do with it, after you examined it?"

"I don't know, I guess I chucked it out. What was I supposed to do, gift-wrap and hand it to the poor lady?"

She chortled at her own sick vision right into a sputtering cough. Another drag on the cigarette quieted her.

"If it was me, I'd want to see what was growing inside my body."

"You would, you reject," Nancy yelled, out of sight but continuing to eavesdrop from the living room. Grandma flapped her hand in an "ignore her" motion.

"What else, Grandma?" My pump was primed and ready for more. She rested her elbow on the table and held up her chin with her thumb, the index finger positioned under her nose. Her other hand gracefully balanced the smoldering cigarette, a striking elegance. The way she looked at that moment is the image I use when I need to remember her.

Her smoking career began when ads pushed cigarettes as a wholesome habit. She never managed to conquer the addiction, not even after seeing damaged lungs like dirty sponges and patients smothering from lung cancer. And smoking didn't kill her, a bus carrying fifty tourists did.

"Now which was worse... okay, the leg one," she thought out loud. "Didn't I tell you this one before? the leg one? I'm almost positive I did."

"No, I'm positive you didn't."

"If you say so. It's not that terribly gory but it gives me the creeps just thinking about it..."

"*What?*" I figured she was trying to stretch it out for the full shock effect.

"It was a lady I knew from high school, a Mrs. Mortimer... no, Mrs. McDonald, I always mix them up. She was in her late thirties, like me at the time, and developed serious complications with the circulation in her legs. She was diabetic, did I say that? Anyway, one leg had rotted, gone real gangrenous, and had to be cut off below the hip. (At this point I imagined Nancy's head cocking to one side, to hear better over *The Beverly*

Hillbillies laugh track.) With modern-day medicine they could have done more but back then, hacking away body parts was often the only way to keep you alive... I'm going off track. Like I said, it wasn't so gory as it was pitiful. Not only did I assist in the surgery but I ended up carrying her leg to the incinerator."

"In your bare arms?" called out Nancy, "with the toes sticking out for everybody to see?"

"No, silly, it was wrapped but I felt awful, hauling off a part of my old friend and tossing her away like a piece of bad meat."

"Ew, gross!"

"I thought you didn't want to hear this," she called over her shoulder and then looked back at me, the brave one. "It was gross, heartbreaking, and I still think of it whenever I see an amputee." I wanted to ask if the lady died but Grandma looked contemplative, as if she stopped speaking to me but was remembering out loud.

I wonder if Grandma passed any of those body parts while travelling through the ether, if she saw those disconnected teeth and hair and limbs in limbo when the bus hit her and sent her flying, knocking the life out of her.

I heard, or perhaps made it up in my teenage grief, that her shoes hit the ground after her body. Why is it people's shoes fall off when they faint or smash up their cars? Do the feet contract at the moment of trauma? I once rubbernecked an accident at the corner of our street. There was nothing in the twisted pile except one sandal wedged under the gas pedal and the other in the backseat, what was left of it. It gave the scene such a personal touch. I've noticed that same lone shoe next to assorted highway carnage on the six o'clock news. Now as a nurse myself, I see strings of shoeless patients wheeled into Emergency. Unless cut off by paramedics, pants and dresses and jewels are intact. Sometimes purses are still slung over shoulders and baseball caps stuck on heads but the feet are generally sock-covered or bare. Those pictures stay with me like the leg story to Grandma.

Silence. *We're now ready for our descent, ladies and gentleman. On behalf of the staff and crew I'd like to thank you for flying Air Grandma —*

"And the third isn't sad because the young man lived and went on to have a couple of kids. I know because one of the nurses started going with him when he got better. It was the middle of the night and although most patients are asleep, we never had a spare moment with getting meds and basins ready for the morning shift. And of course we always did our rounds. I walked into one room and did a double take." She stopped momentarily to make sure she had my full attention; I opened my eyes wide to keep the momentum going. "Here the poor fellow was hanging half out of bed, with one hand and leg on the floor and his other knee caught in the twisted sheets. His cheek was at the edge of the bed and out of his open mouth hung a beet-red tube of congealed blood the thickness of his throat, all the way down to the floor."

That was enough to bring on a group groan, even from me. "No way, Grandma, you're making it up now," I said. A touch of doubt always helped her part with more detail.

"My dear girl," she began, raising her penciled eyebrows and stabbing her cigarette into the swan-shaped ashtray. "Given reality like that, why would I bother to make it up? The fellow was unconscious so with my fingers I dug that red rope out of his airway before he suffocated. His lips were already a shade blue. I don't recall much after that except for a few minutes of pandemonium on the ward. It was a long time ago." She picked up her cigarette pack but tossed it onto the cut-work tablecloth when she remembered it was empty.

"I never admitted it to anyone but I felt like I was drawn

to his room." She turned from elegant to gypsy, needing only a crystal ball under her blue-veined hands to complete the illusion. "For some reason I skipped over three or four in my path to go into his room first. Like divine providence... ach, listen to me, maybe just good luck for the fellow. I sure hope his kids didn't grow up to be child molesters or I might not be so proud of myself."

"Don't dismiss it like that, Grandma," I said. "He might be alive today only because of your sixth sense."

Nancy snorted. "You and your intuition, everything ESP and paranormal. Why can't you accept that the guy lucked out? Period," she said, deciding to rejoin us at the table. I didn't bother to argue, mainly because her credibility plummeted several notches that afternoon when I discovered a copy of *Tiger Beat* stashed under her school books, an issue dedicated to the Monkees. This from the same Nancy who showed off by quoting snippets of Tolstoy and Dylan Thomas. Nancy loved to bicker, you'd say white, she'd yell black. Our definition of a good time was as diametrically opposite as sisters could get.

Grandma knew I wouldn't waste my energy arguing and I knew Grandma was spiritual even if she didn't make a point of discussing it. She hadn't gone to church since my grandfather died but she had more moral fibre than anyone.

"Hey, this will make you laugh, Susie. For all I didn't mind giving people enemas or changing their dirty bedpans, heck, I didn't even mind washing their sweet petooties, but how I hated to touch their false teeth."

I choked, sending a piece of unchewed apple sailing past her. "False teeth? Whadya mean?" In the framework of hospital gore, the category of dentures hardly made it onto the charts.

"Well cripes, digging out false teeth from old turtle mouths and picking at the smelly gunk before shoving them back in... yuch, even thinking about it makes me squirm. And you stop smacking your lips, you little monster." She leaned over and aimed her fork at my neck, threatening, which made me laugh even harder. I found her Achilles' heel and my mind reeled with future gag gifts. Good thing she kept every one of her own teeth, strong but stained a nicotine yellow after smoking more years than I've been alive.

"You two are warped. Change the subject?"

"What would you rather talk about, Nanc," I said in a butter-soft voice, "Davy Jones? or maybe Peter Tork?"

She blanched like I'd caught her in the act of inspecting her privates with a hand mirror, an embarrassing moment that once happened when she thought she was alone in the house. Now she let out an angry hiss and again left the table, slamming her bedroom door and noisily hooking the lock she installed herself.

Nancy kept me locked out most of her life, despite my earnest attempts to get closer. I cajoled her into being my matron of honour even though she didn't involve me in any of her weddings. I tried to confide in her when my short-lived marriage lost its steam, explaining how I didn't have anything left over for my husband after caring for patients all day. Nancy always listened and nodded at the right moments but if I didn't keep in touch, there'd be no contact even though we lived fifteen minutes apart.

That changed. I heard the phone while unbolting the backdoor with an armful of groceries. The last person I expected was Nancy. Her voice sounded strained and I experienced a shudder of pleasure — for once she needed me, calling to say her newest relationship had fallen apart, or her government contract didn't get renewed, or maybe her apartment needed fumigation and could she stay for a few days.

"What's wrong? You sound weird like you've been crying."

"Did I get you at a bad time?" *She was never this polite.*

"No, I just walked in the door. Like I said, what's wrong?"

"I've got it, Susie."

"What have you got, cockroaches? herpes?" The stupid words tumbled out before I could stop them, and me a nurse.

"The big C, I've got it."

"Cancer? Are you sure?"

"Yup. I've had the mammograms, the biopsy, all the tests, even a second opinion."

"But now they can operate with a wonderful success rate and if giving up a breast or uterus means —"

"Too late to give up anything. It's already metastasized to my lungs, from my breasts."

"That's impossible (but I was scared when I heard metastasized, the word too big coming from a woman who worked for Revenue Canada), there would have been lumps, there would have been signs before this."

Nancy said nothing for a few seconds, a lifetime. "There were. I told myself they were cysts like half the women at work get and then worry themselves sick for nothing. I'm so smart, hey Sue? I fucking knew everything."

She'd already worked through denial and was into anger by the time she involved me. I felt bad, sad, helpless, and bitterly cheated. It took me only seconds to make the next move and Nancy surprised me by agreeing. Of course, that's why she called, she needed me for the first time.

I took a leave of absence from my job and moved in with her, even before Nancy required permanent help. Too much time had been squandered and I wasn't going to miss a tear or anecdote or sigh if my life depended on it. It wasn't long before her life depended on me. Even though I have great respect for hospital care and most of the health profession, I agreed she should be at home for as long as possible.

Remember how I said diametrically opposite? We were different in almost every way. While I made a career of dealing with sickness and injury, she was phobic of anything inserted, lanced, and especially removed. She didn't talk about it but her actions gave her away, like refusing to go to the hospital when she fell face-first down a toboggan slide and ripped a patch of flesh from her chin. She chose a ragged scar over a couple of stitches. And like the time I thought she'd curl up and die from a bladder infection instead of seeing a doctor. When I threatened to call an ambulance she took off and stayed away most of the night, showing up the next morning with cheeks the colour of flour and water.

Where was our mother through all of this and why didn't she gather her daughters in her arms and take care of them? More than caught, she was submerged in the mire of Dad's Huntington's. Unless we stood severed and dripping onto her kitchen linoleum, we didn't get much sympathy.

When I was fifteen and begging to stay home from school, she yanked the covers off and pulled me out of bed by the ponytail. "I can't deal with another sick person in this house, you get going!" An hour later the principal phoned after someone found me shivering in the washroom — I had viral hepatitis.

In the car ride home from the doctor's, she tried to apologize, her eyes red-rimmed and watery while she gripped the wheel, white-knuckled at ten and two positions. It made me feel worse, guilty for getting sick. I tried my best to act normal but my body turned traitor with the whites of my eyes yellowing like Grandma's teeth. And I disturbed her many nights with my moaning, wanting to peel back my skin and scratch the vague itch meandering through my bloodstream.

Grandma, who lived with us, was a saviour during our teenage years. Although she felt awful about her son-in-law, she kept better perspective and reminded Mom there were two young girls much alive and needing attention. Since Mom's best wasn't good enough, Grandma stopped harping and took us under her own wing. It was probably because of Grandma that I chose the path to nursing. I feel good about helping people; you have to if you plan to keep your wits among sickness without letting it suck the life out of you.

I helped Nancy turn on her side, her sharp hip bones extruding like a *Schindler's List* survivor. Except I knew my sister wouldn't survive — so I did my best to keep everything lighthearted, like I had nothing better to do than stick my finger up her backside.

Not a sound, until it's finished and she's tucked under tight sheets with hospital corners.

"How can you do that? It amazes me. Here you're on a first name basis with my asshole and I can't even wash anyone's hair."

"You could, you don't give yourself enough credit."

Then we began to talk about dreams and feelings, like normal sisters. She was the one who had to start since I'd done my fair share long before her cancer. We developed a lifeboat mentality knowing each sunrise might be the last. I hung on her every word while trying to act casual.

"You think this is bad? This is a cakewalk." Nancy flashed her famous you're-a-sicko look but I kept talking. "Remember when I got my first job out of school? in the senior's home? Since I was low nurse on the totem poll, I got stuck cleaning up after every one of those old people. The nurse who did the disimpacting, Christ, I figured she was the lucky one. That Christmas we made her a plaque that said Golden Glove Award and gave her a box of rubber gloves with all the index fingers cut off."

I thought Nancy was crying but she was holding her concave stomach with sputters of laughter. "Stop, it hurts... Susie? You sound exactly like Grandma." She didn't speak for several minutes while I rubbed lotion on her arms. "She always loved you more."

I stopped and tightly held her hand. "What are you talking about? Is that why you always seemed angry with us?"

"No seeming, I *was* angry. Mom was too wrapped up with Dad or her bottle of cognac when I needed her, and Grandma and you had your own private club."

"Grandma loved us both," I said, leaving Mom out of it, having already come to terms with her mothering skills that rated three on a good day.

"I know she loved us both but she loved you more. Her eyes lit up when you walked in the room. And she talked to you, really talked."

"We had the same sense of humour, and maybe a little more in common, that's all."

"Yeah, you're both warped!" I sat on the edge of her bed, now so big compared to her shrinking body. With neither needing to make the first move, we hugged and wept into each other's shoulders, both for what was about to end and for what we found in the process.

She used to think there wasn't any rush in getting to know me better, that it would happen on its own at some point. That was before getting sick. Why does it take tragedy to bring people together and force them into honesty? Nursing aside, I've gone to more funerals than weddings. I'm bloody tired of running out of sunrises.

While cleaning out Nancy's bedside table, I found an envelope with my name written in green felt pen and outlined with a puffy heart. Inside was a homemade card, intentionally left for me to find. She had drawn a musical scale with words underneath:

To Susie —

On a scale of 1 to 10, you're an 11! I guess I had to lose you before I could find you.

Love always, your sister.

Sitting on her stripped bed, I was surprised how I could still turn on the waterworks. No matter how much time there is to prepare, no matter how much warning, you always feel swindled.

I was a wreck after Nancy's celebration of life where all my friends from work showed up with their kind nurse faces, the faces they reserve for people they know. Putting the card in the zippered compartment of my purse to keep it safe, I flipped through the last of her mail before driving to the hospital.

Even after being away for many months I didn't miss it, surprisingly. As a matter of fact, I made the decision on the spot to hang up my own golden gloves and felt a huge relief, almost bigger than the relief of Nancy letting go, her dry fingers slowly relaxing in mine. I could be brave for Nancy, for Grandma, and most of all, brave for me. I could move on now.

I planned to see the administrator and give her my decision but first I headed to the maternity ward. After all the sickness and dying I had to look at new babies and watch grandparents being introduced to fresh grandchildren. Shaky fathers would stand by, beaming proudly. Most of all, I needed to see exhausted but thrilled mothers padding through the ward in new housecoats and slippers, thoughtful gifts from the same families who arrived carrying flower arrangements in blue or pink ceramic baby shoes.

Nancy was born in this ward, me too, and I wanted to look through Grandma's eyes since I would never experience it first hand, with Dad's genes and all.

For a long time I leaned against the glass window and watched the newborns. Amazing, that these small bundles could demand so much attention. I watched them sleeping, squalling, and simply being until my throat tightened. Remembering the card, I touched the side of my purse and decided to stay a little longer.

Are you the next New Muse Award Winner?

Are you a writer without a first short fiction collection or novel published? The annual New Muse Manuscript Award is looking for book-length short fiction manuscripts. The annual New Muse Award winning author will have their winning manuscript published by Broken Jaw Press.

New Muse Award winners
1998 Shannon Friesen, *Like Minds* (fiction)
1997 kath macLean, *for a cappuccino on Bloor* (poetry)
1996 Robin Hannah, *gift of screws* (poetry)
1995 Tom Schmidt, *The Best Lack All* (poetry)
1994 p.j. flaming, *voir dire* (poetry)

Guidelines
• Entrants must not have published a first fiction collection or novel (UNESCO minimum of 48 pages literary content). Individual stories may have been published in magazines, anthologies and chapbooks.
• Short fiction manuscripts of 100-140 pages, double-spaced, typed on 8½ x 11 or A4 letter-size paper. Manuscript title and page number must appear on every page. Author name and address is not to appear on the manuscript. No simultaneous manuscript submissions please. Manuscript must be available on disc in an acceptable format.
• Include author name, address, phone numbers, manuscript title, and a literary bio note on a separate sheet of paper.
• $20 Canadian/USA or £10 entry fee. Cheque or money orders payable to Broken Jaw Press only. No cash, please.
• Manuscripts will be returned if accompanied by sufficient Canadian postage or International Postal Reply Coupons (IRCs). Or, enclose a #10 letter-sized Self-Addressed Envelope with Canadian postage (no USA stamps) or an IRC to receive pre-publication notification of the winner.
• Judging is at the discretion of Broken Jaw Press, the premier literary imprint of Maritimes Arts Projects Productions.
• All entrants will receive a copy of that year's winning book upon publication.
• Annual deadline: postmarked 28 February.

NEW MUSE AWARD
BOX 596 STN A
FREDERICTON NB E3B 5A6
CANADA

A Selection of Our Titles in Print

96 Tears (in my jeans) (Vaughan)	0-921411-65-0	3.95
Best Lack All, The (Schmidt)	0-921411-37-5	12.95
Coils of the Yamuna (Weier)	0-921411-59-6	14.95
Cover Makes a Set (Blades)	0-919957-60-9	8.95
Cranmer (Hawkes)	0-921411-66-9	4.95
Crossroads Cant (Grace, Seabrook, Shafiq, Shin, Blades (ed.))	0-921411-48-0	13.95
Dark Seasons (Trakl; Skelton (trans.))	0-921411-22-7	10.95
for a cappuccino on Bloor (MacLean)	0-921411-74-X	13.95
Gift of Screws (Hannah)	0-921411-56-1	12.95
Heaven of Small Moments (Cooper)	0-921411-79-0	12.95
Herbarium of Souls (Tasić)	0-921411-72-3	14.95
I Hope It Don't Rain Tonight (Igloliorti)	0-921411-57-X	11.95
In the Dark—Poets & Publishing (Blades)	0-921411-62-6	9.95
Invisible Accordion, An (Footman (ed.))	0-921411-38-3	14.95
Like Minds (Friesen)	0-921411-81-2	14.95
Lad from Brantford, A (Richards)	0-921411-25-1	11.95
Longing At Least Is Constant (Payne)	0-921411-68-5	12.95
Notes on drowning (mclennan)	0-921411-75-8	13.95
Open 24 Hours (Burke; Reid; Niskala; Blades, mclennan)	0-921411-64-2	13.95
Poems from the Blue Horizon (mclennan)	0-921411-34-0	3.95
Poems for Little Cataraqui (Folsom)	0-921411-28-6	10.95
Milton Acorn Reading from *More Poems for People*. (Acorn)	0-921411-63-4	9.95
Rant (Fowler-Ferguson)	0-921411-58-8	4.95
Rum River (Fraser)	0-921411-61-8	16.95
Seeing the World with One Eye (Gates)	0-921411-69-3	12.95
Speak! (Larwill; *et al*)	0-921411-45-6	13.95
St Valentine's Day (Footman)	0-921411-45-6	13.95
Strong Winds (Hyland (ed.))	0-921411-60-X	14.95
There are No Limits to How Far the Traveller Can Go (Gates)	0-921411-54-5	4.95
Under the Watchful Eye (Deahl)	0-921411-30-8	11.95
Voir Dire (Flaming)	0-921411-26-X	11.95

Available from **General Distribution Services**, 325 Humber College Blvd, Toronto ON M9W 7C3: Toronto, ph (416) 213-1919, fax (416) 213-1917; Ont/Que 1-800-387-0141; Atlantic/Western Canada 1-800-387-0172; USA 1-800-805-1083. Sales representation by the Literary Press Group of Canada, www.lpg.ca ph 416-483-1321. Direct from the publisher, individual orders must be prepaid. Add $2 shipping for one book ($9.95 and up) and $1 per additional item. Canadian orders must add 7% GST/HST.

MARITIMES ARTS PROJECTS PRODUCTIONS
BOX 506 STN A
FREDERICTON NB E3B 5A6   Ph/fax: 506 454-5127
CANADA   E-mail: jblades@nbnet.nb.ca

CU00872342

STRANGE CORRIDORS

MARK SLADE

ILLUSTRATED BY
CAMERON HAMPTON

FOR TRACEY, ZOEY, CHACHI, AND OF COURSE FOR BETTY JANE AND GIZ. I MISS YOU BOTH. TO MARY AND TIM FOR HELPING OUT WHENEVER IT'S NEED (SEEMS MORE FREQUENTLY THESE DAYS).

THANK YOU CAMERON HAMPTON FOR CREATING ART FOR MY PROJECTS.

Strange Corridors

Written by Mark Slade

Illustrated by Cameron Hampton

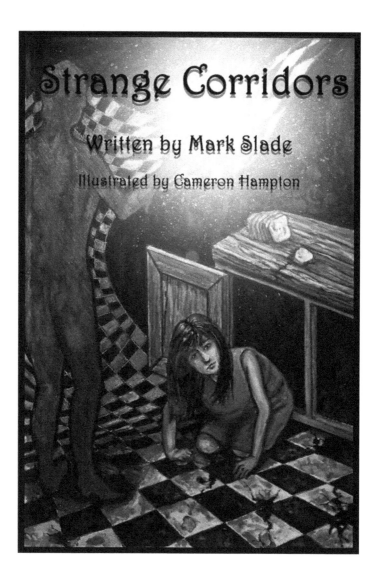

EMMA HEARD THEM FIGHTING. Then it was very quiet.

She knew what type of night it was going to be after her stepsister, Lydia, brought her home from a long weekend at her place. When no one answered the front door, Lydia just turned the doorknob. No one had bothered to lock it. Stepping over several empty wine bottles and cushions lying on the floor, Lydia sighed and angrily closed the door.

"Stay here," she told Emma, and walked away, calling Emma's mother and Jack, the new stepfather. Lydia went into their bedroom, closed that door. Emma heard angry muffled voices.

Emma secretly wanted to live with Lydia and her boyfriend Tom. They were nice, well-behaved, and their apartment didn't always smell like rotten eggs. They ate out at restaurants. They watched TV, and they would take walks in the park. Tom would get his camera and have Lydia and Emma play dress up.

Emma fixed the cushions back on the couch and sat down. She took a book out of her back pack. A Wrinkle in Time was handed to her by Mrs. Gordon. "I think you will like this," Mrs. Gordon told Emma with a huge smile. She was a very nice teacher, but didn't really have much control over her class. Emma's classmates were very rowdy, and most of them almost never completed their work. Lunch and playground time meant more to them than any boring school work. Of course, as Lydia had pointed out. Mrs. Gordon was very old. Lydia had her when she was in the fifth grade.

"Why doesn't she retire?" Emma had asked once.

"I'm pretty sure Mrs. Gordon can't afford to retire," Lydia answered.

She began reading silently to herself, still mouthing each word carefully to make sure she understood the sentences. That's what Mrs. Gordon told her to do whenever she read anything. Get a feel for the words, roll them around her tongue, and take a second to make sure she understood what she had just read. Emma didn't always like doing that because classmates sometimes made comments that her lips moved when she was reading. One girl even said that when a person reads like that, that means they are slow.

Emma didn't know what that meant. She didn't think that she moved slowly. She was always aware that she didn't move fast either, that she moved somewhere in the middle. Normal. At least she hoped she was normal. Because she knew her parents were not normal. Her real father died two years ago in a truck driving accident. That's what she heard the adults say. She knew he had been a truck driver, he delivered a lot of different things, and he drove all over the place. When he died, most of the money went to his new wife and new family. Some of it went to Emma and Lydia. He was Lydia's father as well, even though he hadn't been married to Lydia's mother.

Emma had come to the conclusion that her family was more than a little odd and very confusing. There were brothers older than her she'd never met, and an endless stream of cousins, aunts and uncles, and two or three (maybe) of grandparents she'd never met as well.

Lydia came out of the bedroom, walking very fast. She looked upset. Emma could always tell when her sister was upset because Lydia curled her upper lip and her nostrils would flare.

"What's wrong?" Emma asked, dropping her book on the couch and rising quickly. She placed herself in front of Lydia so she would not ignore her.

"Emma," Lydia said sternly. "You should go to your room. It's past eight o' clock and soon it will be bedtime."

"What's wrong, Lydia?" Emma screamed. Lydia just stared at her. "I'm not moving out of your way until you tell me!"

Lydia grunted and rolled her eyes. "Okay! Mom and Jack were fighting. Both are drunk...the fight is over with. Mom was in the closet when I walked in. Jack...he was trying to pry the door open with a broom and it broke. The idiot fell on his back...so once again he's thrown his back out. I was talking to them afterwards and they both lay on their bed and passed out in each other's arms. There you have it, kid. The newest scoop on your very dysfunctional parents."

Emma began to tear up. "I wish I could live with you......" She hugged Lydia tightly.

"God," Lydia struggled, pretended not breathe. "What a grip you have. Well," she pulled away from Emma. "Looks like it's for the best that you do stay with me and Jack for the rest of the week."

Emma squealed and did a little dance.

"Okay, okay," Lydia laughed, tugged Emma's sweater. "Get your back pack, girl. Tom is going to have to drop you off at school this week. He's on vacation and I have classes early every day this week. Come on. Let's get going before they wake up, start crying and apologize for everything under the sun, including JFK's assassination and Hitler."

Emma ran and grabbed her back pack and book. Lydia opened the front door and both of them went out.

"Who's Hitler and what's a JFK?" Emma sked.

"Never mind," Lydia sighed and rolled her eyes. She eased the door shut, as not to wake either of the two sick people in the bedroom.

———

Emma woke up that night and heard the saddest song she'd ever heard.

It wasn't exactly a song, nor was it singing. More like a wailing. Reminded Emma of the video her class watched about whales and how they called out for their mates. That's what it sounded like. Anyways, someone was very sad. It echoed throughout the apartment.

At first, Emma thought her Mother's boyfriend had left the TV on again. She rose from her bed and tip-toed into the living room. No one was up. Still, that song was ringing in her head. She went to the kitchen to see if her mother was up. Maybe she was cooking late at night and listening to the radio, Emma thought. Her mother sometimes did that.

No. No one was up.

Suddenly she heard footsteps. Her mother's bedroom door opened and her mother appeared from the dark hallway. She asked Emma why she was up and did she know what time it was? Emma shook her head. Emma tried to explain that she had heard a song. Well, not exactly a song---

"You were sleepwalking", is what her mother told her.

Emma knew she had not been not sleepwalking. She tried to for a valid argument, but mother wasn't having it. She sent Emma back to bed, and told her not to get back up unless the sun was up.

Emma went back to her room. She lay in bed, listening to that sad song.

———

A few weeks later, Lydia dropped a bombshell.

She and Jack were moving. Jack got a promotion, but in order to get that promotion, they had to leave. Emma was very upset. Sure, her mom and Tom were normal again, and had been for two weeks. Still, that could change at any time. Who knows if they could stop drinking long enough for Emma to grow up and get out of the house?

Who knows even if they stayed together, and it were just Emma and her mom back at Aunt Shirley's house once again. That situation was not much better. Emma and her mom slept on a couch and there were already six people in that house, including four grown-up cousins. Emma never felt comfortable taking a shower there. She couldn't put her finger on it, she felt weird at Aunt Shirley's.

Emma spent one last night with Lydia. She helped her pack while Jack was off, getting a moving truck. They cried a lot. Lydia tried hard to convince Emma everything would be okay, and mom and Tom wouldn't be sick all the time.

"Yes, they will," Emma said, wiped tears from cheeks. "They drink too much and they will never get better."

Lydia couldn't argue with that. She hugged her little sister and kissed her head. "Still," Lydia rubbed Emma's back. "You have to be hopeful. Not just for your sake, but for the sake of their health."

Emma nodded. She understood that. "I still want to go with you and Jack," she sobbed.

"I know honey," Lydia whispered.

———

Emma heard the gossip at school.

Paul Butterling had gone missing. His mother said she went to work on Sunday evening. Paul was left home by himself with instructions not to open the door for anyone or any reason, nor to go outside. Not even to take the dog outside. She told him she would be home by eight that evening. When she came home at eight-fifteen, Paul was gone. The TV was still blaring cartoons and the microwave door had been left open and a plate of pizza rolls untouched.

Some said that creepy old man that lives behind Klosky's department store had climbed through an open window and stolen him. Others said Paul's father came to the apartment and convinced Paul to leave with him, not caring to tell his mother. Emma overheard one girl had said the police had questioned the father and he didn't know where Paul was.

Emma didn't know what to think. She didn't have many friends at school and usually ate her lunch by herself.

Emma tried to tell her parents but they wouldn't listen. They were too tired, they said. It was two in the afternoon on a Saturday and Emma's mother was supposed to be at her job as a cashier at the department store. Tom had been to work. He did nights as a porter at the hospital. He had already passed out when Emma began talking. Her mother shooed her out of the bedroom. When Emma complained she was hungry, her mother told her to make some toast.

Later, the phone rang.

It was Lydia. Emma was so excited she squealed and Tom screamed for her to shut up. She told Lydia about Paul Butterling. "He just disappeared, without a trace." Emma heard a man on TV say that.

"I'm sure they'll find him," Lydia said.

Emma went on to tell her all the rumors. The latest was that a traveling freak show came to town and snatched Paul.

They forced him to wait hand and foot on all the freaks, even cleaning up after the Monkey boy who crapped everywhere.

Lydia laughed. "Where did you hear that word? Crap?" She laughed again. Emma loved hearing her sister's laugh. She sounded like a parrot squawking.

"It seems everyone on the playground has their own theory," Emma said.

"So what's your theory?" Lydia asked, curious to know what her sister's thoughts were on the matter.

At first, Emma was at a loss for words. No one had ever asked what she thought about anything. Most adults just patted her on the head and never listened. Well, except Lydia. Emma's mother never paid attention to her unless to bark a specific order. Her mother's boyfriend, Tom, never even acknowledged Emma's existence, only referring to her as "the kid", whenever he wanted to be alone with Emma's mother.

"I..." Emma began, cautiously. "I think.... he ran away."

"Is that so?" Lydia steered Emma along.

"Yes," Emma said solemnly in a very grave tone. "I think Paul Butterling opened the front door of his apartment, walked outside and never looked back. Not caring if anyone cared where he went."

"Where do you think he ended up at?"

Emma thought some more. She sighed and answered: "He's still here.... but everyone refuses to see him."

———

Emma couldn't sleep that night.

She awoke with a very dry throat. She made her way to the kitchen to get a glass of water. She noticed the cabinet door slightly jarred. A stream of light had petered out and shone on the tiled floor. Emma was caught off guard, nearly dropped her glass. That cabinet was where canned foods were usually kept. That is, if her parents remembered to buy any food at all. This last bout with the bottle had taken a terrible toll on their minds as well as their bodies. Emma's mother and her boyfriend Tom, didn't even remember to bring in the mail.

The door swung open slowly and the stream of light widened. Emma took a step or two back. A black gloved hand appeared out of the light grasping a Marotte or scepter, a staff, with a shiny crystal ball on top. Then a strange figure followed, just showing the front half of his body. The stranger wriggled out of the cramped cabinet and crawled on to the counter where the dingy microwave sat near the kitchen sink. He was dressed as jester, only his outfit was mostly black lace and black leather pants. The black lace covered most of his chest, but not his forearms, which were littered with many tattoos of skulls, dragons, and Chinese writing. He wore a mask that resembled what people wore at Mardi Gras. Emma had seen a photo of the celebration and felt a little frightened. Why did they need to wear masks? What were they hiding? She would often ask the grownups around her, but no one could ever satisfy her with an answer.

"Don't be frightened,' the stranger said. "Let me introduce myself." He took a bow. "I am Giraud, master entertainer and guide extraordinaire...."

Emma was too frightened to speak. She nearly burst in tears, but held them back. Her lips trembled, and her widened eyes produced a ring of water at the bottom.

"Speak child," Giraud said, adding much needed sugar to his slithering words. "There's no need to be afraid. I assure you."

He spun in a circle, his closed fist extended in air. He spun again, tapped his scepter twice on the floor. He brought his fist down slowly and revealed a dove sitting perfectly in the palm of his hand. He smiled hugely as he brought it closer to

Emma's face. He folded his hand over the dove and tapped the scepter twice more. Giraud opened his hand to reveal a chocolate bar, which he offered to Emma, and she reluctantly took.

She did, however, show a hint of interest if not a bit of awe at Giraud's conjuring.

"Now, my beauty.... what is your name?" He said as syrupy as he could, and still bearing all of teeth the way an alligator shows its prey.

"Emma," she said, quietly.

"Oh! I love that name!" Giraud exclaimed and spun around once more, taking a knee along with another bow. "M'lady's name has such an alluring ring to it." He announced.

Emma peeled away the wrapping paper from the chocolate and nervously took a bite.

"Could this be your home, Emma?" Giraud took short strides into the living room, examining the bottles and clothing littering the floor.

Emma shook her head. "No," she whispered hoarsely. "Belongs to a neighbor, Mr. Suskind. My parents pay him to live here."

He stopped and watched the television screen of several large men and women sitting around a long table discussing the state of the world. He pointed at the glowing box and quietly chuckled. He gave Emma a salacious smile. "If they only knew," he said with a grievous brow entering his face forehead.

"I have to be serious with you for a bit, my little Emma," Giraud motioned for her to come him as he sat on the arm of the sofa. Slowly, Emma stepped toward him, finishing off the chocolate bar. Giraud smiled at her again, staring into her face. He touched her stiff shoulder with a hand. He spoke deliberately, choosing each word carefully. "You don't really like living here, do you?"

Emma shrugged. She didn't know this Giraud at all. Why should she tell him such intimate things? By the way, why was he here? How in the world did he get in our cabinets, with it being such a cramped area? Most importantly, what in the world did he want?

"Ohhh, dear darling. I shall answer all of those questions in good time," he said. "Just as soon as you answer my question. Do you like living here with your mother and her boyfriend...and the fact that they do not pay attention to you? They are always .... sick? Why...I bet you have not had a home-cooked meal in weeks!"

"Yes, I have! We had hot dogs the other day!" Emma interjected. She was fuming now. How dare he suggest they were terrible parents!

"I did no such thing, my dear darling. You did."

"I didn't say anything."

"Ohhh," Giraud wagged a finger. "Yes, you did....you just didn't use your mouth. Can I tell you a secret?"

Emma nodded cautiously.

"I can hear your thoughts."

Emma looked at him incredulously. "No, you can't." She stated in a huff.

"Ohhh, but I can. As a matter of fact, dear darling, we can speak to each other without moving our lips."

See. I know you are hoping I will leave soon. You think I am a little bit scary and a little bit silly.

How...? How did you do that?

Oh, dear darling...it is easy when you are me!

"I am talented that way!" Giraud laughed heartily. He leaned in and lowered his voice as to be more comforting toward Emma. "There really is no reason to be afraid of me, dear darling," Giraud entangled his fingers in the strands Emma's light brown hair, brushing through them gently, not pulling at all. "I can tell you this, Emma. I can provide a much more...stabilizing... erm....fun atmosphere for you exist in." Giraud exhaled dramatically. "I come across many, many children such as yourself...and it breaks my heart to not help in any way I can......all you have to say is.... 'I want to go away with you, Giraud.' That is all you need to say...and I can provide you with anything you wish."

"Can you take me to live with my sister, Lydia?" Emma looked in Giraud's deep blue eyes to see if he was about to tell a lie. Strange thing is, his eyes kept changing color. Blue, brown, hazel, even a flash of red, before settling into a milky black.

"Dear darling...I can take you on the most magnificent adventure there is!" Giraud proclaimed. But Emma wasn't buying it.

"I just want to go live with my sister," she said, sternly.

"Well," Giraud shrugged, then gave a saccharin, wide smile. "If you promise to help me and some friends get a farming business back on track..."

"A farm? You want me to work on a farm?"

"Of course not! That would be horrid! No! A young girl working on a farm....no. You see...a terrible came through and...wrecked the place. I just need you to help for one day to...clean up all the debris...you know? Like move the damage...tree limbs and parts of the.... barn room from the farm itself. Maybe help care for the animals?"

Emma liked that idea. She started to bob her head up and down as her feet left the living room carpet. "Yes, yes, yes!" She squealed with uproarious excitement.

Giraud placed a crooked, gloved finger on Emma's lips. "Shhhhh," He defused her screeches. "We do not want to awaken anyone. I'm afraid they'll only put a stop to our plans, darling dear."

Emma's eyes turned to the bedroom where her mother and Tom slept. Very little movement could be heard. Still, for a second, Emma was afraid one of them would come out of the bedroom and put a stop to, as Giraud put it, 'their plans'.

"What do you say...Emma?" Giraud took her hand and led her into the kitchen. The cabinet door was wide open and a blindingly bright light excelled into a spiral on walls.

Emma paused and thought. She thought hard. She didn't like living with her mother and Tom. She wanted to be with Lydia and Jack. She didn't like going the school here and wanted a chance to meet new kids.

I can make that happen.

She heard Giraud's voice in her head.

But what about Mom and Tom? Won't they be worried about me?

Do they look worried about you now?

Emma looked back at the bedroom. No movement from anyone.

He had a point, Emma thought.

They can always come and visit me when I'm living with Lydia.

Then, you'll come with me?

Again, she heard Giraud's voice in her mind.

Emma nodded.

Giraud smiled at her. "I need to for you speak the words, darling dear."

"What words?"

"Say: 'I want to go away with you, Giraud'. As simple as that."

"I want to go away with you, Giraud." Emma said in a quiet, shaky voice.

Emma was enveloped in a sphere of bright lights. So bright, she had to shield her eyes with her hands. Before she knew it, Emma was already in the cabinet, crawling behind Giraud. It was cramped, weird, and too claustrophobic. For fear of being left behind, Emma had to crawl faster to keep up with Giraud.

It seemed to take forever, was really just a few minutes, and Giraud stopped at a wall. He turned to Emma and smiled. "Here we are, darling dear," Giraud with understated malice. "This is the path that will change your life."

Giraud pushed a block of the wall and a stream of white light appeared. He pushed further and the block became a cabinet door that swung freely. Emma watched Giraud climb down into an infinite wasteland. To Emma, it resembled the

Sahara Desert she'd seen on TV. There was a permeant gray sky and specs of dust flying around from a wild breeze.

"Come along, darling dear," Giraud offered an encouraging hand. "No time to waste. My friends need all the help they can get on that farm.

Emma wasn't sure if she wanted to follow Giraud. Suddenly she regretted allowing Giraud to take her on this escapade. She already missed her mother and Tom. Plus, she had no idea what lay ahead of her. That was the most frightening thing about her predicament. What if Giraud had lied about the promise he had made? What if.......?

Well, she heard his voice inside her head once again. You have already made your choice, darling dear. There is no turning back.

Emma's stomach hurt. A realization came to her.

Giraud just might be right.

EMMA CLIMBED out of the cabinet door, placed her tiny feet on the barren landscape. She felt hot sand between her toes and hard rock under her naked heel. She turned to see what her surroundings was. In either direction there was nothing but gray skies and one dead tree. The only difference was that, to the right, a woman in black was kneeling at a grave. To the left was a tree with moss that ran down it like a waterfall and tiny flies swarming around a hole at the top.

Giraud encouraged her to come with him to the left, but Emma was intrigued by the woman in black.

"Don't go that direction," he commanded. "That's the wrong way to the farm. It is this way," Giraud pointed to the dead tree with the swarming flies.

"I just want to say hello. You did say this was an adventure, so I'm trying to make the most of it." Emma said, pacing herself as she approached the woman in black.

Giraud seemed nervous. "Look, there's no need to speak to that woman." He was getting agitated. "I assure you, speaking to her is a waste of time!" Giraud called out to Emma.

By this time, Emma was no longer listening to him. She'd

made her mind up to talk to the woman in black, and that was that!

You are making a grave mistake, Giraud invaded her mind.

Emma had grown to dislike that part of their relationship. It had become very annoying, so she didn't answer him in words, but in pictures. She shot him an image of a bear eating a fish that he had caught in a stream. This angered Giraud.

Emma! Dear darling, that is uncalled for. You must only answer me with words. Not images.

Emma felt devious. So, she sent him an image of a toilet covered in diarrhea.

Now, that really was childish!

"After all," Emma said, giggling. "I am a child. Do I need to remind you?"

"Of course, darling dear. I do, sometimes, forget," Giraud said sweetly. "Now...please come with me, so we can get started on our path..." he pleaded.

Emma ignored him.

She stood at the woman in black's side, watching her. The woman was indeed dressed in all black: Long flowing black gown, black mesh veil, and soft, frilly, knit gloves. She was whispering a prayer as she dropped a dead rose upon the grave. The headstone was weather beaten. The name was so badly scratched up, no one could make out the name. The only thing legible was the date. Born Nineteen seventy, died 2006.

"Why are you here, child?" The woman croaked.

"I was brought here," Emma said. "Who are you mourning?"

"Ohhh," the woman moaned and the whole area moaned with her. "Someone who refuses to believe they are dead," the woman answered, tears fell from her mysterious face, each drop burning the soiled grave with touch. "Someone who ran from death. And death will undoubtedly catch him......and I will mourn him no more because his bones will be at rest."

Emma wasn't sure how to feel about all of that. She'd only had one person in her family die and that was her grand-mother. She was very sad when she was finally able to comprehend the situation. Of course, Emma was only six at the time. But she handled it well. Much better than her mother, as Lydia explained to her, "Grandma may have been the reason Mom is so sick a lot of the time and she's not coping with her death very well."

"Well," Emma touched the woman on her shoulder. She was ice cold and Emma recoiled. Inside, Emma felt as if she'd had one of night terrors. Especially the ones where she was falling and there was no end. She caught her breath and calmed down. Gathering back some of her composure, Emma said, "I hope things work out for you. I have to go now."

"Pay heed, young girl," the woman in black croaked and the empty valley croaked with her. "Make sure the path you are on is of your own making."

"I don't understand," Emma said.

"Confusion can be a long dark road. Awareness can be a weapon as sharp as any blade, as long as you keep your wits about you. Pay heed." Another dead rose appeared in her hand and she dropped it on the grave just as the petal fell, turning to dust, swallowed up by the soil. "I will make you a promise," the woman sighed and the world sighed with her. "If you will promise to bring me the one who refuses to have passed on. I am old, and I am tired. I cannot go on mourning him."

"How will I know who that is?"

"Ohhh," the woman in black wept, the tears burning into the barren ground under her. "You will know him when you recognize him."

Emma shrugged. "I don't think I'll run into him," she said, glancing over at Giraud, who was now motioning for her to hurry to his side.

"I'm pretty sure you will. These strange corridors are narrow and small. They always lead back to where you come from."

Emma had no idea what that meant. So, she backed away from the old woman slowly, softly as not to disturb her mourning. When she arrived next to Giraud, he was wearing a different mask. This one was of a face that had blacked out, hollow eyes and a sad, thin mouth. The nose was just two holes.

"You changed your mask," Emma said. "How come?"

"I felt like it," Giraud began walking and Emma followed. They were headed in the direction where the dead tree leaned over a small pool of gray water. "There's often no rhyme or reason why people do things."

"That's an excuse adults use when they want to hide something." Emma said.

Giraud giggled. "That's very astute of you, darling dear."

"What does 'astute' mean?"

"Never you mind," Giraud patted Emma on the head. "We need to get to the farm quickly. No interruptions."

They came upon two round boys playing in that pool of gray water. A few seconds before that a door in the opened and Goop and Gop fell to the barren wasteland. Both boys were dressed alike; black and yellow polka dot sweaters and beanies too small for their large heads. The shorts they wore were shaped like pantaloons and had large rips in the seats that had been sewn up many times.

"Who are these guys?" Emma was slightly scared to approach these odd fellows.

"Nothing to be afraid of, darling dear," Giraud said proudly, sniffed the air. "Gop and Goop are just my helpers."

Goop had placed his hand in the gray water and created several swirls. When he pulled his hand out, a small blue person was attached to each finger. Gop had grown bored with kicking the dead tree, came over to see what Goop had found. Goop had shaken off the four blue humans to the dried, cracked ground. Goop inspected one to see if the tiny bald blue person could withstand being crushed by his thumb. The answer was no. The small blue person shifted around wildly, screaming as yellow liquid drained from its broken body.

"I didn't say they were the smartest, nor had the best attention span," Giraud shook his head at what he'd witnessed. "Did you find him?" Giraud disturbed the boys torture time.

Gop took one of the small blue people and positioned it in his pocket. Goop finished pulling off another tiny blue person's head, tossed it aside. "No," he said, his facial expression contorted whenever he spoke. "We couldn't find him."

"We went west in the corridors like you said," Gop sputtered. He usually stuttered when he spoke by himself and to have a full conversation always took a few hours when normal human interaction would only take fifteen minutes. Together the bother boys could speak properly and normally.

"Why am I saddled with you two?" Giraud sighed.

"You're blessed with us!" Goop and Gop exclaimed.

"You two need to find the boy and bring him back to the farm!"

Emma saw anger rise up in Giraud and it made her a little worried that she'd made a mistake leaving with him. He gave her a brief, consoling smile. "I'm very worried about the child. He wandered off one day and hasn't returned. It can be very dangerous out here, you know."

"We've looked everywhere," Goop said.

"Even behind the burning bushes," Gop said.

"Well look again!" Giraud shook his fist at the twins. He lowered his fist, and once again flashed a smile at Emma. "You know how children can be," he said in a smooth, calm voice. "They forget they are playing and before they know it, they are lost. Hasn't that happened to you, darling dear?"

"No," Emma told him. "I know where I am all the time."

"Now, off you two go. And please bring the boy back safely. I will be at the farm, showing Emma around."

"Aye, aye, Kaptitan!" Goop and Gop saluted Giraud and waddled off as fast they could, knocking each other down like bowling pins. They recovered and ran as fast their little thin legs could carry them.

Giraud and Emma went in the opposite direction. In the distance they could see something hanging from another crooked tree. There was a rope attached to whatever it was, and the gentle breeze blew it around and around in long, slow motion circles. On the very top limb sat a large crow, cackling away.

The closer Giraud and Emma got, they could see it was a man hanging from the tree. The rope had been tied with huge, professional knot, tight around his bloated purple neck. From the look of his attire, the man had been a cowboy. Dirty dungarees' cut close to the boot, spurs barely hanging at the heel, and a torn shirt ripped open at his back with several long gashes embedded in his skin. Seemed to be a possibility of what the poor man had gone through before his hanging. There was a message on his forehead written in blood.

Thief.

Giraud and Emma stared at the hanged man a few minutes before the crow spoke to them.

"He's not what you think he is," the crow said.

"We don't think anything of the dead man," Giraud said. "One way or another."

"I've never seen anything like this before," Emma said, a little apprehensive to speak a first. "I've never seen a dead person before."

"No reason to be frightened child," the crow said, and cackled. He couldn't help himself. The cackling was a nervous reaction to the fact he was readying himself to speak. "This range rider is only dead at the moment. Pert soon he'll be out of that noose and going into town to gather the townspeople's sins."

"That's a bit strange," Giraud scratched the top of his head.

"So says a man who wears masks to hide who he is," the crow cawed, then cackled.

"No reason to be insulting, friend." Giraud shot back. "My choice to wear the mask."

"My choice to insult you," replied the crow.

At this point the dead man stirred. He kicked his legs, caught a boot on the side of the tree, held on to the rope, and lifted the noose over his head. He fell to the ground, picked himself up and started walking toward a strange sundown that seemed to going on for an eternity.

Emma gasped. "Where's he going?"

"Ah," the crow cackled. "Once a month, Jocko goes into town to steal sins."

"You can't steal a sin." Emma replied. "You have to be forgiven."

"These are unforgiveable sins, little girl," the crow said, changing positions on the dead branch. "Those are the ones that can be stolen."

"Then what does he do with them?"

"He brings them to me," the crow said proudly.

Her curiosity was angering Giraud. He wanted to hurry to the farm. He had so much to do. Giraud opted out of the conversation, going over the list in his head. First and foremost was finding that boy. The boy had something important that belonged to Giraud. Well, actually, it belonged to the Drake sisters. Still, he considered it his, and he considered that hideous creature that produced such valuable commodities, his as well.

The Drake sisters were small timers. They didn't think big enough. They captured that creature, and kept him prisoner on that farm. But what have they done with the commodities so far? Trading them within the Corridors? Big deal. Giraud had travelled through the known worlds in these Corridors. He'd explored, gotten to know its inhabitants and their needs.

Oh, how silly those two old biddies were, Giraud thought.

With the commodities, he could rule the Corridors. Giraud laughed malevolently.

"Something funny, clown?" The crow asked Giraud.

"Only the lack of glow on your feathers, bird." Giraud raised his dark eyes to the crow. The crow shuffled on the dead branch uneasily.

"Even Napoleon had doubts, clown." The crow crooned.

"What does that mean?" Giraud struck back

"In spite of popular belief," the crow cackled. "People are not so easily lead into chains, my friend."

"I wonder what he's going to do," Emma said, her eyes transfixed on Jocko, as he disappeared into the hazy horizon.

JOCKO AMBLED INTO TOWN, looking for sins to steal.

On his path, he discovered a herd of dead cattle littered in the dry, yellow grass. From the smell of their death, he could tell they were poisoned. When Jocko knelt to examine the cattle further, all the flies abandoned their mission to feed off the dead, already overtaken by rigor mortis. Jocko closed his eyes and heard the confessions of five men who had ridden off to their ranch, and wallowed in their glory as they slept peacefully in their individual bunks. In the distance, Jocko could also hear the tears of the wife of the owner of the poisoned cattle. A few miles down, Jocko found the owner of the cattle. His body was riddled with bullets, his face frozen in a grim smile, as if he knew his fate beforehand.

Night had fallen over the town by the time Jocko shuffled in, bringing the beginnings of a dust storm. The street was quiet. Even the cicadas stifled their usual nighttime concert. The horses in the livery stable complained, called out for help as Jocko passed by.

Jocko entered the crowded saloon and the patrons noticed there was a sense of purpose. All activity ceased, and every noise was stifled. The only sound was that of Jocko's boots on the wood floor and his spurs rattling. He went to the bar, catching a momentary glimpse of his own ravaged face in the mirror that hung behind the barkeeper. All eyes stayed on Jocko, but the frivolity of the evening no longer lingered. A few cowboys took their saloon girls upstairs, a few others called it an evening. The card game continued, but no words were spoken.

"What can I get you?" The barkeeper nervously asked. He kept one hand on the counter, the other gripping a Colt that lay on a shelf by the corn liquor.

"Whiskey," Jocko answered, his voice raspy from the rope burn and crushed vocal cord.

The barkeeper hurriedly poured the liquid into a filthy glass, using one hand. Jocko drank the whiskey in one gulp, slammed the glass on the counter. He smiled at the barkeeper, nodded or him to pour another. The barkeeper put his hand on the glass and Jocko placed his dead cold hand on top of the barkeepers. The barkeeper felt a chill move through his body.

"You can take your finger off that sixgun, mister," Jocko said.

"I-I don't know what you're talking about," the barkeeper stuttered.

"I'm not a fool, mister," Jocko's eyes glowed a sunburned hue, the pupil dilated a deep black that the barkeeper had never seen before. The barkeeper could feel his hands as well as Jocko's, rise up in temperature, almost to the point boiling heat. The barkeeper winced. "I ain't got words with you," Jocko said. "But I sure can mince some if you like."

"Yeah," he barely managed. "Yeah .... you got it, mister." The hammer on the Colt was released, and Jocko's eyes returned its dead, familiar look. He removed his hand from the barkeeper's, and this time, the drink was poured with both hands visible.

Jocko chuckled. "Boy," he threw his head back and gulped down the whiskey. "This place has changed since I was last here. Kinda dead, huh?" He chuckled again.

"When were you last here?" The barkeeper slid the question to Jocko, not meaning to continue the conversation, except he was afraid what would happen if he didn't.

Last spring," Jocko croaked, his voice sent shivers up the barkeeper's spine. "The day after Holloway killed his wife."

The barkeeper stopped wiping down the counter. He sniffed the air. "Is that a fact? I wouldn't know. I was in the next town, down the valley. Calverton."

"Let me ask you something," Jocko motioned for another whiskey to be poured. The barkeeper obliged, only slightly more nervous than before, more whiskey was spilled on the counter than Jocko's glass.

The barkeeper broke a momentary smile. "Shoot, mister."

"You know a lot about poisons? I mean...more than what you serve?"

"I'm not too sure what you're getting at, mister." The barkeeper laughed nervously.

"I've walked a many a mile to get here," Jocko said.

He had a sick smile on his face. He felt the heat rise up inside him. It starts in the pit of his belly, and comes up, nice and slow, through his chest, where his heart becomes inflamed. The tips of his fingers begin to tingle. There is a low humming in his ears. His tongue, which was brittle, stiff and pale white, turns a blood red, vibrates against his puffy cheeks. By this time, his eyes were already glowing red.

"I hate to inform you wrong, mister, but I don't know what you mean...."

"I was coming through this Godforsaken valley," Jocko cut the man off.

In the back of the Saloon, three men entered the room, two from upstairs, where they had left their chosen saloon girls peeking around a corner of the stairs; the other man, obviously the ring leader, came in from the street, drunkenly shuffling his feet.

Jocko continued. "I passed by several cows and a few horses that lay dead on the ground. I could smell how they died. Poison was in the air. Sick...strong smell of Grainberries."

The barkeeper chuckled. "Now, everybody knows Grainberries don't grow around these parts. Come on, mister. You're reaching."

"You're reaching," Jocko snarled. "And if you don't take your hand off that Colt, I'm going to melt your face right in front of these good people."

The barkeeper pulled his hands from under the counter and raised them up in the air, showing Jocko he wasn't anywhere near the gun. "Okay, okay." The barkeeper chuckled and shook his head.

The three men nodded to each other and slowly moved toward Jocko's back, their hands close to their sheathed six guns.

"Grainberries grow in Calverton," Jocko grit his teeth. "You helped destroy the Cobb family for a few silver dollars."

"I've never met..." The barkeeper didn't finish his sentence.

Jocko's glowing hands had reached inside the man's chest, disappearing into his shirt, the flesh of his chest cavity and stayed there a few minutes.

Just as the three men unsheathed their six guns, the barrels caught on fire and melted into their hands. They screamed in unison, stumbled to each other and immediately burst into flames. The saloon was in chaos. People screaming, knocking over chairs, tables, each other. Clawing, crawling, pulling the person in front of them down on the floor and trampling them. Clothing being ripped off.

All because three human bodies were on fire and posed no danger to the building or people.

In mere moments, the saloon was empty except for Jocko and the barkeeper. Jocko left the saloon, a sphere of light in his hands. He walked off into the darkness, the townspeople staring nervously at his back. A few people wandered back inside the saloon, confused as to why the events happened and why the building was not ablaze.

They found the barkeeper sitting in a corner, drooling on himself. He was still alive, but his mind wasn't.

"What was it that Jocko was carrying in his hands?" Someone asked.

After a few minutes, someone else retorted: "The barkeeper's soul."

Jocko returned to the dead tree where Giraud and Emma stood talking to the crow. They stared at him as he smiled and caressed glowing ball in his hands. The crow flew down from the dead branch and landed on Jocko's shoulder. Jock offered the glowing ball to the crow and the crow began to feed from it.

Giraud shrugged, said to Emma: "I think we should keep moving, darling dear. The farm is not far from here."

The farm was beautiful.

Large, green trees dwarfed the burnt orange wheat in the back of the land. To the side were grapevines. A hundred yards or so from that, corn stalks reached to the skies. Two rows ahead were vegetables of every kind imaginable. All ready for picking, which several children were working very hard on in the hot sun. None of them were laughing, smiling or singing, like Emma had imagined.

They looked miserable.

To the left of the main farm were shacks. Several of them.

And to the right was this beautiful, three story white house with a balcony on top, and a white gate chained together. Two dark figures appeared in an open window, glaring gloomily at Emma. She felt a chill run up her back. Just as she was set to hide behind Giraud, she heard that song again. But she also realized, that song was only in her mind and no one else could hear it. Or so she thought.

Helppppp! Help! A voice invaded her mind, part singing the word, part speaking it. Helppppp!

Don't pay attention to that noise, she heard Giraud in her mind.

What is that? Emma answered.

Just nothing but noise, Giraud thought.

It sounds like someone singing.

Dear child, hear me! It is nothing but noise. An illusion. Your mind is playing tricks on your ears because you are not used to the dense air the farm produces.

Uncertain, Emma was not ready to believe Giraud's premise.

Really? She asked.

Really, Giraud answered.

So, why do I have a headache then?

The pollen from the trees, dear child. Once you come inside my room and eat something, you will be fine.

I don't know, Emma sent him the message back.

She could see Giraud was getting agitated. He wasn't used to being told no.

Dear child, I know you are weak with hunger, and tired from the trip. All you need is nourishment and rest. All will be right as rain, he messaged her back and gave a reassuring smile.

Emma wasn't sure if she should.

"No," she told him. "I just want to do my part to help the

farm so you can help me find my way to my sister and her house."

Giraud held out his staff, the ball on top spun counter-clockwise. Emma's eyes screwed up and focused on the ball, from which an illuminating glow eminated, with harsh outlines. Emma's concentration became one track, as her body felt limp, wanting to float in the air like large kernels of popcorn.

"Come, dear child," Giraud's lips widened in that sick smile of his. "Lie on my bed and rest a while. Eat from the food from the plate of the house of the most wonderful host-esses, the Drake sisters, which provides all provisions to the dutiful children that finds their way to us." He offered his hand and the locks unlocked, and the chains fell from the gate. Emma took Giraud's hand as the gate creaked open, slowly.

"You'll not regret this a bit," Giraud whispered. "Even if you remember it."

Giraud heard heavy, running footsteps. He turned and saw an overweight child being chased by Goop and Gop.

"I'm going to fricassee his head!" Goop licked his bloated lips.

"I'm going to sauté his fat little toes!" Gop screeched, trailing Goop by a hair.

The noise broke whatever spell Giraud had cast on Emma. She recognized the overweight boy as Paul Butterling, the boy who had gone missing. He was trucking fast toward Giraud, who no chance of moving out of the boy's path. Paul huffed and puffed, gained speed just as he hit Giraud. The two of them fell hard on the ground and tumbled away from the gate, stirring up a large cloud of dust.

Paul emerged from the ground, the staff in his left hand. Goop and Gop stopped in their tracks and immediately broke into a roaring laugh, holding their sides and slapping each other on the shoulders. When the dust cleared, Paul was sitting on Giraud's face. Paul realized where he was, what was happening, and quickly jumped to his stout feet, trotted to Emma.

He grabbed her by the hand and pulled her as he his feet kicked up another burst of dirt clods. "Come on!" He screamed at her.

"What?!" Emma tried to pull away. "Why?" But Paul was stronger, and in order to keep her balance, Emma paddled her feet on the ground, racing alongside of him.

Goop and Gop stopped laughing momentarily, straightened up, and cleared their throats. "We found him!" They bellowed.

"You don't want to stay here!" Paul yelled back to her. "Not unless you wanna be a slave forever!"

Giraud recovered, sat up on his heels and pointed a warped finger at the two children gliding away from him. "Get them!" A cobbled scream ripped from his throat.

Goop and Gops' eyebrows lowered, and a vicious smiled curled their lips. They ran to Paul and Emma, pushing each other off one another's feet.

Suddenly, a door appeared in front Paul and Emma. The door slid open and a patch of blue sky hanging over the top of trees formed. Paul looked back at Goop and Gop, who were gaining on them. "Quick! Jump through the door!"

No time to react, Emma did as she was told. The door closed behind Paul and disappeared. Goop and Gop stopped running, turned to Giraud and shrugged concurrently. They shushed a brief giggle.

Giraud beat his fists on the ground and let loose a fierce scream skyward.

EMMA AND PAUL were walking in a forest discussing their predicament. The trees were many and towered over them. The bushes were thick and looked like they went on forever. Leaves crumpled under their soles as they headed east. A direction not premeditated, but taken by chance.

"So he lied to me?" Emma asked, looking down at her shoes. She was a little embarrassed that she believed someone's lie and was led astray.

"Giraud lies to all the kids," Paul said, marching a bit uncoordinated and trying to twirl the staff like a baton. "No reason to mope around. Anyway, what did he promise you?"

"He would take me to my sister's house if I helped on the farm. What did he promise you?"

"I could eat anything I wanted, anytime I wanted," Paul said. He dropped the staff. It bounced and landed by a tree with several holes. He trotted over and retrieved it.

"So," Emma picked a red and light blue leaf from a tree that had its limbs curled up in knots. The leaf shriveled up and turned to dust in her hands. She knew not to pick anymore leaves from that tree. "He makes all those poor kids slaves? How come he didn't make you a slave?"

Paul shrugged. "I ran away, I guess."

"Funny how those two dummies couldn't find you. Or Giraud."

"Yeah. I'm real good at hiding. One time I hid in a grocery store and nobody could find me. I was in a shelf with a stack of paper towels covering me. Not even the manager or my mom could find me until a lady bought one of those paper towels. Boy, did she scream when she saw me," Paul laughed and twirled the staff again, dropping it. "My mom sure was mad at me, you know." This time, instead of falling to the ground, the staff stopped in midair and rose above his head. It twirled on its own and then levitated into Paul's waiting hands. "Wow," he marveled at the staff. "I bet I can make this cane do whatever I wanted to."

"Why did you want to leave home?" Emma asked. She noticed some movement inside the tree, and went to investigate.

"My mom was never home. She worked two jobs. When she was home all she did was yell at me for eating everything in the refrigerator."

"So why do that if you knew it made her mad?"

"Sometimes I can't help it. I just get hungry. The TV and food made me feel less lonely I guess."

"Hey," Emma took a step back. "There's something inside this tree."

"Just a squirrel," Paul dismissed the warning with a wave.

"I don't think so, Paul. A squirrel can't make the tree move like it's going to fall," Emma said.

Through two oval shaped holes in the tree, Emma and Paul saw two large eyes staring at them. Paul screamed, fell backwards, only his hands keeping the seat of his pants from touching the ground. Emma jumped when Paul screamed, and she danced in a little circle before hiding behind another tree. The tree with the holes in question, tore itself from its roots and dragged the trunk across the ground. A high-pitched bellow came from the tree as well as several grunts and fearful pantings. .

Emma saw a long, multi-colored rattlesnake tail protruding from the trunk of the tree. She also noticed that whatever was inside the tree was more afraid of them than they were of the thing which was now running away.

"Hey!" Emma yelled to Paul, laughing. "Whatever it is, it's scared of us!"

"Hmmm...." Paul pulled himself up to a standing position, surveyed the situation. "You're right," Paul folded his arms, shook his head and sighed.

"Well," Emma stood beside Paul. "We can't let it get away without knowing what the heck it is."

"Yeah," Paul agreed. "We'll be wondering the rest of our lives."

They both took off in a sprint after the tree. Emma being faster than Paul, was able to catch the thing inside the tree only because it was ready to pass out. The tree came to a fast walk, huffing and puffing.

"Hey!" Emma called to it.

"Hey!" Paul echoed her, albeit from ten paces behind, he himself ran out of breath quickly.

"Stop! We won't hurt you!" Emma placed her hands on the tree and blocked it from moving any further.

The tree stopped and wobbled bit. Wheezing and coughing was heard. Paul finally caught up, doing the same. Like a sock barely hanging on to a foot, the husk of the tree slithered off to reveal a very large, robust monster ready to pass out. He tried hard to catch his breath, large black eyes keeping a nervous watch on Emma and Paul. The rack of horns on his head seemed to weigh him down. Snot ran from his flattened nose, and a long stream of slobber had attached itself to his chin. He was a very hairy monster with hooves on his muscled hind legs, which was no problem for him to not stand upright, when he wasn't worn out. His long, spotted, spiked tail flipped and flapped on the grass with each short, sharp breath taken.

Paul was afraid of the monster, but Emma was curious. She did not hide, or back away from the creature. She felt sorry for it. She walked over and took the monster's hand, which dwarfed hers by comparison.

"Are you okay?" Emma smiled.

Finally, the monster caught his breath. He nodded slowly. The monster returned the smile, showing two large fangs that accommodated several smaller teeth. He reminded Emma of a Husky a neighbor once had, always happy, ready to please its owner.

"What's your name?" Emma consoled him by using her other hand to pat his forearm.

"Orgo," he said, shyly.

"Orgo, this is Paul," she pointed in Paul's direction, who was trying to hide behind a tree, just in case the monster decided he was hungry and wouldn't spot him. "I'm Emma. We're glad to meet you."

The poor creature struggled to get his thoughts together, hemming and hawing when suddenly he belted out: "Orgo glad to meet you." He smiled sheepishly and did a small energetic dance.

Emma laughed. She turned to Paul and saw he was still hiding from Orgo. Emma took Orgo by the hand and led him to where Paul was.

"Paul," Emma had the same tone in her voice that his mother had when she was about to command him to do her bidding.

Paul sighed and relinquished all control to whomever the dominant female in his life was. "Yes, Emma?"

"Shake Orgo's hand," her dark eyebrows narrowed down

in the shape of a v on her small, pale forehead. "Do it NOW," Emma demanded. Slowly,

Paul offered Orgo his hand. Orgo lifted his hairy hand toward Paul and buried the boy's hand in his palm, shook it gently twice.

"Good," Emma smiled, proud of the peace-making achievement. "Now you two are friends."

"Friends...." Orgo nodded.

"Emma? I have to tell you something." Paul rubbed his midsection.

"What's that?" Emma asked.

"I'm hungry," Paul said.

Emma rolled her eyes.

"Orgo hungry, too," the creature lamented.

———

They were sitting around the fire, eating meat of some kind that Paul conjured up with staff and Orgo had cooked over the open pit fire. In spite of the ball on top of the staff falling off, the magic conjured the food with no problem. When the ball fell off, it rolled to Orgo. He picked it up in his huge, hairy hands, cradling the shiny ball and carefully offering it to Paul.

"That's okay, Orgo," Paul said. "Keep it. The staff works fine without it."

Orgo smiled and grunted. He found a pocket under several layers of hair and placed the shiny ball inside. He felt a tingling sensation throughout his body. And suddenly a door opened in front of the three of them, disappeared just as quickly. Paul pointed the staff and the door appeared again. Orgo rubbed his pocket and the door disappeared. This went on for a few minutes, and all three had a great laugh about it before they grew tired of the trick.

The meat, fastened to sticks, was shaped like hot dogs, but Emma wasn't sure if it was from pork or beef. No matter, she thought it tasted good. Paul and Orgo acted as if they had no table manners, and at first, it amused Emma. Toward the end of the meal, the act just turned her stomach. She was feeling annoyed, and considered the annoyance was due to lack of sleep. Wherever she was, in the corridor (as Giraud called it), that led to the other world, Emma knew the concept of time was not an agenda with the inhabitants. She had no idea how long she'd been away from her parents and the outside world.

Emma wanted to talk more. Sitting there listening to the two of them scoff down their meal was not only disgusting, but boring. And Emma's mother always used to say: If no one spoke during a meal, the food wouldn't settle in their stomach.

"Have you always lived here, Orgo?"

Orgo stopped eating. His eyes rose to meet Emma's. He swallowed slowly, shook his head no. "Orgo come from another place," he said. "Been so long, Orgo don't remember too much." He closed his eyes and mouthed something as if he were getting his thoughts together for a speech.

"Orgo had job once," he said with much difficulty, sputtering and stuttering before and afterwards. He gathered his thoughts again and this time there was no difficulty in what he had to say. "Orgo lived in a house. Lots of houses around. Lots of people. Lots of buildings," he closed his eyes. A painful memory brought on a painful headache. "Too noisy. Too crowded. Orgo liked money too much. Orgo work too much...Orgo mean sometimes... Orgo hurt loved ones, sometimes. Orgo not faithful to one he loved most," Orgo let out a deep sigh. He stared at the fire, sorrow entered his dark eyes. "Orgo woke up one day, he was here. No more house...no more money...no loved ones...no LOVED one... Orgo lonely."

Emma patted Orgo on the shoulder. "Not anymore, you aren't," she said and nodded to Paul. Paul shrugged and continued eating. "Orgo, you can come with us. We're trying to find our home. If I find my sister, you can live with us."

Paul was shocked. Wide-eyed, his mouth hung open, and tiny bits of meat fell from his lips. "Emma...are you sure..."

"Yes, I'm sure!" Emma screamed. "Orgo is my friend and he can live with me."

"Okay, okay," Paul said. "Sorry I said anything."

"Tomorrow we set out to find our homes. Paul has a staff that can create doors to other worlds. We go through a long corridor, until we find a door that appears."

"Orgo not sure," the creature looked up at the dark sky and twinkling stars. Then he looked to right and then to his left. "Orgo will miss the woods."

Emma yawned, lay her head on a log. "Well, you can sleep on it and decide in the morning."

———

A grey cloudy sky hovered above a house below. All along, in a long line were houses the same as the just described. A ranch style with another level built on and a front porch with picket fences. A paved street that led to a cul-de-sac was occupied by either SUV's or mid-sized four door cars.

In the sky, a door opened. Three faces appeared, looked out the door. Emma scowled. Orgo grunted, shook his wooly head. Paul shrugged.

"Orgo don't like cities. He likes forests."

"I don't want to go there," Emma said. "It doesn't look like my home."

"You live in an apartment like I do," Paul said. "No houses where we live."

"Yeah," Emma rolled her eyes. "But my bus goes through streets like this."

"Oh, yeah," Paul said. "Mine too. But what if one of those houses belongs to your sister?"

"No. She doesn't live here."

"How do you know?" Paul asked.

"If she was down there, I'd feel it. That's how close we are. It doesn't feel right."

"Oh," Paul resigned. "Yeah. That makes sense."

"Let's keep moving." Emma ordered.

Orgo closed the door.

Dee hated yard sales.

Her mother, and her younger brother Ben, were all dragged to a yard sale the week before Thanksgiving by her Aunt Flora. They had to move in with Flora while their father was away, stationed half-way round the world. Flora was alright, just a little odd, too odd for Dee's nine- year-old sensibilities. She cooked breakfast for supper almost every night, and played opera music while taking a shower. Even dressed her Pomeranian, Gus, as famous presidents. Flora had a strange habit of videotaping cooking shows she never watched. She said she was saving them for when she had more time to study the chef's expertise.

Every item they came across, Flora would sigh or become over-excited. Dee's mother talked Flora out of buying these items. If she hadn't, the car would've been full of Tupperware and men's clothing. Ben also showed enthusiasm for board games. Already he'd spent five dollars of his allowance, of which he'd saved thirty-five dollars since last spring. That really irked Dee. She couldn't save a dime. Dee always seemed to buy too much Goobers or buy the newest video game for her DS.

Mother only bought a red scarf. Dee could tell she missed Father. Mother had several red scarves, and always when Father was away. Dee heard Mother, a few nights before, telling the story of how she met Father. She was standing on a bridge watching the moon reflect off the water when the wind blew her scarf from her hair and she chased it until a sailor caught it for her. That sailor, of course, was Father.

They were almost out of the yard sale when Aunt Flora saw the item that made her heart skip a beat. Dee was first to the car when she heard Flora cry out. Dee put a hand on her head and made a grunting noise.

"I can't believe I found it!" Flora exclaimed. "I need this for my collection."

What she held in her hands so delicately was a porcelain Elephant with white tusks. Yes, Flora did have a very large collection of porcelain figures, mostly of animals or circus related items. The worst of those were the clown figures. Dee hated those things. They unsettled her. Once in a while, when she was in the living room by herself watching Animal planet, she would climb on top of the couch and turn the clowns around facing the wall. Flora always asks who did that, no one would answer. Flora also had a terrible habit of naming her porcelain figures.

Aunt Flora placed the porcelain elephant on the mantle next to her two porcelain circus tigers. She stood back and admired it. She looked at Dee and said, "Little Tusk. That's what I will call him." She cackled and Dee plugged her ears with her fingers. Then Flora saw that her collection of clowns was facing the wall again. She was infuriated. "Who did this?" She exclaimed, her eyes shifting to all in the room. No one said a word. "One day," She said. "I will find out who does this -- this -- terrible act!"

The next day, Dee awoke to a car hissing by her window. It sounded like a cat trying to sing. She wandered into the living room, eyes half closed. She stepped over Ben, who was lying in the middle of the floor, eating brownie cakes and watching Iron Man cartoons on TV. The house was very quiet. Dee spun around, trying to find the source of her confusion.

"Mama's gone," Ben said, entranced by the screaming voices and exploding cars and buildings.

"Gone where?" Dee said in a drone voice. She was making her way slowly to the kitchen for a bowl of corn pops and raisin bran mixture. Dee was a genius of creating new cereals.

"Last night Daddy called. He said his boat--"

"You mean ship, doofus."

"Ship — whatever!" Ben raised his hand at Dee, then continued. "His ship, is close by, so Aunt Flora is driving Mama to the airport."

Dee placed her hands on her hips. Her eyebrows lowered, her lips tightened up. "Why am I always the last to know everything? I'm the oldest. She always forgets to tell me first! It always comes from you — and wait! If his ship is close by, then why is she catching a plane to meet him?"

Ben wiped crumbs from his mouth. He said calmly, "Why you're always last to know is because you're always late home or always asleep, and you're a brain fart. I don't know why she has to catch a plane. They didn't tell me."

Dee walked up to Ben, placed her dirty foot, which she hadn't washed in a day, in his face. She held it, began to push, while he screamed as if he had just been stabbed. There was the sound of keys rattling in the front door. The door swung open and Gus ran inside, immediately peed on the floor. Aunt Flora stepped inside and slammed the door shut.

"Ah hah!" She screamed. Dee quickly removed her foot from Ben's face and jumped away from him. Ben wiggled around on the floor sputtering and moaning about germs in his mouth. "The adults are away and we can play!" Aunt Flora bellowed, then cackled.

Ben crawled all over the living room floor, coughing and spitting. He pushed the cushion from the couch and bumped the couch, which bumped the wall and shook the wall. The shelf attached to the wall above the couch rattled. Aunt Flora's statuettes moved slightly, several hung on to the edge of the shelf. Flora screamed as if something cataclysmic was happening. Dee smiled. Ben was about to get into trouble. Serves him right for calling her a brain fart.

Ben saw the porcelain elephant fall from the shelf. It tossed and tumbled through the air. He placed both hands out, just as he'd seen a wide receiver in a football game on TV. The elephant fell directly into his hands. He cupped the statuette in both hands and rolled across the couch.

Ben looked up and saw Aunt Flora was in pieces. Then she ran to him and knelt down to kiss him.

Ben had saved the day!

Dee snarled at him as Flora doted on him, telling Ben he could have all the candy and soda he wanted. Ben smiled hugely at Dee.

Ben turned the porcelain elephant on its back in his hand. He eyed a few words that were not recognizable. "Timbur... Ork...Roknal?"

Suddenly, the elephant jumped out of Ben's hand. It landed on the couch, upside down. Ben looked down at it. He noticed the elephant was moving. Its trunk wiggled. Its eyes blinked. Its mouth opened and closed as its tiny legs kicked in the air. Now it was right side up, standing. Ben bent down, eyes wide with disbelief. The elephant sounded off in his face. Ben fell over backwards away from it.

Flora dropped to the living room floor. She passed out cold. Dee ran behind the TV set and peeked from behind it, watching the tiny porcelain elephant sprint back and forth on the couch. It was stuck, thinking at first there was no outlet. Gus took off to Flora's bedroom to hide under the bed.

"This is the craziest thing I've ever seen!" Dee exclaimed.

Aunt Flora regained consciousness just in time to witness the small elephant scale down the arm of the couch, walk across Ben's head, neck and arm, to the living room floor, where it promptly pooped.

"Oh, stop that thing!" Flora cried out.

Ben threw both hands out for it as he leaped at the small elephant. The elephant sensed the position of Ben's hands and thrust forward its tusks. One of the tusks pricked Ben on the palm of his right hand. Ben yelped and withdrew. The wound only bled slightly, but he felt a surge of pain that caused him to weep buckets of crocodile tears. Ben ran to Flora, hoping for motherly attention, only to receive expressions of confusion.

"Look!" Dee said, pointing and laughing.

The elephant was using its trunk to swat the TV remote control like it was hitting a hockey puck with a hockey stick. It was running wildly up and down the living room, all four powerful small legs pumping furiously. It was moving so fast it became a blur. Finally, as it approached Ben and Flora, it took one last swat, sending the remote high in the air. The remote caught Aunt Flora right between the eyes. She fell on her back on to the floor, once again losing consciousness.

"You jerk-head!" Ben screamed at it. He began chasing after the small elephant. Lamps, books, DVDs, pictures from the wall ... after the great chase, the level of destruction the two mounted was impressive. Even the TV, which was hiding Dee somewhat, was overturned. The chase headed to the kitchen, where loud crashes of dishes fell to the floor along with pots and pans. Back into the living room, more destruction mounted. The two chairs were pushed over. Aunt Flora's collection of statuettes was among the victims. The circus animals, even her beloved clowns. All fell to their porcelain grave.

Dee had found a new hiding spot behind the couch, had a terrible vision of Ben and the pint-sized elephant in her room causing all kinds of chaos and destruction. She had an idea. She called over to Ben. He stopped in his tracks, turned to her, huffing and puffing. She reached over at the hat rack where her mother's new red scarf dangled from a wooden hook.

"Here," she tossed one end to Ben. "Grab hold of that and drop to your knees when I say go.

The elephant avoided hitting the wall for the thousandth time and turned right at broken vase. It was heading right to Ben and Dee. The elephant put its head down and gained more speed.

It was right there at that point Dee screamed out *go*. Ben and Dee dropped to their knees. The scarf formed a goal of sorts, like in a soccer game. Ben smiled at Dee, Dee smiled at Ben. They knew they had the elephant.

The elephant rushed through the scarf, its tusks cutting the scarf in two pieces, like a ribbon being cut to introduce a new building. Ben and Dee looked in bewilderment at the piece of material they had in their hands. The elephant passed by them several times, still running at full speed.

Dee stood and threw down the shredded scarf in anger. "That's it, Elephant," She said. "No more Mr. nice guy." Dee had a backup plan. She wasn't sure if it would work, but it was worth a try. Her eyebrows lowered. "Timbur...Ork...Roknal!" Dee yelled.

The tiny porcelain elephant stopped dead, its legs froze up. It blinked its eyes, then they froze up. It raised its head and it froze up. It stretched its trunk out, sounded off as the rest of it stiffened up

Dee sighed, flopped down on the couch. She felt something squishy under her bare feet. She knew what it was, but was afraid to find out for sure.

Aunt Flora awoke, rose up, saw the damage. She was fine until she saw all of her porcelain statuettes were in pieces. She placed her head in her hands and burst into tears. "All gone." She said. "All gone."

Ben slowly approached Aunt Flora. "Well..." He said in a consoling voice. "You still have Little Tusk." Ben handed the porcelain elephant to her. Flora shrugged and accepted the gift. She hugged Ben, turned to Dee.

"Now we have to clean this mess up," She said.

ORGO HAD TROUBLE SLEEPING, so he decided to take a walk. The moonlight was bright, so he had no problems finding a clear path, avoiding bushes and trees. He also made sure didn't wake the children. They were very tired, having explored several corridors in one day, trying to find their way home.

Orgo had walked more than halfway through the forest when he heard footsteps breaking twigs. He turned quickly and found no one behind him. He grunted to himself, then carried on. Orgo saw small pieces of dust flying around him. He sneezed, shook his head to clear his mind. Then he heard buzzing at his ears. Orgo stopped walking, grunted to himself.

He was curious about the noise, but his attention was soon drawn to his left arm. He felt several stingings up and down his arm. Orgo flung out his left arm, and then his right arm when he felt the stings there. He held his arms out in the moonlight. That's when Orgo saw tiny humans with wings holding electric lances in their tiny hands.

Orgo felt the stings all over his giant hairy body. He screamed out as he fell to his knees. A net the size of a small hut fell on Orgo, trapping him. Orgo struggled, slapping at the nylon net and screaming for help in his native tongue. He tired himself out after a few minutes. He just lay in the net and wished the children were there to help him escape. There was an intense humming sound all around him. The net lifted Orgo into the air and by the light of the moon, he could see more than a thousand of those tiny winged humans exporting him through the forest.

Orgo moaned, decided to go along with the ride, hoped he'd discover a way to escape. The cool air and fluent ride through the air made Orgo sleepy. He closed his eyes fell into a deep slumber.

———

When Orgo awoke, he was lying on a bed of rocks, covered in soft animal furs. A stable fire burned brightly with embers falling at Orgo's side. He looked around and gathered he was in a cave. Several drawings donned the pale, white marble. Most were of hairy beings discovering fire, killing a giant shadow creature and dancing around a totem pole made of heads. A bowl of ground up meat and obliterated rice sat in front of him.

Orgo looked around, made sure no one was near him to cause any trouble. He picked up the bowl with one hand and began shoveling the bits and pieces of meat and rice into his mouth with his other hand. Grunting and smacking his lips, more food ended up in the fur on his neck than in his mouth.

A medium sized boulder had been moved, scraping the granite floor of the cave. Moonlight shone in a slither at first, then as a window when another hairy being stomped inside. This being stood there a moment, admiring the fact that Orgo looked just like him. Orgo stopped eating, slowly placed the bowl back on the ground.

Orgo growled, curled his upper lip to show a fang.

The other hairy being did the same. "You Orgo," he said.

Orgo nodded.

"Me, Torro," the creature said, tried to smile, but a fang got caught under his top lip.

"Torro," Orgo repeated, nodded again.

"Orgo King," Torro said, handed Orgo a shiny golden crown.

Orgo shook his head. "No, not King. You King." Orgo pointed to the other hairy one.

"No," Torro growled. "Old King dead. We need new King. We see you in Forrest. We see you look like old King. You our King...or we not do good .... we need new leader....You are new leader."

With great reluctance, Orgo took the crown. He placed it on his head, this tint five-pointed hat that sat sideways. Orgo smiled. "King," he nodded. A few moments later, the cave was filled with giant hairy creatures that looked just like Orgo. They were all happy to have a leader again. They hooped and howled, slapping each other on the back. One even shouted, "Party, Party, Party! Party!"

Orgo had a thought. He stood, quieted his new followers. "We do something good," he shouted. "We help friends!"

OUT IN THE forest just a mile or two outside Gorak city, are a row of trees that house the Fraks.

Fraks are small people of about three-foot-tall, fat and round in shape. They have no necks, just heads that swivel and sit on their bodies. Fraks live simple lives. They build their modest homes inside the tree trunks, harvest berries from the trees above, which are the main ingredient for every kind of food and drink they make.

All the men from the age of sixteen, have to go into the city to work in the plastics mine to pay the very high taxes on their homes. If the taxes are not paid, the Imperial Army takes the head of the household to jail, where he sits in a cell for five years. So out of the thirty-five-hour day, twenty-two of them are spent working. The Gorags are taller people and are also a bit more oppressive to the Fraks. The thought in the intellectual community is that the Fraks are not as bright as the Gorags, because of their height. The women are not allowed to work because of religious laws of the Gorags, which the Fraks are not believers of that religion at all. The Fraks are believers in a Forest God that takes care of everything, as opposed to the Gorag belief system of a family of divine beings that wills the world to turn on its axles. Thus, it is not in the Fraks mentality to question anything, even if it is a collective thought by the community that they are mistreated.

Dumml-dee was a child of twelve and very precocious. He never listened to his mother. In these difficult times for the Fraks, it was detrimental that the children cause as few problems for their parents. He'd been told time and time again not to explore the forest when the Imperial Army was doing their training. But Dumml-dee cared nothing of what his parents said. He continued to go out in the forest, even while the Imperial Army was firing their muskets and preparing for an enemy that did not exist but only in mythical tales, told to all as a way for the Imperial Senate to keep their citizens in check.

The Imperial Army was on a hunt. They were looking for that invisible enemy, which now had become tangible. He was called the Krete. He was a ten-foot skeletal metal man that ran off the energy of a glowing sphere that usually sat in his chest cavity. The Krete had escaped the factory it he had been created in. At the time of the great hunt, the Krete was inoperable, for the sphere had fallen out of the skeletal metal body and rolled to a tree, where it sat, no longer glowing. The Krete stood motionless not more than a few feet from the sphere.

Dumml -dee found the sphere on one of his walks. He thought he'd found a new toy similar to the ones sold in the shops in the city. A toy that bounced when thrown against a building or even trees. Dumml -dee was so happy at his new find that he jumped up and down and clapped his hands. He bent down and picked up the sphere. Immediately it began to glow a soft orange in his hand.

Dumml -dee was dismayed. He nearly dropped the sphere when he felt the warmth of the object. Then he heard a loud humming. He looked up and saw the Krete standing in front of him, his arms stretched out, ready to strike. Dumml -dee leaped out of the way just in time. The Krete's fists slammed into ground, creating two wide trenches. He thrust forward at Dumml -dee, missing him by inches with those massive steel ribbon fists.

Dumml -dee used the Krete as a stepping stone to the lower tree branches and climbed higher to the top. Every branch he stepped upon, the Krete smashed. And every tree Dumml -dee leaped to, the Krete destroyed.

The Captain of the Imperial Army noticed that trees in the forest were disappearing before his eyes. He thought that was strange. He soon realized he may have found what he was looking for when he heard several trees fall in a row. The Captain knew for sure when he saw Dumml -dee swinging from a vine, laughing and waving the glowing sphere. There was the Krete, not too far behind Dumml -dee. The Captain screamed orders at his army. He told them to ready their guns. The soldiers lined up, all thirty of them, muskets aimed at the Krete.

Dumml -dee swung high above the metal creature. The soldiers fired their muskets. Their barrels exploded, a cloud of grey smoke surrounded them. The little black balls were propelled toward the Krete, doing no damage at all, just bouncing from his metal skin.

That angered the Krete.

He turned his attentions to the soldiers. With one swipe he sent four of them miles away from where they stood. Several began to run in spite of the Captain's orders to stay their ground. The Krete crushed ten in his left hand, another ten in his right hand. He tossed the dead from his fingertips without a thought, lift his right foot and crushed another ten underfoot. The last of the soldiers scattered, dropping their weapons. They left the Captain of the Imperial Army by himself, staring at this horrible creature his superiors had created.

The Captain fell to his knees and prayed to his Gods. The Gods must have laughed.

The Krete took the small human in his hand, examined him, and closed him tightly in a fist. The Captain of the Imperial Army was nothing more than dust that the Krete sprinkled over the downed trees at his feet.

Suddenly, the Krete was still.

The sphere had fallen from Dumml -dee's hands, rolled across the ground to the Krete's metal feet. Dumml -dee lowered himself from a tree to check things out. He made sure the metal giant wasn't moving. Moments later, it struck him as to why he wasn't moving. It was the sphere that made him move. Dumml -dee looked behind him, saw the city gates.

He reached out, grabbed the sphere. The Krete moved, the humming resumed.

Dumml -dee smiled. "Let's go into the city." He told the metal giant. "We have got something to do there."

JORY LOVED TO DRAW HOLES.

He would sit on the windowsill of his apartment, high up on the fourth floor and draw black circles all day. Sure, he drew other things. Knights on their steeds, trampling monsters under their large hooves. Beautiful maidens with monsters as pets. He even drew his mother's cat, Oscar, eating one of the bullies in his second-grade class.

"Nasty," His mother would say. She would only glance at the drawing of Oscar. Continue to prepare dinner.

He showed it to his father, who never looked up over his gardening magazine. "Well, Jory. You are becoming a wonderful artist, aren't you?" His father would cough, then tap his pipe on the ashtray and return the pipe to his chapped lips.

Jory did not like not being tended to.

He went back to his bedroom, opened the window and climbed on to the windowsill . He pushed out his bottom lip, and began drawing holes again. He often wondered what would happen if he tossed down one of those drawings of holes while people walked up and down the busy street under his window.

Always, as he was about to do this, his mother would call him.

This time it was for dinner. Yesterday, it was to go to school. Last week, it was because his baby sitter was over. And the week before, he had to go to the park with his grandpa. Dreadful situation. His curiosity had become so great, that it prevented his nights of restful sleep. In class, while the teacher told the story of a fox and a turnip, Jory's thoughts turned to the holes.

Could it be, he often surmised, that the holes lead to other worlds? Maybe. But he really wanted to know, if he were to drop a drawing of a hole under someone's feet, would they fall into that black spot and disappear?

That thought always made Jory smile.

Of course, while he was smiling at lunch, that bully Martin Best, pushed Jory out of his seat at the lunch table. The boy was twice as tall as Jory, and twice as wide. He had a screwed down red square box for a haircut, small eyes and big wide mouth, which always sat open in a maniacal grin. Martin was forever wearing those horrible red and black striped tee shirts and shorts just past his knees.

Jory reached up to the table and snagged his notebook. He sat under the table and drew a hole. Using his 2b pencil he'd gotten from the art teacher's desk when she wasn't looking, he drew a large circle and shaded it black. He sat under there the whole time Martin ate his two hoagies and Chip Ahoys.

In between eating, the boy would giggle in a husky voice, his whole body shaking the table above Jory.

When Martin rose from his chair to throw his lunch bag away, Jory placed the picture of the hole in front of Martin's high-top sneakers. He took one step, and WHOOSH! He was gone in a flash. Jory crawled out from under the table. He inspected the black circle on the plain white paper, turning it over and over, holding it up in the sunlight.

Jory left the Lunchroom with a huge smile on his face.

Saturday came quickly, and the rest of the week was a piece of cake for Jory since there was no bully at school. He even got to be the Teacher's helper the day after he made Martin Best disappear.

Saturday he and his father went to the park and flew their remote-control helicopters. Later, they ate at the corner Deli and went to the car wash. Jory's Mother had peanut butter cookies she had baked waiting for them on the table. Jory took his bath later that evening with no fuss. He went downstairs to watch the game show network and discovered his parents were going out.

Sandy was over to watch him. She was the teenager next door and Jory definitely did not like her at all. She was bossy, controlled the TV, and never wanted to have fun. One of Jory's recurring nightmares was that he would go to bed one night, wake up in the morning only to discover his parents had given him to Sandy.

The first time she watched him, Jory thought she was nice and very pretty. She played Madden with him, and made great nachos. She even let him stay up past nine o' clock. The next time Sandy watched Jory, she barely paid any attention to him at all. She even made him go to bed too early so she could stay on the phone with a boy.

Now she was downstairs watching a boring reality show on his TV, waiting for him to come sit with her. His parents told him to be good as they went out the front door.

Jory wasn't interested in anything Sandy had for him. Snacks (Cheetos, root beer) Games (Uno, Madden) TV (Cartoon Channel, Nickelodeon,) Books (Charlie and the Chocolate Factory). Instead he wanted to throw fits, scream, kick and make faces at her. He was sent to his bed early.

Jory hated Sandy. He told his Batman action figure. He told his comics that he scattered around the room. He told the walls. He even told God and wished for him to turn Sandy into poop.

Jory sulked in his bed for an hour.

He nearly fell asleep. But a brilliant idea suddenly woke him. He sat straight up in bed and kicked off his blankets.

"The holes," He said to himself.

First, he had to think of a plan. He couldn't get rid of her in the house. His parents would be suspicious, get the cops involved. Couldn't have that. He was too young to go to jail for letting people disappear in a hole.

Jory waited for Sandy to go to the kitchen during a commercial break of one of her boring reality shows and slipped outside.

It was slightly chilly outside. Actually, it was very cold to be out there with no shoes and just in your pajamas. He had his drawing of a hole in his hands. Jory needed to find the right spot to place it. He remembered that over the summer, back when he liked Sandy, she never walked on the sidewalk. She always walked in the grass.

Perfect.

Jory placed the piece of paper with his drawing of a hole right between the two hedges to the left of his front door.

Just then, the front door opened. Sandy appeared, her hands on her hips and a very sour look on her face. "I thought I heard you talking to yourself. What are you doing out here? You'll catch your death?"

Sandy stepped outside and reached out to take hold of Jory. He was quick. He sidestepped towards the drawing, slipped. As he was falling, Sandy caught the collar of Jory's pajamas.

Jory's arms fell on the black hole he'd drawn hours ago. It was like some imaginary force was pulling him inside. His head, his shoulders, and arms slipped in. Mere seconds, Jory was falling into a spiral of light and darkness, Sandy clinging to him. In the spiral were many other black holes of various sizes. What felt like hours of free falling, was actually seconds.

Jory found himself lying on a pile of hay in a barn inhabited by chickens and cows and horses. Jory had the biggest headache ever in his life, similar to the ones he'd get when the seasons changed and loads of pollen was floating in the air. He noticed he was still in his pajamas, though they were torn and frayed at the bottom of the legs.

Jory didn't feel quite himself. He felt itchy and something kept swatting him in the face. He scratched his arm, noticing that it was very hairy. What kept swatting him in the face was a long, thin tail. Jory touched two fangs on each corner of his mouth. He moved a hand to touch the shaggy hair on his head and two pointy ears.

That monster — in his drawings — he'd turned into that monster he had drawn several times.

"That can't be good," He tried to say, but it came out in gurgles and snorts.

Oh great, Jory thought. Now no-one will understand me.

The barn door creaked open and a bit of sunlight appeared, as did a woman in a long flowing silver gown and a pink pointed hat on her blond hair.

She had the ends of her gown in her hands as she stepped toward Jory. He was baffled. The woman not only resembled the princess in his drawings, but she was definitely Sandy. He tried ease himself up to greet her, only there were chains attached to his arms and legs.

"I'm very angry with you," Sandy said. "You ate three of my best chickens --- while they were alive."

"Let me go, please, Sandy," Jory snorted and his throat gurgled.

"No way, you wretched little monster." She pushed Jory back on the pile of hay with her foot.

"You will stay here until you learn to be a better pet." With that statement, Sandy turned on her heels and marched out of the barn with her nose in the air.

Jory lay on the pile of hay and cried for hours.

During the night, Jory discovered something.

The chains that bound him were attached to a very loose piece of wood in the stable. He realized this as he was trying to stop his tail from smacking him in the face, catching his tail above his head. The chain on his left wrist ripped away from that stable shutter immediately. Jory looked at it in amazement. He knew exactly what to do next. He pulled his right arm and the slender column holding up the rest of the stable shutter fell to the pile of hay.

Overjoyed, Jory made loud grunting noises from his diaphragm. He got to his feet in one bound, scurried toward the barn door in a crouched position. He pushed open the barn door, his long yellow nails scraping the weather rot wood. Again, loud grunting noises came from his throat.

The moonlight was bright, burning away most of the darkness in the tiny kingdom. It was Jory's chance to flee. So he ran as far his little hooves could carry him.

From the top of her tower window, Sandy screamed for the guard to catch Jory. A knight on a huge black and white steed was soon on Jory's heels. The knight removed his helmet to reveal he was Martin. Sandy wasn't too far behind. She was waving her arms and calling out all kinds of threats to Jory. Behind her was a giant cat that resembled Oscar, trailing her.

They reached the forest where trees lined up like gates to hide the kingdom. Just as Jory entered the forest, a black spiral opened up and swallowed him. It grew larger, tearing the forest apart, swallowing up the knight and his steed.

Sandy, the knight, the cat, Jory, all of them swirled inside the spiral.

Finally, it expanded and the whole kingdom was engulfed in complete darkness.

Jory found himself being placed in his bed by Sandy. Her eyes were screwed in to show confusion, anger at Jory. She pulled his covers over top of him. They heard voices downstairs. It was Jory's parents. They seemed in a good spirits, laughing, whispering as they came upstairs. Jory saw a body sprawled out on the floor in a sleeping bag beside his bed. It was Martin fast asleep, snoring.

Sandy sighed, looked at Jory. She placed a finger on her lips and shook her head. Which meant tell no-one of what happened.

His parents entered the bedroom and Jory bounced out of bed, hugged and kissed them both. They placed him back in bed. Sandy explained Martin's presence, which was fine with Jory's parents. Father thanked Sandy as she went out the front door. He turned to Jory's mother, perplexed.

"I must be tired," He said, as he took Jory's mother by the arm and led her up the stairs. "I could have sworn Jory had a tail when he jumped out of bed to greet us."

Goop and Gop suddenly found themselves in the pages of a comic book. They exchanged confused looks, then shrugged, continued on their journey through a dark and dreamy world where everything resembled nightmare images. Buildings built sideways, and cars driving backwards. People walking down the street in 1940's attire, speaking without mouths or seeing without eyes. They walked down an alleyway and saw the bricks disintegrate and reform as wooden walls. They realized they were in a house now. A beautiful, well-kept house with many trinkets and paintings on the walls.

In a dark corner, they saw a woman sitting in a chair. Her face was hidden in the shadows and her gnarly hands rested on the lap of her velvet ball gown. Two German Shepherds sat on either side of the chair. The dogs were concerned. Their ears were perked up, and their eyes watched Goop and Gop intently. The woman leaned in out of the shadows. She had a strange grin on her wrinkled face. Goop and Gop noticed she had no eyeballs in her sunken eye sockets.

"You've come for them?' The woman asked.

Goop and Gop exchanged nervous looks.

"Yes, ma'am." They answered her in stereo.

"I would like to find someone as well," the woman said. "Do you think you can help me if I help you?"

One of the German Shepherds started roving around, smelling the pristine, shiny tiled floor. He inched his way over to Goop and Gop. Picking up on a scent, he kept his nose to the floor. Every time Gop would flinch, the dog would stop and look at him. A low rumbling came from the back of the dog's throat. The other German Shepherd watched the scene unfold. He was very anxious to follow his brother, but knew he had to stay where he was to protect his mistress.

"We're not sure," Goop said.

"We don't really know people," Gop lied.

The woman chuckled. "He's trained you well. Could you be a dear and open that cabinet for me?" She said to Goop.

He hesitated, took a step. Both dogs showed their discomfort with him. Their loud, intense barking echoed in the house. The old woman quieted them down with a shush. Both dogs obeyed her immediately.

"Go on," she encouraged Goop. "Open the cabinet, please."

Goop did as he was told. The cabinet door was difficult to open. Gop pulled on Goop, and the door flew open as they fell on their backsides. Both dogs roared, stood at attention, ready to attack.

"Behave!" The old woman screamed. The German Shepherds became silent. They heeled, sat motionlessly without a sound.

Inside the cabinet was a dusty crystal ball. Beside it was a jar with different eye shapes and all eye colors. Goop and Gop were befuddled. They stared at the jar eyes, which stared back them.

"Bring the jar of eyes," the old woman's voice creaked. Gop wasn't sure if he wanted to, but the old woman raised her voice. "Bring the jar of eyes!" Gop instantly reached inside the cabinet and removed the jar. All the eyes floated around in hazy, dirty water that swathed them. He saw the old woman had stood and was pulling an old flimsy card table to her chair. Both dogs nervously walked in circles until the old woman sat down again. He sat the jar of eyes on the card table. The table started to buckle, but held its composure in the end.

"Bring me the crystal ball," the old woman commanded.

Goop shrugged, grabbed the dusty glass ball and took it over to a table beside the old woman. Again, the table wobbled, bent in the middle, but its sturdiness was definitely an enigma. She adjusted her chair to see the crystal ball better.

Her twisted fingers unscrewed the top of the jar with ease. She placed a hand in the hazy, dirty water and caught a pair of deep blue eyes. She fished them out of the jar carefully, as not to damage them. She held them in the palm of her hands and let the water drain back into the jar. The pupils shifted slowly, from left to right, trying to catch a view of where they were. One by one, the old woman placed the eyeballs into her deep-seated eye sockets. Blurry at first, eyesight came to the old woman like a flash of lightning.

The image of Giraud appeared in the crystal ball like images from an old TV set, the vertical lopsided, Horizontal wavy. Giraud was fraught with depression and anxiety. He didn't know what to do with himself, pacing his bedroom from one side to the other. He'd undressed, but not taken his makeup off, and had been ready for bed. But worrying over his scepter and what Drusilla and her sister would do to him because two children had escaped, had magnified his problems tenfold.

"He seems upset," the old woman stated. "Deservedly so. He has not fulfilled his promises to you, has he?"

Goop and Gop exchanged looks. At first sad, but after thinking things over, their expressions were sour, angry.

"No," Goop said.

"We don't like being lied to," Gop said.

"He promised you this," the old woman waved a hand and the image changed. Goop and Gop were standing on a balcony. Millions of people pushed and shoved in a massive crowd to get a look at their newly crowned leader. They screamed and shouted Goop and Gop's names. Women threw themselves at the two men, fainting if even Goop and or Gop blew them a kiss.

"He promised," Gop said in a huff.

"He said he'd give us one of the dimensions to rule," Goop screeched as he clasped both hands together and began to wring them.

"Show me who he really is," the old woman said. "And I promise you'll rule any dimension you fancy."

OTTO KRANTZ STEPPED OUTSIDE of his diner for a breath of fresh air, only to get a lungful of dust as the wind kicked up small clusters around him. He coughed feverishly, smacked his barrel chest a couple of times with the palm of his hand. He caught his breath after a few minutes, sighed, and turned to look at his diner. A yellow and blue square shaped building with a bright red triangle roof. In Otto's eyes, it was a thing of immense beauty. The sign on the front of the building moved side to side with the hard wind, then fell to the ground, barely missing him.

The sign was lovingly hand painted, with much care and detail. A woman in shorts and army shirt tied at her waist, exposing her midriff, stood to attention in the most alluring way. She had a cigarette hanging from her lips and wore an airman's cap. She was saluting the American flag, which prominently overshadowed her. In bold red, white and blue colors to the left of the woman was the name of Otto's diner.

OTTO'S ASTRONOMICAL FOOD.

He stared at the sign, nodded. "I guess I could have thought of a better name for you, huh, baby?" Otto said to the diner.

Otto loved his diner. He loved the smell of the cheap, highly toxic paint he recently slapped on her walls. He loved the futuristic look of the new slope on the roof he commissioned last week. He loved the smell of the burgers, eggs, bacon, stews, that he cooked on her stoves and in her ovens... He loved watching Val, his waitress, glide around in that tight white uniform across the diamond-shaped tile floor he installed last year.

This was a love affair that would never die.

Every day at three p.m., Otto was outside the diner admiring her, remembering five years back to the day he signed on the dotted line to buy this magnificent building, turn her into the dream he had since he was sixteen. Otto was from San Heranado, not far from Joshua tree, California. He moved to the flatlands after a five-year stint in the army. Val, too, was not from there. She was from New York, which Otto figured from her tough talking act and the confident wiggle in her walk.

"Otto?" He heard Val 's voice from the screen door of the diner. He saw a tall, leggy brunette with giant hoop earrings standing on the deck, her hands on her hips. "We have customers to feed, Otto, or have you forgotten about them?" She pranced down the creaky steps and trampled innocent pebbles in the parking lot with the thick heels of her platforms. "What is it about this place that makes you so lovesick, eh?" Val chewed her gum swiftly between each word.

"I just want to stop a few minutes each day and be thankful for what I have. Nothing wrong with that." Otto said.

Val gave him the wife look, a combination of bewilderment, head cocked slightly to the side, and of course, disappointment. She shook her head. "You're such mook." Val took Otto by the hand and led him up the creaky steps.

"A mook? What's a mook?"

"Never mind, dim wit," Val cackled. "The flatlanders are in there and demand our services."

"For crying out loud," Otto protested, pulling away from her. "I hate cooking for those screwballs."

Flatlanders were the town people and ranchers. About three times a week the ranchers came out to eat along with their employees. The cowhands, or some were sheep-hands, would get paid at the end of the month, go to Shemp's bar just in town and get tanked. A few of the fellas and sometimes gals, would end up incarcerated in Sheriff Goldie's damp cell for the night after a big fight. This was just once a month. They head into Otto's diner that lay just outside town a mile or so on Highway 45.

The flatlanders for the most part were okay in Otto's eyes. When a family of three would occasionally wander into his establishment and order a sandwich, split it three ways, Otto would chip in drinks and a side order of fries for free. The three of them usually couldn't finish their fries and would have to take them home for a meal later.

The ranchers, well, they caused mayhem because they had no other way to wind down. The worst of them was Curley Brown. Curley was cow punch for Deanna Grosse's ranch. From all accounts he was good at his job, twice had been her Forman, three times fired for various reasons, mostly for being a stone cold drunk. Curley had eyes for Val. Val had eyes for no one in particular, but enjoyed Otto's company and without Otto noticing, had begun to develop strong feelings for him.

Otto and Val walked into the diner that was now seated with about twenty-five customers, twelve tables filled mostly with ranchers, bar filled with townspeople. Otto snatched his grease stained apron, threw it haphazardly over his neck when he heard Curley call him out.

"Hey, fancy pants, you need help with that," Curley said

and the room shook with laughter. Curley was a big man at six-three and an even bigger mouth with a small vocabulary.

"Curley, it's always good to see you. I see from your outfit the Sheriff let you out of jail recently," Otto said.

For some reason that got a great response, and again the room became panicked with catcalls, whistles, bellowing laughter. Curley didn't like being the punch line in a joke. His oval-shaped face turned beat red, his nostrils flared. He looked like Yosemite Sam ready to blow his stack.

"Quick wit, eh, boys. Quicker mouth. Hey Otto, you sure make a lot of those hamburgers. How come I never see any dogs running around in town? Must be a key ingredient."

"Curley, you are by God the smartest man in the flat-lands," Val said, handing a menu to an elderly couple. "If even I was sure you were a man."

The room roared again, fists banging tabletops. Curley grew angrier by the moment. He sputtered, screamed at his buddies to shut up. The room quieted down.

"Oh, don't worry, Miss Valerie, you will soon know my manhood." Curley retorted.

"Is that what they call it now a days at the doctor's office? No thanks --- a disease is a disease, I always say."

"That hurts, Val. I might have to see you later, after work," Curley said with such conviction and a stare that made the hairs on the back of Val's neck stand up.

"Val," Otto called out to her, eyeing Curley from the kitchen. "I have an order up. Would you get it?"

"Yeah, sure, Otto," She said, nervously pushing past Curley.

Otto went to Curley. They were facing each other, nose to nose, eyes locked on each other. Otto could smell the whiskey on Curley, nearly knocked him down.

"You ever say a thing like that to my employee and I'll give you a fight you'll never forget." Otto said. "You don't understand, I'm not a flatlander like these others in town. I don't shiver when you whisper."

"Oh," Curley let out an effeminate giggle. "I forgot you was a doughboy at one time."

"I was never a doughboy, cheese head. My great grandfather was a doughboy. I served in Afghanistan and Iraq. I've seen Iraqi women that could wipe their asses with you. Just remember what I said." Otto walked away. But Curley wasn't done.

"Otto, doesn't scare easy. I know his customers would be frightened to death if they ever found creepy crawlies in their soups."

Otto turned quickly to Curley. He smacked the kitchen door. His lips became tighter, trying not to rattle off the first thing that came to his mind. Otto's pace picked up as he drew closer to Curley. Again, they were face to face.

"You start spreading lies like that, Curley Brown," Otto whispered, gritting his teeth. "I'll make sure you're not only dead, but I'll be the one digging your grave, and pissing on it at your funeral."

"Only joshing," Curley laughed. "Just joshing, Mr. Otto." He shrugged.

The door opened to the diner and a young man in ragged tee shirt and jeans stepped inside. He looked like he had had rough times. His face had dirt caked on, and the smell of body odor was so bad, most in the diner made a sour face. The young man shook slightly, his attention span was short, turning to see whatever noise or movement made. Val found his appearance repulsive, strange, nevertheless she approached him.

"Would you like a table or sit at the bar?" Her hands danced around to show the young man and his eyes followed closely. He just smiled, nodded. Val eyed him a second or two before encouraging him to follow her to a table in the back near the ranchers. She urged him to sit, handed him a menu. Then Val realized the young man didn't understand to read the list and tell her what he wanted.

"Why don't I bring you half a sandwich," She said and sighed. She snatched the menu from his docile hands, leaving him to stare at his fingertips as if he was reading a book.

Val pushed open the swinging door, stepped inside the kitchen. Otto was busy cooking hamburgers, setting more fries in the vat, shaking a little Cajun seasoning on a basket he had already prepared.

"What's up?" He asked.

"Another derelict out there. Looks like this one fell out of a boxcar. He's not all there." Val said, crossing her arms over her breasts.

"Don't look like he can pay, huh?" Otto slapped a burger on a plate, dumped some fries beside it. "Give him this."

"No, Otto. Those people are going to drive you out of business." She pushed the plate back in Otto's hands. "This one ---- this one is creepy."

"Creepy or not, a person has to eat. Where's he at?" Otto demanded.

" It's your diner," Val threw her hands up. "Table ten. In the back."

"You put him with the flatlanders? Val! Especially with Curley Brown out there, you know that's bad news!"

"I'm sorry. I forgot your rule." Val rolled her eyes. "Listen to me, Otto. I have a bad feeling about this one. "You should put the food in a bag and send him on his way."

"I got it, Val. Everything is going to be okay." Otto patted Val on her ass and she rolled her eyes.

Otto took the plate of food to the young derelict, who was at his table surrounded by three flatlanders, one of which was Curley Brown. Otto shook his head. He knew he should've kicked Curley out earlier in the day.

"Hey, boy, I know you're from somewhere," Curley said, repositioning himself on the table. The derelict kept nodding his head and giggling.

"Something ain't right with this one Curley," One of his buddies said.

"That's because his mama and daddy were cousins," Curley replied. His buddies guffawed, smacking each other on the arm. "That right boy?" Curley raised his voice slightly as if the young man was deaf. "You the product of kissing cousins? Huh? It's okay. It's against the law, but that don't stop some family from being too friendly with each other."

Otto had heard enough. He walked over to the table, elbowed one of Curley's buddies out of the way, and slammed the plate down. "Here you go, pal," Curley smiled at the young man. "It's on the house. Where you from?"

The derelict nodded, smiled. Picked up the hamburger and bit into it with the side of his mouth that still had teeth, though they were brown and ready to fall out anytime.

"Otto, why can't we ever get a free meal?" Curley asked. "I'm just as needy as this fellow."

"You are indeed needy, Curley. I have to say, I think this young man is definitely smarter than you."

Curley lowered himself off the table, and not in the most agile way. He moved slow and concise like he was a gunfighter. He looked around the room to see who was snickering. Whoever it was, would get it later.

"You can't talk to a customer like that, Otto. A good one too. I've bought a many a coffee and hamburger when I could have spent that on real food."

"You mean whiskey, don't you?" Otto said. He was more than ready to flatten Curley that day. "Now, you and the rest of the flatlanders have eaten. So get out of my place."

While everyone was preoccupied, the young derelict had found a steak knife wrapped in a napkin along with a spoon and fork. He took the knife in his right hand and held it to his left wrist. The jagged blade slid across easily, breaking his dirty pale skin. The blood trickled down his arm, then flowed like a river that been damned up. A strange thing happened. Before the blood drops hit the table, they morphed into tiny, fat, white roaches. There were hundreds that ran free on the table top, and in mere moments, they were double that. Before anyone noticed, a thousand of those white devils had run rampant at Otto and Curley Brown's feet.

Curley squealed like stuck pig, and ran in a circle with his hands in the air. Panic broke out in the diner. Curley's screams were not in vain. Several of the white, black dotted roaches, about the length of anyone's forefinger, raced up Curley's pants leg. Rushing up his body, many of the roaches began to cover Curley's legs, and midsection. A strange milky substance had also been passed out ofthe black dome.shaped end of their bodies , which began to burn part of his clothing away like boric acid on plastic.

Curley took off, sprinting through the diner's exit door, screaming, "Lord-God-Jesus-help me!" He was out in the street, swiping the roaches from his body and face, waving his arms like a lunatic.

The rest of the customers followed his example. The absurd moment was exactly that: an absurd moment in everyone in the diner's life. Otto saw the roaches, began to take the offensive by stepping on the ones that had been at his feet. But the bugs seemed to only be interested in Curley Brown. When he left, they went with him. When Otto realized this, he tried to call everyone back inside, in spite of a hoarse voice, no one listened. They converged out in the parking lot, facing Highway 45.

Otto threw his hands up, still lost in some sort of bewilderment.

Val ran out of the kitchen to investigate the commotion.

"What just happened?" She asked, looking out the window at all the people in the parking lot.

"I don't know exactly," Otto started to laugh. "But the craziest thing...."

The derelict had his head laying on the table, eyes closed, mouth slack.

"He's not dead, is he?" Val touched the young man's shoulder and he bounced up giggling.

The front door opened and a man in a black overcoat and a black homburg appeared in the doorway. He stood there a second, taking in Otto's establishment. The man scrunched up his nose, screwed his eyes down. Otto's diner was not to his liking.

Otto noticed that. Otto took in a deep breath. "Can I help you, bub?"

The man forced himself to smile. "Yes...I'm here to pick up my son---Oh, there you are," He said, and went to the young derelict. The young man laughed, pointed at Otto, the diner, then outside.

"Yes, yes," The man said, helping the young man from the table. "That was very droll, son. Come along Wilford." The two of them pushed through the exit door. "Mother has been very worried about you."

The man's overcoat rode up revealing a long, black, dome shaped shell. Otto and Val were stunned. They exchanged glances.

Val shook her head. "This place gets weirder and weirder."

Defeated, Otto slowly moved to the diner's entrance, turned the sign over from open to closed. He sighed and nodded. "Yep. You're right, Val," Otto said and smiled. He grabbed her by the waist and kissed her. "That's what I like about it."

———

Goop and Gop stood in front of Otto's restaurant staring at the old building. A memory had stopped them from going inside. It was the day they met Giraud. The problem was, the memory kept changing. Other memories morphed into another memory. Or were they lies? They weren't sure. All they knew was that when those "memories" came to them, they just stood still and thought about those happenings all day long. They played out the instances in their minds as if they were starring in their own TV show. The scenes played out over and over....

Until something interrupts.

Still, those "memories" haunt Goop and Gop every day and whatever they are in the middle of, never gets resolved.

THEY WERE SITTING in Smokey's having coffee, not saying word, staring at each other like staring at their own reflection. Jeff and Kyle had grown up twenty miles from each other, different parents, different friends, owning the same face. They were dressed similarly, blue suits, white ties. Jeff had gold cufflinks, a present from the Insurance Company for the most sales in a year, that was the only difference.

"I guess I should break the ice," Kyle said, after a lengthy silence.

Jeff smiled. "I guess you should," He took a sip of his coffee and waited. When Kyle didn't continue , Jeff held his hand up, asking Kyle to continue.

Kyle laughed, shrugged. "It was a little strange when you called."

"It was stranger whom I passed on the sidewalk two weeks ago. It's not every day you see someone with your FACE attached to their body."

Their waitress showed up again, arms folded. "Can I get you two anything else?" She looked unhappy, even though there was a forced smile on her face. Actually, it was a strain. She looked as if she'd lived a hard life, but Kyle didn't want to jump to conclusions. He still thought maybe she'd been a junkie at one time.

"I do believe I would like a piece of cherry pie," Jeff spoke up.

The top of the waitress's head opened up like the trunk of a car. Out of the pitch-black inside, two hands rose up holding a pen and a notepad, immediately wrote down Jeff's order. "How about you, doll?" She said to Kyle.

"Oh...sure. Cherry pie is fine." He nodded.

The hands wrote down the order and disappeared in the in the dark corners of her mind. The top of her head closed slowly. "Okay. Two cherry pie slices coming up," She said as her salt shaker shape body walked away.

Kyle spied a group of Mimes sitting at a table across from them. They all sported fur coats and rings on every finger. One Mime had a steak knife, cleaning his fingernails, while the other was cleaning his 45. The conversation from the group turned very loud and intense regarding their "stable" of women that earn their living on the streets.

Kyle looked away. Jeff tapped the table with a finger. "Have you been listening to me?" He said.

"Oh! Yes," Kyle cleared his voice. "You, uh, said your father was a pharmacist?"

"Yeah," Jeff sipped his coffee. "My mother drove a bus. What did your father do?"

"He owns newspaper companies. Print is dead, it's sacrilegious to him."

"And your mother?"

"Mothers."

The salt and pepper shakers levitated and floated around their heads.

"Oh," Jeff raised an eyebrow.

"My father was married four times. This last one has lasted ten years, she's only six years older than me."

Jeff snickered. Soon the waitress brought the slices of pie. She set the plates down gingerly, waddled away.

"What do you do?" Kyle took a bite of his pie, chewed, and then made a sour face. He put his fork down and pushed his plate away.

"I'm a salesman." Jeff broke off huge chunks of pie with his fork.

He was pleased with his pie and it showed in the enthusiastic way he was eating.

"What is it you sell?" Kyle so wanted a cigarette, but would not risk being shot on sight by a policeman if he lit up in a restaurant.

In the corner of the restaurant, in a booth, a woman and a wolf were making love very loudly.

"Body parts," Jeff said nonchalantly. "You know, mostly kidneys, arms, livers. The occasional brain, but I don't think those transplants really work."

"Yes," Kyle sighed. "I suppose they don't."

"What about you?" Jeff asked.

"Nothing." Kyle shrugged.

"Oh, come on. A person has to do something," Jeff chuckled.

Kyle shook his head. "Not me."

"How do you live? You need---"

"Money. I live off my Father. He has plenty. And I found out recently, that if you have influence, you can do whatever you want." Kyle said.

Outside on the street, a gang of headless thugs chased a man down and tore him to pieces. They took the pieces of flesh and stapled them to the restaurant's door, wrote graffiti with his blood.

"What do you mean by that?" Jeff had a sheepish smile on his face.

The walls began to breathe in and out, leaving a low moan as with mood music.

"Well. I was driving through a sleepy desert town at two in the morning last year and I swerved into someone's yard, a ratty place, full of old tires stacked to heaven and broken-down cars everywhere. I swerved and killed a young boy. I wrote a check out to the parents for ten thousand dollars. Then I called the family lawyer and he called the town mayor and the family was moved out of their home that they'd lived in for twenty years. The place was condemned. Bulldozed over, and land sold for a shopping center."

"That wasn't very nice. They got to keep the money though."

"No," Kyle said, "I had the father arrested for forgery."

"You are a rotten person." Jeff proclaimed.

"So I am told very often." Kyle admitted.

"Well, I must be off. Meeting my girl outside." Jeff stood, looked out the restaurant's window. A woman and her Siamese twin attached at the shoulder was waving at him. Jeff waved back.

"Is that her?" Kyle asked.

"Yeah," Jeff nodded. "Maybe I'll see you around."

"More than you know," Kyle replied. Jeff turned and was out the door. He took his girl's arm and headed down the street. Kyle began to laugh, everyone in the restaurant joined in.

Kyle closed his eyes. When he reopened them he was alone, leaning against the wall of his white room, trying to get comfortable in his straight jacket.

JIMMY MARTZ WAS NOT the smartest guy in the world, but he ran one of hottest companies in the electronic trade. He didn't even come up with the idea. He just read an article in a magazine he couldn't remember on a flight headed to San Antonio to deal with a divorce. Some guy in Atlanta had built a touch screen tablet that ran both Apple components and Microsoft. That wasn't even the kicker. He had put a chip in it to make cell phone calls from any company for free. Martz only had to pay a small fee to the cell phone companies.

Martz had met the Holland Wilkes in Atlanta at a hotel room where Wilkes resided. It was there that Martz had his team of lawyers work up a contract that virtually cut Wilkes out of any royalties and the only money he was to receive was a one-time amount of five thousand dollars to be paid out over ten years. It turned out Wilkes was bat-shit crazy and money was not a concern. He was worried about little green men with their black gloves removing his soul was his testicles.

Martz couldn't be happier as he boarded his plane back to Miami with the plans to a new tablet.

Gladys was extremely happy to have money again. His

divorce from his third wife was messy and expensive, working for a toy company executive that made playdoh knockoffs did not keep them in good company at the club.

Once STELLAR Tablets took off, Martz was on everyone's list to play croquet. Money was not a problem. So he and Gladys invested in real estate. Buying up several buildings along the Fourth and Habeas Street to knock down for a mini mall.

There was a problem on the third building. This building had been an apartment complex for low income people. Then it was condemned. Nearly abandoned. The Foreman tearing the buildings down had gotten rid of almost all who were there.

Except one.

This old man was cunning. He'd somehow gotten past all the construction crew to the bulldozer and stolen the keys from the ignition. A thug the Foreman had hired to take the old man out anyway he could had fallen out of the three story building window, breaking both legs.

Martz decided to handle this himself.

Years ago, on the streets of L.A., Martz had kept some tough company. Even participated in some gang activity until an incident of three dead rival gang members who were executed before his eyes. Martz felt it was good time to get out of town. So he felt as though he could take on an old man, no problems.

"Hey, you have to get out of here! I own this place now," Martz banged on the door of the apartment with both fists. The door fell off the hinges, disturbing a vast amount of dirt on the floor. "What the—and they couldn't get inside the place? somebody was bull crappin' me."

Martz stepped inside, looked around. "Jesus...at least the old man has decorated." It looked like a junkyard. TVs scat-

tered throughout, toilets set up like furniture and old adver-
tisements from billboards were used for wallpaper.

In the middle of other junk and empty food containers
were shopping carts with missing wheels, fastened together
with blades from lawnmowers. An extension cord was
connected to ten computer towers, which were linked
together with hundreds of wires. The craziest thing was that
all the lights on the computer towers were blinking blue. And
an old printer from the early nineties was printing out on
teletype paper.

Martz looked at the print and it was all nonsense. Symbols
and math equations. He followed the trail that led to a
bedroom, piled with more junk. Busted microwaves and
stereo parts. Books, were stacked above his head, reminded
him of the ruins in Rome.

Martz was ready to give up on talking to the old man
when he heard movement from a corner of the bedroom near
some chairs stacked on top of each other. He walked over and
discovered nothing was holding them together. He touched
the chairs, they wobbled, but stayed in place. He heard heavy
breathing, then saw a man lying on a bed made of magazines.

"Hey, you know you can't stay here," Martz said, shuffling
to the old man, who barely moved, except for his eyes rolling
around in a powder-white head. Several sores were puss-
bound on the old man's misshapen face. Martz kicked at the
old man's leg and a hand took hold of his pants leg. Martz
shook the hand away, cursing loudly. "Listen you old fucker!
No tricks, get out now!" The hand grabbed Martz again by
the pants leg and brought him hard to the floor. There was a
stream of pain from his back to his neck.

Before Martz could say anything, the old man pulled him
closer to him by his jacket lapel and placed both hands on his
forehead.

In a rush of visions, Martz saw the old man as a young

man building the contraption that was in the other room. He saw the young man reading data from the printouts, stating a report that in fifty years' time a colossal explosion will end humanity. A threat from an alien species, millions of light years from earth, called the Torgias. The old man had finally contacted the Torgias with terms of foregoing the attack. The old man explained he was from a distant planet in an alternate wormhole that protected smaller planets from that viscous alien species which destroyed planets, unless payment was received.

"Here," The old man handed Martz a gold coin the size of his palm. "Go to 54th Street, where the solar clock stands in the park. At exactly noon today, place it in the upper right corner where it looks like a crack, it isn't. It has always been there for that reason. A beam of sunlight will send the message back to the Torgias. Your planet will survive."

"I-I don't think I can--" Martz tried to tell the old man, but he ceased to exist.

The old man's eyes were still, and now his hands fell from Martz jacket. His mouth became slack. There was a low-sounding gurgle.

Martz held the coin in his hand, swallowed hard. He had to do it. He had no other option. He jumped to his feet and ran out of the apartment, kicking empty containers out of his way. He looked at his gold watch and saw it was eleven forty-five. 54th Street was across the street. He ran out of the building and down the sidewalk. He ran across the street and avoided several cars from taking him out of commission. He pushed open the gate to the park where a guard screamed at him to pay up. He ran past barking dogs and their concerned owners, past ducks trying find pieces of bread in the grass.

He'd made it to the solar clock. It towered over him by at least six feet and just as he was feeling the bricks that held the contraption together, he heard voices behind him.

Ten men in gang-related garb had surrounded him. Martz swallowed, looked up at the solar clock. Two minutes to noon.

"We just want your wallet, asshole," A smaller gang member said and stepped forward. He showed Martz his nine-millimeter. .

"Look," Martz held up his hands. The gold coin caught their eyes. "You don't understand."

The gun went off just as the clock struck twelve. A bullet caught Martz in the chest and went right through. He fell to the ground under the solar clock. The coin rolled to the one holding the gun. He bent down and picked up the coin. They heard sirens and scattered.

"You...don't understand...you don't understand..." Martz said as he slipped into unconsciousness.

Footsteps plowing away at the street took Goop and Gop away from those memories. Suddenly, they realized they were not standing in front of Otto's restaurant anymore. Goop and Gop had moved through the corridors again and ended up in a small town with several small buildings and a main road that was not paved.

An odd old man shuffled past them. He had a bottle tied around his neck. He seemed to be hurry.

Goop and Gop exchanged glances.

"Hmm," Goop said, raised an eyebrow.

"Very strange," Gop said.

They both shrugged and found an opening in one of the buildings that led to the corridor. They walked through the opening and disappeared, just as the opening did.

THEY SAW him coming down Main Street kicking up dirt behind him; doing a sort of power walk. Leonard was the first to notice the man in the checkerboard sports jacket, ball cap, and tennis shoes with holes in the sides. He was approaching fast, past the barber shop and the school house. Bob noticed something around his neck, swinging back and forth with every step the stranger took. Sol pointed out that the man must have been on the road a long time.

"See the dust flying off of him," Sol said.

"Pitiful sight."

Bob shook his head, rocked a little more in his rocking chair, as he carried on whittling a stick he'd been working on for a week.

Leonard laughed. "He could be one of your cousins, Sol."

Bob joined in, his laughter more like a squeak.

They were the eyes, ears, and mouths of that town called Leering. They'd gather at Sol's store around two pm, sit on the front porch, and spin stories and gossip about the town's residents till around six. All three had lived in that small town all their lives. All three had never once set a foot outside the state of Virginia.

Bob ran the garage, and had been a grease monkey from the age of twelve. Leonard called himself a farmer, but never really grew anything. He made his money doing odd jobs around town, and once in a while did maintenance on the school house and football field.

"Look at that idgit go." Bob shook his head again.

"Where in the hell did he come from?" Leonard posed to the others.

The three of them exchanged confused looks, shrugging their shoulders.

The stranger came closer, stumbling as one foot tangled with the other. He fell to the dusty street in front of the store. The three of them jumped up and ran to the stranger's rescue.

"Whoa...buddy." Leonard put a hand on the man's torn jacket to lift him up by its shreds.

Bob helped by pulling on the bottle around his neck attached to a gold chain. It fell off with ease, hitting the pavement. The bottle bounced then rolled to Sol's feet. He bent down and scooped it up. Sol made a face. While this was going on, Bob and Leonard had gotten into a heated exchange about clumsiness.

"Weird," Sol said, turning the silver bottle around and around in his hands. "This thing is warm...feels like a beating heart..."

Bob and Leonard left the stranger in the middle of the street to see what Sol was talking about.

He lay down, turning his face skyward to let out a long sigh before promptly ceasing to exist. Bob and Leonard rushed back over to the stranger's side.

"He's dead..." Bob gave Leonard a confused look.

"What the hell?" Leonard shook his head, a whining whistle leaving his lips as he did so. "I never in my life...Sol, this man is dead...Sol?"

Sol was still intrigued by the silver bottle. He held it up in the sunlight. He read the inscription on the side that had been engraved in old English lettering.

"Whosoever holds this bottle, once owned by COMTE SAINT-GERMAIN, will live as long as he is its curator and defender...la vie éternelle."

Bob and Leonard looked at each other. "What did he say?"

Leonard made a face.

"You okay, Sol?" Bob rushed to his old friend's side.

Leonard trailed him.

Bob took Sol by the elbow. "Let's get you out of this heat, old boy."

They pushed him forward a few steps.

"What about the dead guy?" Leonard nodded towards the body.

"Go tell Bill about him," Bob yelled out.

Leonard stood paralyzed for the moment, seemingly confused, then, as if something had just occurred to him, he ran across the street to the jailhouse.

Later that evening, after Bill, the town sheriff, took care of the stranger and the locals' statements. Leonard, Bob, and Sol gathered at Sol's store.

They sat out on the porch to watch the sun set. It was Leonard and Bob doing the talking mostly. Sol was on the other side to them with the empty beer kegs, mumbling to himself. In an instant, Sol let out a blood curdling scream. Bob and Leonard jumped from their seats. They held onto each other.

Sol's face was frozen in agony.

His mind was taken back in time. A stone hammer pounded nails into a hand that was now bound to one side of a wooden cross. Another flash, another vision came and the imagery changed. The cross had been driven into the ground hours ago. The glaring sun cast a shadow on the man's body as clouds darkened the sky above. Below, on the ground, a woman holding a silver bottle caught blood dripping from the cross.

Then Sol snapped out of it.

"La vie éternelle," Sol said.

Bob and Leonard were bewildered when they finally noticed they were holding each other tightly. A feeling of embarrassment came over them. They pushed each other away.

Sol got up and left.

They watched him scuffle down the street toward his house, kicking up dust behind him.

"What in the world..." Bob scratched his head.

"I think Sol is sick, Bob," Leonard sighed.

"What's Jane going to think of Sol and his bottle?"

Leonard looked at Bob, clearing his throat. "I have a bigger question for you."

"What's that, Leonard?"

"What's in the bottle?"

———

Bob and Leonard were at Sol's store.

Bob tried the front door, exasperated. "It's still locked."

"Ain't seen him in two days. I'm worried, Bob."

"Me too, Leonard. Me too."

"Hey!" Leonard screamed, pointing to a man shuffling his feet through the street, cars dodging him. "It's Sol!"

Leonard started off the front porch of the store, Bob grabbed hold of his shirt and pulled him back.

"We gotta get him!" Leonard cried out, shaking off Bob's grip.

Bob shook his head. "Let him go," he said. "He obviously has something important to do."

I moved a hand over my chest where a newly created tattoo of the sign of Mogul rested. The sign that will protect me till the end of my life and well into my afterlife.

Spying through the trees, one can see a man in a black hat and trench coat walking the solemn streets of an idyllic American neighborhood. From a distance he can be tracked happily wandering aimlessly from one side of the street to the other, wobbling in a frantic shuffle. He can be seen whispering to himself, his eyes widening with every syllable spoken.

Finally, he stopped in front of a house that was obviously built in the nineteen-fifties with a modern porch built on. The man extended his arms, sighed. He had found his journey's end.

The strange man murmured to himself, giggled. He opened the screen door to the porch, eloquently, if not prissy, walked to the front door. He rang the doorbell, jumped as if a hand had touched his shoulder. He looked around, giggled, whispered to himself, pointed up to the sky. He rang the doorbell again. He took a step back and removed his hat before bowing.

He giggled, stamped his foot.

The front door opened. A woman in her mid-fifties appeared. She looked hurried, harassed. "Yes?"

She spoke softly, apprehensively.

"I beg your pardon, madam. I am looking for a Meg Hopewell?" The man's eyes lit up as he spoke the name.

"She's not home," The creases in the woman's face tightened after taking a long hard look at the strange little man at her door. "What is it you want with Meg?"

"I only wish to speak with her. My employer wishes to offer her something--"

"She's not here! I told you."

"I'm sorry, madam..?"

The woman wasn't sure if she should reveal who she was, then thought, why not. I have the upper hand. "Mrs. Hopewell. I'm Meg's mother."

The man bowed again, giggled. He shook his head, stamped his foot. "I am very pleased to meet you."

"Look, mister, I don't have time to chat with you. What do you want?" Mrs. Hopewell put her hands on her hips.

"Oh, I only wish to give Meg a present."

"Do you know my Meg somehow?"

"Oh...yes...in a way...I surely do..."

The strange little man took from his trench coat a gold colored gift box with a red bow tied around it. He bowed his head. "Please," he said. "This is for your Meg. My employer wishes her to have this..."

Mrs. Hopewell looked perplexed. She wasn't sure if she should take the box, but felt propelled to do so. Hesitantly, she took the box from the strange little man, who immediately began to laugh. It was glowing. The box felt warm, breathing slightly. She saw Meg's name embroidered on the box. Mrs. Hopewell gasped, tried to hand the box back.

The man was gone. She stood in the doorway, lost in thought. She looked out in the street. The street was empty except for a young boy riding his bicycle. Mrs. Hopewell shivered. She closed the front door, sat the box on the hutch in her foyer

———

"I did as you said," The strange little man said. He was sitting at a long table in a dark room, a flickering candle the only light. Across from him was a shadowy figure, a woman by the grace of her mannerisms. "I only hope for my reward---"

"That is all you can hope for!" The woman screamed. Her voice echoed in the near empty house.

"I have followed this girl from her school in Vienna to this little shit hole town! This better be the right one..." The woman rose from the table. Briefly the little man caught her visage. A weather-worn face living well beyond her years.

"Madam Guneer, I assure you, the girl is last one for your time to be young...forever." The little man giggled. Quickly he shut himself up. "I have found you six others from your class over the last three years...SHE is the seventh and last one."

"You said that about the last girl," Madam Guneer said, coldly.

"Minor complication. I did not know she was not a blood kin of the woman she called Mother."

"I am well versed in the spell, you little toad!" Madam Guneer spat in his direction. "The only daughter of an only child---seven I need to regain my youth. There's a reason Gypsies should be wiped off the earth."

"Madam, I too, am running out of time..."

"Oh yes," Madam Guneer walked toward the little man. "The cancer that you have."

"Yes...the cancer that is eating me away..."

Madam Guneer bent down over the little man. "And now...your prize." She lunged at him, elongated fangs protruding from her pale broken lips. The first feeding was Zen for the little man. Blood dribbled down his neck, his gaze fixated on the burning candle. His thoughts went to all things he would do as he lived forever. Then something went terribly wrong.

The pain was immense.

The second feeding was a feast. Madam Guneer tore his throat apart, chewing flesh as if it were chewing gum. She swallowed, lapped up his warm blood gushing to the floor.

"My prize...my prize..." were the little man's last words.

———

Mrs. Hopewell sat on her couch, listening to her daughter enter the house. Suitcase on the floor first. Coat next to it. Left shoe, then right shoe in the middle of the foyer. Meg came in the living room like a whirlwind and jumped on the couch next to her mother.

"Hello," Meg smiled.

A smile from her father, Mrs. Hopewell thought.

"Hello, pet." Meg laughed, threw her arms around Mrs. Hopewell's neck. She kissed Meg on the cheek, hugged her close. "I've missed you."

"Missed you, too, Mommy. What's been happening here in perfect little boresville?"

"Oh, you joke, Meg. Someday you'll miss this town."

"I already do, Mommy. I went to see Daddy's grave before I came here. You pinned my drawing of him on his gravestone."

"He always liked your drawings."

"I know. Wish he knew I made it to Vienna."

"He knows, Meg. I tell him every night before I go to sleep."

"Yeah. I know you, Mommy."

Meg saw the gold box on the coffee table. She draws a breath. A hand crosses her chest, she glances at Mrs. Hopewell. She looked back at the box. "She said she would send it to me. I...I didn't believe her." Meg wiped tears from her cheek.

Mrs. Hopewell bit her lower lip. I'm not judging, she thought. "Who did, Meg?"

"Mrs. Guneer. My teacher in life drawing, Mommy. Remember? I wrote you about her." Meg said.

Mrs. Hopewell had a funny look on her face. Finally, she nodded her head. "I remember."

"She lives in the most extraordinary castle, Mommy. Very dark...brooding. You'd love it." Meg picked up the box. It began to glow in her hands. "This jewelry case...is so beautiful. The last day I was there, Mrs. Guneer said she'd give this to me. I admired it so much...didn't have to ask for it...she knew I loved it."

"A strange little man brought it here just yesterday." Mrs. Hopewell said.

"Is that right? I once saw a peculiar man in a black trench coat leave her castle. She sounded very upset with him. Her dogs chased him away." Meg laughed. "Who wears trench coats anymore? "

"Meg?" Mrs. Hopewell touched her daughter's hand. "You're causing your hand to bleed---please Meg..."

Meg had been clutching that box so tightly her hands were sinking into the corners of the gold box. Mrs. Hopewell pulled her hands from the box. The box fell to the floor. Mrs. Hopewell took her daughter to the bathroom upstairs to tend to the wounds. The box seemed to soak up the blood that fell from Meg's hands.

———

Night fell fast. A blanket of darkness covered the town and no stars lit up the sky above. Inside Meg's room, she lay adrift in deep sleep. Furiously tossing and turning in her bed. Dreams were fast moving and vivid. Images flashed, people moved in and out of frame in fast cuts. One image kept appearing. That of a man hanging from a noose and two rabid dogs sniffing at his rotting corpse.

The box sat on a book shelf in Meg's room, between Neil Gaiman's *Coraline* and Alan Moore's *Watchmen*.

The glowing box was breathing, the pewter moving and expanding like flesh in unison with Meg's irregular breathing. Suddenly, a sharp cry came from Meg's sleeping lips. The box sighed.

———

The next few mornings Mrs. Hopewell was doing laundry. She noticed a few spots of blood on one of Meg's nightgowns. She examined it closely, thought a few minutes. She heard footsteps on the staircase.

"Mom?" Meg called out to her.

Mrs. Hopewell went to the living room and saw Meg lying on the stairs, passed out. She cradled her daughter's head in her lap. Meg's nightgown had fallen off her shoulders. Mrs. Hopewell saw the two little punctures in Meg's neck on the right side. Mrs. Hopewell gasped, her hand drew to her parted lips. She whispered in Meg's ears, Meg stirred, just enough to get to her feet. Mrs. Hopewell leveled her daughter's right side on her, helped her to the bedroom.

She lay the sick girl in her bed, covered her up and said a prayer.

"Soon, the Doctor will be here," She told Meg.

———

Mrs. Hopewell sat at her daughter's bedside. She kept thinking about what the Doctor had said. He couldn't find much wrong with Meg, except the loss of blood, how pale she was. At the clinic, Meg was normal. In the daytime, for the most part, she was normal, apart from being seemingly weak when lifting certain things.

I just don't understand it, Mrs. Hopewell thought.

The Doctor went so far as to suggest there was a mental problem regarding Meg. Last two nights, it's the same thing. Meg screaming. She's out of her bed, on the floor, begging someone to not hurt her. Mrs. Hopewell helps her to her bed, she sees the little holes in her neck, the blood streaming from them. In the morning, Meg remembers nothing.

———

Meg was restless. The covers and sheets were like chains bound around her body. Her hands were twisted in front of her face. She mumbled, "No...Please!"

A white noise could be heard, growing louder and louder, a droning hum. The box sat on her book shelf, glowing red, like a heart beating faster and faster.

A woman with long, blond, tasseled hair, faded into existence. In her long, white, flowing gown, her bare feet rose above the floor. Her whole body eased toward Meg as if a wind blew her there. Meg screamed again. Her hands were grabbing at the air, her fingers writhing. The woman hovered over top of Meg, baring slender white fangs from under broken lips. The woman lowered her face to Meg's snow-white neck.

The woman jolted upright. She turned quickly, still hovering in the air. Mrs. Hopewell was in the doorway of the bedroom. She stood there, fear had turned her into stone, momentarily. The woman reared her head and growled at Mrs. Hopewell. Mrs. Hopewell snapped out of her trance.

She produced a cross made of silver. The points on each cross end as sharp, it let off a bit of light from the nightlight in the bedroom. The woman threw her arms over her face, hissed. In one smooth lunge, the cross was buried in the top of the glowing box, blood gushing from its wounds.

The woman no longer hovered over Meg. She gradually faded out, leaving nothing behind to suggest she had ever existed, for the box turned to ashes.

Mrs. Hopewell rushed to her daughter, caressed her.

Meg woke, rubbed her eyes. "What's wrong, Mom?"

Mrs. Hopewell sighed. "Bad dreams. That's all."

———

In the early morning hour, that small sleepy town could hear a harsh cry echo along the horizon. In a dark house hidden in the middle of other sleepy houses, at the top floor, the bedroom of Madame Guneer was empty. Her bed showed signs of presence. Small, black specks of ashes of a body lay in that bed, until a breeze from an open window carried those ashes off and sprinkled the town's green idyllic hills.

HE WAS TALL, very tall, the man they called Gerin. He stood at the exit of the train cart and glanced over at several corners of the train station. He was mustached, balding on top, hair parted in a ridiculous school boy fashion. His face showed of a man very serious and stern. His suit was a bland gray with a fat blue tie that most definitely didn't match.

Gerin found a cab parked a few feet away from the newsstand behind the train station. The only cab not bothered by anyone. He walked up to the cab, opened the door to the left rider's side and slid in on the noisiest vinyl covering he'd ever come across.

The cab driver was in the middle of his lunch. A messy hamburger where the sauce sat comfortably on his chin. "I'm not on duty," The Cabbie said, his mouth spitting out chewed bun on his shirt. He casually wiped it off. He was looking at Gerin in the rear-view mirror.

Gerin sighed. "Look I need a ride into Vandy. I'll pay double the rate."

The Cabbie finished his burger in one swallow. When he was done, he laughed. "My God, friend. No one rides into

Vandy. Not the least it's a good fifty-six miles from this train station. It's also the most boring town in America."

"As you say, sir, I need the ride. It includes the tip." Gerin avoided the Cabbie's gaze in the mirror.

"It would have to, friend. On top of the fare and double the rate." He started the engine and the cab coughed and spat out a dark cloud of fumes that nearly choked Gerin to death. "And away we go." The Cabbie said in a sing-song voice. They drove a few miles down a road that took them across a hill of green grass and cows with eyes the color of the black hole. Still, Gerin would not look his driver in the eyes. This annoyed the Cab driver to no ends.

"For you to pay this amount of money, not rent a car, must be pretty important to go to Vandy." The Cabbie said.

Gerin thought a moment. He kept his eyes on the scenery. "Yes, I suppose it must be." He retorted.

The Cabbie waited a few minutes. He laughed, looked in the rear-view mirror. "Why the hell didn't you rent a car, friend?"

Gerin breathed through flared nostrils. "I can't drive," He said.

"You're kiddin', at your age?" The Cabbie turned around briefly to see Gerin's reaction.

"Business there?"

Gerin thought again. His eyebrows lowered. "I'm not sure why I'm going there." He said. He saw a pair of confused eyes in the rear-view mirror. He looked away. "Yes. Business."

The Cabbie felt the iciness of Gerin's voice. He shrugged, said, "I don't care what you do."

The ride was a long one for both driver and rider. Still, almost any conversation would end with a false start. The jazz that came from the radio annoyed both, so it would get switched off several times. Gerin nearly fell asleep staring out the window a number of times. He wasn't sure, but he felt whenever his eyes were getting tired, so too were the Cabbie's, as the car would jerk back and forth on the road between lanes.

In two hours by the back roads, they reached Vandy. The cab pulled into a town reminiscent of white picket fences and clean roads, the stuff only existing in most minds in TV land.

The Cabbie seemed to get excited. "Man, I haven't been here in years."

The cab pulled into the parking lot of the only hotel in town. Gerin paid the Cabbie, the stack of bills rested in the palm of his hands, then rolled them up in rubber bands and placed them in a cigar box under his seat.

"Hey, you have nice visit, mister," The Cabbie turned to Gerin, who had already slammed the door to the cab.

Gerin walked into the lobby. A group of elderly people dressed in black parted in the middle for him to pass. He stood at the desk, waiting for the two clerks to acknowledge him. One clerk, a woman with dyed black hair fashioned in a bee hive, looked at Gerin as if she'd seen the taxman at her doorstep. The other clerk, a man dressed in a black tuxedo, had eyes that bugged out of his head and was constantly blinking.

"Excuse me," Gerin said. "Could I have some service, or do you have to be a member?

They exchanged looks. But the male clerk stepped forward. He blinked twice, said in a high-pitched voice, "Very droll, sir."

"I'd like a room," Gerin said.

They exchanged looks. Whispers came from the circle of elderly people. The male clerk blinked twice. "I'm afraid I haven't any rooms available, sir." He blinked twice more.

"Oh, no," Gerin gave a tug at the lips of what resembled a smile, but could also have been gas. "There are very few vehicles in the parking lot. This, what I believe, is the only hotel in town."

"That matters not," He blinked twice. "The parking extends down the street, sir. We have a town pageant, sir. Folks from the adjoining counties are also here for the occasion." He blinked twice more.

"I was not aware there was holiday--"

"Good day, sir." He blinked twice, went back to the female clerk and their conversation.

Gerin was dumbfounded. He'd never experienced such rudeness. As he left the hotel, he glanced back. The circle of elderly folk was staring, one lady had her head bowed, mumbling a prayer.

Gerin had no idea where to go next. He decided to walk toward the courthouse. In a long row of houses he'd seen a cafe in the tradition of a malt shop. He'd passed a drugstore where four men, dressed in black and blue suits, sat in rocking chairs.

"Excuse me, gentlemen," Gerin stepped toward them. They exchanged uneasy looks. "Could any of you point me in the direction of a bed and breakfast?"

"What in the hell would you want with a bed and breakfast room," One of them said in a shocked voice.

"That's a silly question," Gerin fired back.

"I'll tell you, son, but I don't think Halley will give you a room." Another said, stubbed out his cigar.

"Why wouldn't she rent me a room?" Gerin was exasperated.

They exchanged looks.

The third man sighed. He stood, pointed. "Go a ways two blocks up this road. You'll see a sign for Lafferty Ave. Take that. The third house on the left. You'll know her house, she's got a sign that says Halley's place."

"How convenient," Gerin said sarcastically. "Thank you,

gentlemen." He walked away knowing they were staring at him.

Gerin knocked on the door of a quaint two story house that was painted powder blue. The curtains in the front room moved slightly, placed back carefully. The door opened and a woman in her early fifties, dressed in black, appeared, smiling.

"Yes?" She said in broken English. She focused her eyes on the man standing at her door and her breath exited her body uneasily. She stepped back and tried to close the front door.

"Wait!" Gerin caught the door with a hand. "Please! I'm only here for a room."

They struggled with the door, the woman finally winning the battle. "I have no rooms left!" She screamed and slammed the door shut.

Gerin walked away, running a hand across an exasperated face. "I only want a lodging for the night," He said to no one in particular.

"What's a matter, friend? Can't get a place to stay?" Gerin looked up and it was the Cabbie who brought him to town.

Gerin smiled slightly. "It seems I rub people the wrong way," He walked up to the cab that was idling in the street. He leaned in, resting his arm on the side mirror. "You haven't left yet?"

"Naw, I'm enjoying this place. People are friendly...well, to me. Food here is wonderful. Gee, mister, I don't know what you did to these people, but they treat me like a king." The Cabbie thought a second. He slapped his hand on the steering wheel. "I got it! Come with me and I'll get you some food and a room."

Gerin was more than willing. Like a child who'd received the best Christmas present ever, he giggled as he jumped in the backseat of the cab.

An hour later, Cabbie and Gerin were parked along a curb by the empty school grounds.

Gerin was slumped over in the backseat with his hand casually draped over his face. The Cabbie fiddled with the car radio. Neither were saying much. Cabbie couldn't stay quiet for long.

"Like I said, I don't know what you did to these people---" Cabbie said, almost in a whisper.

"I didn't do anything to these---oh, hell with it." Gerin kicked the backseat.

"You want me to take you back to the train station---say... where are you from?"

Gerin sighed. "I don't remember," He said, lost in thought.

"Okay, don't tell me."

"No...No. I swear...I don't remember. I looked in my wallet...it says on an I.D. Card I live in Santa Barbra. I really don't remember..."

Cabbie reached back there, took the wallet from Gerin. He looked through it. "Jon Gerin, 5504 Furor Dr, Santa Barbra, CA. Looks like this is your wife," Cabbie showed him the photo through the plastic casing inside the wallet. A wedding picture of Gerin holding hands with a young blonde woman dressed as a bride, he as a groom. "No pics of any kids. But one of a Great Dane...you really don't remember anything? Job? Parents? Where you grew up?"

Gerin shook his head.

"Geez, friend. You got it bad---hey! The Town Pageant is starting! Let's go look." Cabbie jumped out of the car, starstruck.

Gerin reluctantly followed Cabbie out of the car and down the street. He stood beside Cabbie, and hundreds of onlookers, as a band of people, dressed in black, walked behind an old hearse, led by a horse, and a driver with a whip in one hand, reins in the other. The onlookers were tossing lilies at the feet of a woman walking directly behind the hearse.

"Ain't that something, friend? Right out of a PBS drama, huh? Reenactment of some kind..." Cabbie noticed Gerin wasn't at his side anymore.

Gerin had rushed out in the crowd of marching people in the street, fighting his way to the woman right behind the hearse. When he reached her, Gerin turned her around, tore the veil from her face. It was the bride from his wedding picture. He fell backwards on to the back of the hearse. The horse stopped in its tracks. Gerin peered inside the hearse window.

He saw himself lying there in the velvet lining of the hearse, arms folded across the front of his black suit, eyes closed, resting so peacefully.

IN THE MOUNTAINS of Wise County, ear piercing screams can be heard throughout the hollows and towns below. The screams can be tracked all the way to the Steadman place. A one room shack with a chicken coop out back and cages with traps tied to the wire doors. The torn and ragged bodies of two dogs lay in several pieces by a nineteen eighty-four Isuzu truck. Inside the truck is Horace Steadman himself, his hands frozen to the steering wheel, his eyes bulging out and glazed over with a thin veil of death. Blood had stained his work overalls. Blood that had flowed with ease from a large gash in his throat.

In the dark woods just to the left of the shack, were two glowing red eyes. A content purring came from those red eyes. There was the sound of shuffling feet on dead leaves.

A short, balding man in a crimpled suit that dated back to the nineteen fifties, stepped out of the darkness and whistled. In a blur, the hunched over four-foot tall creature with red eyes scurried to the man, leaped into his arms. The man accepted the creature with open arms and snuggled it closely to his chest.

"You did fine for old Chester Fields," The small man said to the red eyed creature.

"Insult me in front of people, will you Horace Steadman!" The small man placed the red eyed creature on his shoulder and disappeared into the dark.

———

"I hate sitting out here in the truck." Delaney said, rubbing his eyes with a hand.

"We have to do this. Del." Gill sipped his coffee from an old LIL' SUE cup. He hadn't been to a convenience store in months, let alone that one. Not since the miners' strike back in October. Maggie and the kids had to go back to the county and ask for assistance. She had to lie about him living in the trailer and that she was working in the dry cleaners. Well, you do what you have to do. Ten years mining for the Colby family and they try to take benefits from everyone. It started out reducing wages for part timers, then announcing they were raising the copay to visit doctors.

That was the start of picketing, layoffs, and finally, strike. Strike in these parts means war.

That's why Delaney and Gill were sitting outside Mac's eatery, waiting for Jackson Pryor to come out. Pryor was their foreman and very vocal about replacing the strikers with scabs.

"Man, I have to get home," Delanie said. "Janet is babysitting those Guthrie boys and you know how bad those buggers can be---"

Gill cut his eyes at Delaney, his nostrils flared. "What are you so scared of, boy?" Gill grit his teeth, fighting back harsher words. "We need to do this. We need the Colby family to understand we need our jobs back."

"I just don't understand..." Delaney shook his head. "By hurting Jackson Pryor? We went to school with him. I don't much like him----"

"Well I down right hate him!" Gill exclaimed.

"I know, Gill. Everybody in Big Gap, Norton and Wise knows it. You've told everyone since the ninth grade. Yeah, he's a jerk....more than that. But hurting him..."

"Del, listen to me. We were one of the first people to get a job with Colby. We've been there ten years. A long time. We got Pryor the job---"

"And he took that foreman job that you were eyeing. Gill. I can't do this. I don't want to hit him with a tire iron while you spray paint his truck."

"Then I'll do it and you----"

"No." Delaney said. "I'm not doing this. I'm going home and I'll wait out the strike. I'll survive. You'll survive and we will do it without blood on our hands. It's one thing throwing nails in somebody's driveway, it's another bashing his skull in."

Gill grabbed the duffel bag containing the tire iron and spray paint, opened the passenger door. "I'll do it myself then."

"Gill, come on---"

"I got this Del. You go on home. I'll call you later, let you know what happened."

Delaney batted his eyes a few times, smiled faintly. "Okay, Gill. Be careful."

"Will do, buddy. Go get some rest."

Delaney pulled out of the parking lot of Mac's eatery easily. Gill watched the 95 S-10 and its headlights disappear in the dark. Gill's eyes narrowed. "Go on Delaney, with your tail between your legs."

Gill heard rustling behind him and a door slam shut. He

turned to find Jackson Pryor with Matt Rawlings and Frankie Borges. Nothing had changed since high school. They were still Pryor's slaves.

"What are you doing here, Gill? You panhandling now?" Pryor said. He looked to others for confirmation it was funny and they heartily gave it to him.

"Just walking, Jackson. None of your business actually." Gill stepped up to the man, who was a good two heads and fifty pounds heavier than him.

"We know why you're here, friend." Pryor said, placing his hands on his hips and sticking out his chest.

"I'm not your friend," Gill snarled.

"Oh, we know that, Gill. Friends don't screw up each other's property. What's in the duffel bag?" Pryor reached for the bag and Gill motioned to hit him, but the other two grabbed him. There was a struggle, not much of one. The three ended up wrestling on the ground. The bag fell to the ground and was kicked around a bit before Pryor picked it up.

"My, my," He unzipped the bag, looked in. "Looks like you were going to do somebody some real mischief, Gill, my boy." Pryor showed the other two the tire iron, then the cans of spray paint.

"We owe you a beating," Frankie Borges said.

"Let go of me and I'll fight all three of you fair and square!" Gill screamed.

"Hey, fellas," A voice said, and Chester Fields walked from around the corner of the eatery. "Can't you boys keep the noise down? I'm trying to get some shut eye."

Frankie let go of Gill and backed away. Matt followed. "A witch-man," Frankie said softly.

"Hey there Chester," Pryor faked a smile. He dropped the duffel bag and began walking away. "It was good to see you

Chester." He quickly jumped into Frankie's Taurus. "Take her easy, Chester."

"Hey," Matt said as he climbed in the backseat. "What about your truck, Jackson?"

"Leave it! I'll get it later. Come on! Let's go, Frankie!"

Chester laughed, watched them squeal tires and kick up gravel in the parking lot. He bent down, picked up the duffel bag and handed it to Gill. "There you go, boy. Tools of the trade eh?"

"Thanks, Chester," Gill said nervously. He took the bag from Chester gingerly. "Well, so long, Chester." Gill started to walk off. Chester whistled at Gill. Gill turned and gave Chester a quizzical look.

"Come and have a drink with old Chester Fields," Chester smiled. They were yellow, a sick almost brownish-yellow, but Chester's teeth were perfectly straight. This became part of the town joke, though no one let Chester know of the joke, out of fear.

"I need to get home, Chester," Gill faked a smile. "Maggie's going to have my hide, being out..."

"You wouldn't be insulting old Chester, would you?" Chester's small black eyes narrowed into slits.

"Why no, Chester. Not at all." Gill scrambled for the right words.

Chester walked up to Gill and slapped him on the back with a grimy hand. "Good," He smiled carnivorously. "I can help you with your problem."

Chester practically walked Gill into the eatery, holding Gill by the elbow. They went to a booth in the back. Gill was remembering when the eatery used to be a Pizza Hut and it was where he first met Maggie ten years ago. The Pizza Hut was really was just a hangout for young people. There wasn't anywhere back then. Now everyone goes off to Bristol. where the lights shine brighter. Hangout either inside, eat pizza, play Alan Jackson on the jukebox, or drink beer and listen to Black Sabbath in your car in front of the Hut. Gill did both. He was ordering a pizza, waiting in line, when he saw a tall brunette step out of the bathroom. He walked over and pretended to bump into her. He knew her friends, she knew his. Later in his car, just conversing about everything, Maggie confessed she didn't know who her father was. And to this day she was still searching for him. She said she always suspected he lived right in town and was not a roadie for some crappy 80's hair band, like her mother said.

Gill sat across from Chester, wishing he'd come up with a better excuse not to be around the witch man. After a few minutes, Francine slinked over. She was an old flame from high school. Time had not been kind to Francine. After a few years in Memphis, thinking she could make it as a singer in bars and discovering she liked cocaine a lot, two bad marriages, Francine was glad to be back home, taking care of her mother, who had Alzheimer's.

Espresso love by Dire Straits could be heard over the eatery's speakers.

"Hey there, Gill," She flashed a pathetic smile. "How's Maggie?"

"Hey, Francine. She's good. The kids are good. How's your mother making it?"

"Just it," Francine sighed. "Barely making it. You know how it is. Some days are better than others."

"You going to ask me how I'm doing, Francine?" Chester piped up.

Francine went white. She fumbled a hello, then cleared her throat. She was mystified the reason Gill was around Chester Fields. "What I can I get you two?"

"Three beers," Chester said. "Gill here is treating me, on account it's my birthday."

Gill cut his eyes at Chester. He only had thirty bucks on

him. He nodded to Francine, she went away promising to bring the beers directly.

"Nice place," Chester said. "Been a few months since I've been in here---"

"Okay, witch man. Tell me how you can help me," Gill was more than agitated with the way things had gone this evening, now being snookered into buying beer for a drunk.

"I saw and heard your troubles with Jackson Pryor," Chester said. Francine brought their beers, quickly skated away from the table, looking behind her like she was being chased.

"Everyone knows my problems, Chester," Gill sipped his beer. He looked over his glass and saw Chester down the first glass in one gulp.

Chester gave out a sigh of release, slammed the glass on the table. He wiped his mouth with a hand. 'I can get rid of him for you," Chester showed those perfect yellow teeth.

Are those real? Gill thought.

"I think this deal will land us in jail, Chester." Gill told him, drank some more of his beer.

Chester drained his second glass, shook his head. He slammed the glass down. "No police, friend. You know dang well why everyone in town is afraid of me."

Gill nodded. "I'm not sure I believe in all that mumbo jumbo."

"Oh....but you do, boy. Or you would have turned down coming in here with me."

"I'm listening," Gill said.

"I can bring the Scatter." Chester said bluntly.

"The what?" Gill began to laugh. Then he saw Chester's eyes narrow again. He shut himself up. Gill got himself together and shrugged. "You are talking about the Devil monkey, aren't you, Chester?"

"What else is a Scatter, boy?" Chester let out a gravelly laugh. "You ever seen one?"

"I don't believe in them," Gill finished off his beer. He noticed Chester was trying to get Francine's attention. "I don't have any more money, Chester."

Chester shrugged. "I understand. With the miner's strike and all. I understand. You were out at the Steadman place last year."

"So. Yeah, Gill was there, helping with the cleanup. There was so much blood. But he was the only volunteer not out back puking their brains out from the sight of things. "You're saying you did that?"

"I didn't," Chester got excited. "The Scatter did. I can bring him on Jackson Pryor, kill him and everyone in his bloodline living in the county. That's how the curse works. All just by you giving me the word to do it. How's that?"

"Those things don't exist, Chester. Just like Bigfoot, Jersey Devil and Mothman. That Devil Monkey don't exist. We tell those stories to scare our kids to make them behave," Gill chuckled nervously.

"I'll show you the Scatter is real," Chester said and stood indignantly. His top lip puffed out like a little boy that had just been whipped with a holly switch. "Well!?" He bellowed. Everyone in the eatery turned to look at him. "What are you waiting for, friend? I'll show that thing is real?" Chester slammed his fist hard on the table, knocking the napkin holder over. "You-you just give me your word...I will give your job back and he will not be in your hair anymore..."

"What do you get in return?" Gill whispered, looked over his shoulder to see if anyone was staring. They had stopped, gone back to their business.

Chester sat next to Gill in the booth. Gill slid over. Now he was too close to the wall. He hated closed in areas.

"I don't want much," Chester said reassuringly. "Just...you

know...a few bucks from your paycheck each week when you go back to work. That's all."

"How much? Each week?" Gill thought about all those bills and wondered if he could afford this deal. He wasn't entirely sure the witch man could perform this supernatural feat. But a part of him believed a little that Chester Fields was blessed by the devil.

"You know you hate him," Chester said.

Gill nodded.

"Give me your word and you can see for yourself."

Gill swallowed hard. "I give you my word."

————

The door of the double wide trailer opened quickly. Gill appeared inside, his face white as a ghost, his body shaking slightly. He walked past Maggie, who had been on the computer talking to someone on Facebook. He went in to the kitchen, opened the refrigerator and grabbed the last three beers. He opened all three in fast successions. He went back into the living room and sat clumsily on the couch next to the computer.

Maggie looked at him coldly. "Where have you been?"

Gill said nothing. He downed the first beer, then started on the second. "I don't want to talk about it."

"I need to know!" She raised her voice, left the computer and stood in front Gill.

"I was with—Del. We were drinking in his truck. Please... let me just sit here."

Maggie looked Gill in the face. She could tell something terrible happened. She sat beside him, patted his leg.

"I have something to tell you," Maggie began smiling, blushing. "I found out who my father is."

"You what?" Gill barely comprehended.

"I've been talking to Everett. My cousin in Bristol. There was a family secret. He's known all these years, Gill. God, I can't contain my happiness. It's Henry Pryor."

Gill turned slowly to her, mouthed the name back to her.

"Yeah," Maggie began to cry softly. "It looks like Jackson Pryor is my brother. Isn't that something?"

Gill heard the shrill scream outside the trailer. He looked out the window and saw two yellow eyes glowing in the dark.

ELI AND CARRIE had seen the pool glowing at night. They had lived with the Rothsteins only a few weeks. They were lucky to have found a home after the fire took their parents from them, even if it was a temporary one. Eli was eleven and Carrie nine. Carrie didn't say much in front of the Rothsteins. Eli had to speak for her. Carrie told Eli that Mr. Rothstein was scary. He was very tall, had a looming presence about him, and a booming voice. He always seemed agitated. But Mrs. Rothstein was a small lady, and Carrie would often ask Eli why Mr. Rothstein was married to a girl and not a woman.

"Not married to a girl, Carrie. I told you before. She's a real woman." Eli yelled at her.

They were upstairs in the attic of the Rothstein's home, looking through a pile of junk, T.V.s printers and computer monitors, old clothes.

"You don't have to yell at me, Eli," Carrie found a frayed mulch-colored scarf and wrapped it around her neck.

"I'm not yelling at you. I'm kinda tired of explaining things to you." Eli found an old painting of a man with very little hair and tiny eyes that peered right through you. He shivered, hid the painting behind a car stereo

"How long do we have to stay here?" Carrie sat on a paint bucket.

Eli shrugged. "I don't know. As long as they let us."

"Do you like Mr. Rothstein?"

"Stop with the questions, okay! He's alright, I guess."

"I couldn't sleep last night. That light outside was bright." She stood and kicked over the empty paint can. It rolled to the other side of the attic and banged against the wall., which was spotless, clear of anything.

"That was weird. A bright light from the swimming pool next door. Soon those people will have to close it.

"Why?"

"Summer is almost over with. Soon school starts. Nobody has their pool open in the cold days, can't go swimmin' if it's cold."

"Oh." Carrie began to hum to herself as she played an imaginary game of hopscotch.

At dinner time, everyone was very quiet. Baked chicken and squash was on the plate. The adults ate at their usual pace. Carrie and Eli just picked at their food. Out the corner of his eye, Mr. Rothstein watched them mistrustfully. He sat very straight and stiffly in his chair. His movements were robotic. At times he even spoke as if he were a machine.

"How was your day, dear?" Mrs. Rothstein asked, then chewing her food carefully.

Mr. Rothstein groaned. He was staring at his plate now. Mrs. Rothstein placed a hand on his shoulder, their eyes met. A sadness they shared.

Later that night, Eli could hear them talking in the living room. He was supposed to be in bed. The next day he and Carrie would go to the school with Mrs. Rothstein to enroll. But Eli was curious. He sat on the stairs behind the living room. He saw Mrs. Rothstein sit next to her husband on the arm of his chair. He placed a hand on her legs.

"You were thinking of Todd, weren't you?" She whispered.

"Yes," He said after a brief silence. "I'm...always thinking of him."

"It's been two years, you would think the police would have found him by now."

"I should have been watching him more closely. I knew better than to leave a six-ear-old boy on the toy aisle by himself."

"You didn't know he would be taken..."

"You should hate me."

"There is no way I could hate you. Not even for that...it could have happened to me."

"But it didn't. It happened to me."

There was more silence. She stood, took him by the hand and helped him to his feet. "Let's go to bed."

Eli scurried up the stairs and ran into his room. He shut his door gently, he turned to see a shadow looking out of his bedroom window. He nearly swallowed his heart.

"Eli." Carrie said, pointing. "The pool next door is glowing."

"What are you doing sneaking in my room?" He whispered.

"I needed you to see it," She said, wiping her nose. "I can't sleep because of it."

"Well," Eli went to the window and looked out. "What do you want me to do about it?"

"What you said today you would do," Carrie had that stern look on he face the way their mom used to have to make Eli do what she wanted. "You said you would go over there and see why it's glowing." She wiped her nose with a hand again.

"We can't. It's too late at night and your allergies are acting up."

"You said you would. Don't say things like that unless you mean them," Carrie wasn't going to give up.

Eli sighed, rolled his eyes. "Alright! We'll go. But only for a few minutes. We have to wait until they are asleep—that's soon. Go out the backdoor. We have to be quiet. You understand?"

"You don't have to tell me everything. I'm not a little kid anymore."

They stood by the old huge oak tree with the name of the Rothstein's son carved in big bold choppy letters. Carry pointed to the glowing pool of blue in an otherwise dark backyard. To the side of the pool a two story house stood, designed like a Spanish villa. In front of the pool was a statue of a woman from the Roman period of history, she had seven arms, each of them holding a small baby. Eli was scared. But he didn't dare tell his sister. Strange, somehow she seemed to want to wander through that strange dark yard with the glowing pool, as if she needed to.

Carrie started toward the yard without him. Then, turned and said, "Come on. Don't be a scaredy cat, Eli."

He followed Carrie, who walked along as if in a trance.

They were there, in front of the pool, glowing in all its glory. Carrie stood motionless. She was transfixed. Eli tried to control his hands from a nervous twitch by balling them into fists. A golden light shone brighter than any moonlight, giving the two of them a heavenly glaze about their faces.

Eli peered into the pool. Under the soft currents, thirty or more children floated aimlessly, their big black eyes distilled. They were motionless like Carrie, and like Carrie, too, they were under the age of twelve. Eli let out a whimper. He stepped back only to find someone in his path. He turned slowly, gripping at the person's ragged pants.

It was an old man, leering at him, his decrepit claws holding Eli by the shoulders. "Beautiful, is it not?" The old man spoke in an old dialect, possibly from Eastern Europe. My Art...it's taken me a lifetime...to create.

"I—I don't understand, Mister. Are they dead?" Eli barely managed. He tried to break free of the old man's grip, but he had some sort of hold on Eli---it was more than physical.

"Ohh....no. Not exactly...just free of this world." Eli looked away quickly. Don't look into his eyes---he told himself. Those black, milky eyes seemed to shimmer from the light that the pool gave off. Finally, Eli was able to pull away. The old man continued, stepping toward Carrie, who by now was at the edge of the pool. "They were all children who at one time or another needed attention from someone that cared more for them.

"You sound crazy, mister. I'm gonna get the cops---you'll be in a lot of trouble--"

"These children, need protection from the world—from their parents—who care not for them. The Goddess--" he pointed to the statue of the woman holding several babies in her arms. "Leah, would hear a child's prayer to take them away---so they would never be unhappy."

"Carrie!" Eli ran to his sister. He placed a hand on her cold, frigid shoulder. "Carrie, please, come away from the pool. It's bad. Real bad."

She couldn't hear him. Lost in a deep trance, she stared at the glowing pool.

"She is safe with Leah---safe for all eternity." The old man looked up at the statue. "My art...it is beautiful, my Goddess?"

The statue turned to the old man. "You promised more children for me to love...you have broken your promise." The children in her arms squirmed and cried out. The statue hissed at Eli. "This one is too old!" Her face became stricken with ferocious rage. "Get rid of him!"

The old man bowed and the statue returned to her frozen

stance. The old man grabbed Eli by the collar of his pajamas. Eli jabbed the old man in the ribs. The old man only squinted, still held on tightly. Eli elbowed him again and pulled away, dragging the old man with him. The old man took his other hand and began choking Eli. Eli struggled to catch his breath, the pressure on his throat was too much. Everything became hazy. Eli began to black out. When he regained consciousness, he reached out for Carrie. But Carrie wasn't there. She was on the other side of the pool, still entranced by the glowing pool, awaiting the old man's orders to step into the pool.

Eli pulled one last time, with all his strength. The old man skidded. Both of them just barely at the edge of the pool, momentarily, then fell in. Both sank to the bottom, underneath the now moving children's feet. The light from the pool disappeared. The spell on Carrie was broken. She looked down in the pool and called out for Eli. The water bubbled and steam rose and fell. Eli and the old man were nowhere to be found.

The children he had lured and kept in the pool for years, climbed out. More than thirty naked, disoriented children under the age of twelve surrounded Carrie, weeping and asking for their parents. One boy in particular stood out to Carrie. She recognized the Rothstein's son from photographs they kept of him. "Todd..." She whispered.

The boy was shivering, along with the others. He looked at Carrie and said, "Would you take me home?" His voice sounded raw.

The other children said the same thing. It sounded like a noisy schoolroom. At this moment, the pool stopped bubbling, the currents were still. Eli rose out of the water, pulled himself up on the concrete walk. He saw the statue had already crumbled to the ground. Eli tossed some of the smaller pieces into the pool. The other children followed his act, rolling the bigger pieces into the water.

Eli took Carrie's hand. "Let's go home," He said to the children.

The Rothsteins were in shock when Eli and Carrie appeared with all of these children at their doorstep. Dumbfounded when they brought home their son. Eli and Carrie tried to explain to the Rothsteins and the police what had happened. But neither wanted to believe it, it seemed they had no choice. When Eli mentioned the old man, described him, the Rothsteins and the police shook their heads and told Eli, "The old man had been dead for twenty years, and the house next door had been empty just as long."

The Rothsteins tried to keep Eli and Carrie in their home. The paperwork to adopt them was caught in red tape. They did stay for a few months longer than expected. They got to know Todd a little. But he was shy, withdrawn. Carrie thought him a little strange. The boy saw them off on their last day at the house. A brown Sedan came and took them away to their new home.

As he waved goodbye, a thought rushed across his overworked mind. I'll start again, my Goddess. You shall have all the children you need.

I FOUND myself lost in the currents of the black sea, the waves pushing my body here and there. I remembered the vessel that had brought me out here, roasting in the burning sun. The ship was called The Dear Lady. I should have never entered the dark portals, bunked in its nether regions. I was hired on as all other men, deckhands, standing in front of the town court, listening to the Captain and his First mate spout off an advertisement looking for all that would work hard and receive as many shillings as the pocket could carry.

I had nothing to lose. I had no family to speak of, except an uncle and an aunt I stayed with one summer. But I ain't heard from them nigh on a year. Both parents had died of the plague. The only woman I ever loved married a tavern owner and a worse criminal of the soul, selling children off to the textile plants for nothing less than slavery. I had just been released from town jail for robbing a poor sod and cracking his skull in.

Little did I know the Captain had no intention of paying his shipmates. He was no worse than the Devil himself. Rations were a crumb of bread that fell from the man who lay next to you, stealing a crust from the other poor sod that had a fourth of a piece of bread.

The ship itself was exporting barrels of whiskey to the coast of France. Of course, the Queen and all the British Isles were at war with at the time. The Captain, he never gave a damn for allegiance except to himself. He ate well, if you think pigeon is tasty. Well, it was better than crumbs.

Before we set sail, a black cat had jumped to the ship and scattered. We searched everywhere for that little demon. It was as if that creature had turned into a ghost.

It was just a few hours ago when all of us heard the most angelic voice praising the sea. We all heard it. It was to say the least, hypnotizing. We all felt a calm and those black hearts around me had become a shade brighter. It was like a mirage...this vision of a dark-haired beauty, naked, walking on the same waters that carried us closer to the shores of our destination. We were all stunned.

The Captain himself walked off the side of the ship to meet her. More of us were willing to wallow in a deep wet grave to touch this woman who seemed to appear out of nowhere. Alas, a storm brewed and engulfed us. We fought this dark hard storm to a standstill. We lost the battle.

As you can see, I am here, fighting the currents, trying hard to keep my head above it all, surrounded by what used to be The Dear Lady and many bodies of my shipmates. If you must know, really know, I only ask for one last song from that mistress of the sea as I give the sea my last gasp.

I AWOKE in a place of familiarity. Something that happened to me years ago. I was standing in a garden that never ended. Remembering this garden, I began to walk. I was determined to leave, at all cost. I must've walked for hours. My feet were sore, so I sat on the soft grass.

I have a way to go and at every corner of the hedge, there is a new beginning. I started to remember...So I rose and walked out of the garden to the house of my dear Uncle Nave.

I came to visit my Uncle Nave at his brilliant residence, Hobart Manor. When I arrived, the four story mansion was empty. No servants, no Uncle Nave.

I wandered through the place, finding doors open and attics locked. The furniture had all been stacked upon each other as if they towers or ladders. Windows in the house were open and would not let me close them.

Strange, everywhere I went, that black cat was there, either sitting there or crossing my path. Always, its dark eyes looking deep into my soul.

Uncle Nave's study was bare, contrast to last visited. None of the paintings he'd been working on were there, except the one of the garden.

But there hadn't been a garden at this house for years. Since Aunt Lana died. The garden had been her obsession. She had built the garden with her designer from Argentina. Soon after the garden was built, the designer disappeared. Aunt Lana struggled with the upkeep. Soon the sickness came. Everything died in the garden. Soon Aunt Lana passed. The Servants spoke of the garden as if it had been alive. Said it drained Lana of her life.

I didn't believe any of it. Until this morning.

I touched the painting Uncle Nave had done of the garden. I heard my name being whispered. The watercolors were warm, breathing. My eyes were failing me, but when they came back from the blur, I was inside the garden that Uncle Nave had cut down years ago.

At the opening of the garden, was that damned black cat, following me everywhere.

I walked for miles, seeing the same apple trees, dogwood and hedges nicely clipped. At every hedge I turned a corner. A new beginning. I could hear voices calling to each other, crying out for help. I recognized a few as servants belonging to Uncle Nave. I heard Aunt Lana's voice as well. She told us we would never be apart again. Just as I had entered the garden , I thought I saw Uncle Nave walking ahead of me, leading me to every new hedge.

When I turned to find the footsteps behind me, I would catch a glimpse of a man watching, following. Then he would disappear.

I continued my journey to find the end of the garden.

ON MY JOURNEY, I heard the golden voice of her and the garden had begun to flood with the sea, overtaking hedges in the distance. That black cat trailed me a few links. When I would stop, it too would stop, and stare into the depths of my soul. I would feel a chill down my back.

She appeared, standing firmly on the waves as if it were a floor. She smiled at me, this ghostly woman, this dark-haired beauty was the songstress I heard on The Dear Lady. Her skin was so white, it nearly blinded me. She came closer to me, her toes never once broke the currents that kept rising.

Upon her breasts were two small children suckling. Their broken and dried lips were filling with a black milk that overflowed from her long perk nipples. The children dug their claws deep into her sides, their black milky eyes opening and closing as they drank. The children made strange cooing sounds, and she rubbed their hairless heads, softly.

She stood in front of me, smiling. I was engaged in the conversation before she spoke.

"My children are hungry, kind sir. Will not help us?" A pleasant, calm voice came from her perfectly rounded lips.

"How could I help?" I asked. "I have no means of caring for myself."

She touched my face with a hand. I felt a chill come across my entire body. I began to shake. I backed away, but she followed, held my chin in her grip.

I felt the black cat brush my legs. I heard a loud purr. I felt strange, almost as if the world was beginning to blur.

"Please...do not go. I cannot let you leave..." She said, her voice becoming harsher, cutting through me like the end of a bastard sword. "You are cold...so cold. I will provide you with warmth. "

The songstress bent down and kissed me with her blood red lips. I felt the cold leave my body and I shook only from the promise of another kiss from her.

Her children began to cry. A low whine that came from the gurgle of a dying man.

"I will put the children to bed," The songstress pushed open the flesh between her ribs and inserted a child on the left into a pocket of darkness, sealed it up again. She did the same for the child on the right, only this one cried out louder. She struggled at first, but soon the other child was in its own pocket, fast asleep.

The songstress waved a hand and the blue sky became a moonlit night filled with sparkling stars. She lay me down on the currents, a thousand fingers rolling across my back. She lay across me like a blanket and I could feel myself rise. She sat up, took me inside her. Her long, dark locks grew and explored every inch of my body as she moaned and writhed, slightly bouncing, grinding on top of me. The strands of her hair curled around my neck like a hangman's noose. With every gasp, it tightened round my throat, squeezing ever so gently.

A dark veil swept over my eyes periodically and I would dream I was on The Dear Heart again with my shipmates. I could see their dead faces, white as sheets. Their eyes were a milky black, water seemed to spill from their powder white lips. I walked past them to the plank. I couldn't feel my arms, only because they were tied behind my back.

At the end of the plank, I saw the captain of The Dear Lady. The Songstress had him in her clutches from behind. Her teeth were deep into his throat, and a black liquid ran down his shoulders from the wound she made. The more she drained the captain, the more his body shriveled up. His flesh fell from him to expose a rigid skeletal frame. When she was done with him, she removed her grip from his arms and released her teeth from a sagging mound of black puss that was once his neck. The Captain fell limp at her feet.

Her children were feeding from her more than ample breasts. The black liquid they were draining from her nipples was too much for them. In integral moments they would remove their lips and let the black liquid flow like a water from barrels tap; then continue their feeding.

Just on the other side of the ship, where the cabins were, I saw the black cat sitting there, a ravenous smile on its face. Still, it looked deep into my soul, saying: "'Tis, a good day to die...."

The Songstress sang and my shipmates, one by one, pushed me out of the way to be a part of her children's meal. I tried my best to break through the long line to reach the plank. I wanted to die the right way. I wanted to be punished for my crime against my shipmates.

It seemed a fruitless venture.

THE TINY PIMPLY SKINNED creature spied him from behind the rubble. Adolf was aimlessly walking down the street with no intention of a destination of any kind. He was walking, and thinking, definitely not taking his life very seriously. He especially did not care if he lived or his fellow German lived. He did not care whether or not the whole world crumbled underneath him and swallowed everyone up. The world could go straight to Hell as far as Adolf was concerned.

And that was the start of the attraction between Ubel and Adolf.

Adolf had fought in the Great War. He was a war hero, even though Germany and her allies lay in rubble. Adolf had even been awarded many medals for his valor. He suffered trauma and possible blindness from a mustard gas attack. The outside world cared little for this great man.

Adolf had much hatred and drank a cup of bitterness every day.

Adolf was destitute. With no many, no job, no future, he had only his book of drawings and the clothes he made.

From the street, looking past other unfortunates, Adolf found shelter in a hollow, bombed out building that used to be a great hotel a few years ago. The days were becoming colder, and this one was no exception. A slither of sunshine cast little light for Adolf to write and draw in his journal. He was tired as well, which was the reasoning for what side of the building he chose to camp.

A slew of wine crates became Adolf's office and sleeping quarters. He perched himself on two crates and set up three more to rest his journal upon. It was so cold, that later when Adolf found a muddy and tattered blanket, he draped it across his small, frail body for warmth.

That day, Adolf drew very little. He mostly wrote thoughts. Thoughts about mankind, mostly, about politics. But of course, it all began with his life story.

He was thinking of his mother and father when Adolf heard scratching at one of piles of loose bricks in the corner across from him. He slowly ambled over, bent down and removed the bricks. He saw the three foot, milky-green skinned creature, hunched over, nursing a wounded leg. The creature batted its large eyes at Adolf and growled.

Adolf backed away, cursed under his breath.

"I've been watching you," Ubel said. He pointed a claw at Adolf.

"How?" Adolf fumbled his words. "When?"

Ubel smiled. "All of your life."

"What---what are you?" Adolf found a crate and sat beside the creature. He repulsed, yet was curious about Ubel.

"I have attached myself to you," Ubel touched Adolf, stroking his chin with one his claws.

"That doesn't answer my question," Adolf said.

"There are many questions that will never be answered in life," Ubel forced himself to sit on a brick beside Adolf. "To answer one of your questions, I was there when you were born. Your father was not happy with you. Said you were weak."

Adolf snarled. "What does he know, eh?" He looked away, closed his eyes. "I am strong...stronger than he! I fought valiantly!"

"Ah...yes," Ubel smiled. "I was there when the mustard gas exploded in your trench. Did you not feel a hand grasp your uniform and drag you to a place with fresh air?"

"No...I did not...That...that was you?"

"Yes," Ubel looked at his crooked fingers, rubbed his claws together.

They heard a voice in the distance, footsteps echoed in the next room. The voice grew louder and then was split into two. A man's voice, then a scratchy woman's voice.

Adolf went off to investigate. Through a crack in the wall, he saw a man in a tattered suit. The man was much older than Adolf, with a bushy mustache and a longer nose. The man's face was covered in soot, and from what Adolf could tell, he was completely alone, having a conversation all by himself. This man was cutting bologna with a small knife.

Adolf went back to the creature, smiling. "It's only a man by himself. Quite frankly, I am jealous. He is eating bologna and all I've had today is a piece of bread."

Without hesitation, Ubel said, "Go take it from him."

"No," Adolf shook his head. "No, I am not a thief."

"When it comes to yourself, you are what you need to be. One...only one, is the number that counts. It is the human way, my friend."

"No. I cannot do such a thing. He is hungry as well, same as me." Adolf sniffed the air.

"We both know what he is," Ubel said. "The so-called Children of God. The privileged is what they are. You know what he descends from. The Hell that no gentile should find himself in...Not those pits...or his kind will surely disappear. Listen to me. I know. I was once human. And I fell in with the Children of God.

"They are not bred from God's loins. They are Hell spawn! You know what I am. Your mind is in denial...but your heart knows better. I was a lucky man, living in Berlin. I was a wine maker. I eventually owned a gallery. I showed all the greatest living painters in my house. And one day a Banker took it all from me.

"I had nothing for my wife. Nothing for my children's future. So...I did the only thing I could. I took my own life. Just in that instant before I slipped into death, I was visited by something of what I am now. He was kind. He pointed out the real blame went to the Banker. He said, if I were to give him my mortal soul, my children would be protected always.

"I had no choice. I asked if there was room for me where he came from, could I too help others in the same situation? He said yes.

"Here I am, Adolf. Helping you. If you do this one thing to help yourself. You can retain my knowledge, understanding of the human condition. Better yourself, help others.

"The world will be all for yourself...it will be yours for the taking."

"I...I think you are right. I have to help myself if I want anything in life." Adolf walked slowly to the crack in the wall. It was just large enough for his hands to fit through.

The man was eating the bologna fast, but his conversation had taken a nasty turn into an argument with the scratchy female voice he was making. Adolf slipped his hands through the crack, took hold of the man's throat from behind and squeezed. The man gurgled. His body stiffened. Adolf squeezed harder, closed his eyes, wished for it to be over soon.

There was a hush all over the world.

The man went limp, all of life exited his body. Adolf let him fall to the ground. Rubble fell across the dead man's body, covering his face.

Adolf found himself in the next room. He was bent down, removing the knife and roll of bologna from the man's hands. Ubel was standing beside Adolf, sneering. Adolf sighed. He wondered if he had really done the right thing.

"He was a Jewish dog," Ubel spat on the dead man. Ubel looked up at Adolf. "You'll see," He smiled grotesquely. "I will not steer you wrong."

30 April 1945

Adolf stood in his uniform, grasping the gun in his left hand. Explosions could be heard outside the bunker, which had lately become his home, as well as many he trusted, or thought he trusted, and his beloved Eva. Adolf could hear voices in the distance, chattering like black birds on a snowy day. He could hear them say the Russians were near.

Ubel appeared. He took Adolf's hand, pointed the barrel of the gun at Adolf's head. Adolf shook with fear. He closed his eyes and murmured in German he did not want to die.

Ubel sneered. "Have I ever led you astray, dear Adolf?"

GIRAUD STARED at the tiny graves on the hill a few yards
from his farm. It was near sundown, the sky above was a
palette of pinks and blues. Giraud hated sundown. His world
was something he wouldn't wish on his worst enemy. He
looked back to the small house he'd built with his own two
hands. It wasn't much, but it was a roof over his and Helens'
heads. He saw Helen looking through the window at him. She
saw the disappointment on his face and drew the curtains.

    Giraud turned, scoffed at his world. A shadow loomed
over him. He looked up, found it was the scarecrow. He heard
blackbirds calling to each other as two of them flew to the
scarecrow's shoulders. Giraud's eyes returned to the tiny
graves with no markers. Why give them names? Giraud
thought. They didn't even last the night, all four of them.
Wasn't even sure what sex they were.

    Giraud carried himself slowly back to the house, bitter-
ness and all.

    "Supper's on the table," Helen told him as soon as he
walked through the door. She turned toward the bedroom.

    "You gonna eat with me?" Giraud said.

Helen stopped in her tracks. She shook her head no. "Not hungry," Helen went to the bedroom, shut the door.

With no expression, Giraud went to the sink, washed his hands, then his arms.

He sat at the table, placed a piece of bread on his plate. He took a spoonful of peas, placed them next to a small piece of chicken. "Nothing's gonna change," He said drearily. "Unless I do the changing myself."

Giraud chewed his food slowly, the image of the scare-crow, overshadowing him, deep in his mind.

He heard the noises coming from the bedroom. Giraud tried to eat, hoped his teeth grinding the food would drown out Helen's sounds. The sound of the bed springs bopping up and down, creaking, bodies writhing in the sheets. Helen's breathing becoming more and more shallow. There was a low gurgle from a stranger. Giraud closed his eyes. Tears fell from his cheeks. He chewed faster, faster, in rhythm with the bed springs, shallow breathing, gurgling.

Giraud grabbed the table with both hands, turned it on its backside. The dishes and food slid off. A loud crash caused dead silence.

Helen rushed out of the bedroom, her hair a mess, sweat pouring from her red face. She was fastening her robe in a hurry. She stood, looking at the mess, then at Jim.

Nothing was said as their eyes met. Contempt between the two of them.

The sun beat down on Giraud as he plowed the fields. The corn had already begun to grow, on the other side of the hill he had planted tomatoes. Here, below them, he thought of putting to the ground potatoes.

Giraud had decided to take a break when he saw a red pick-up pull in at the house.

He watched a short man in his late fifties get out. Giraud

got off his tractor, walked down the hill. The man saw Giraud, turned on his heels, waved.

"Giraud," He said. "Didn't think anyone was at home."

Giraud met up with the short man in a suit and fedora. It was Garret Barnes. Barnes owned most of the farms in the tree-counties and was recently on a buying frenzy. He'd been after Jim's farm for three years running.

"What can I do for you, Garret?"

"Just came for a visit, Giraud," Barnes smiled. He removed his fedora, fanned himself with it.

"Can I offer you some water, then?" Giraud poured water from a cooler into a plastic cup.

"Thank you," Barnes drank the water quickly. "Getting hot now." He looked around. "How's the farm comin?"

Giraud sipped his water, keeping his eyes on Barnes. "It's comin'," He said.

Barnes nodded. "Expecting a good crop." It was a half-hearted statement. Barnes knew the answer as the question meant nothing to him except a sale, which at the end turned into a statement.

"What do you want, Garret?" Giraud blew air through inflamed nostrils.

"You know what I want," Barnes threw his cup to the ground. "Giraud, you're not doing too well. Let me help you."

"I'm not selling," Giraud turned his back on Barnes.

"That would be a mistake, fella. If you sell this to me, I can help you and Helen. You can move into town."

"Into one of those shanty's you own, Garret? Get a job at the factory your brother owns? Go to church where your son is the minister? Buy groceries from the store your cousins own? And what will Helen and I have?"

Barnes shrugged. "I don't know, maybe...peace of mind. No more worries, friend."

Don't go calling me 'friend', Hoss." Giraud stepped toward Barnes. "I think you ought to go, Garret."

There was silence for a beat. "Look, Giraud----"

"Get off my land, Garret."

Barnes nodded. "Tell Helen I said hello." Barnes ambled to his truck.

Giraud watched the red pick-up speed off. He looked at the house, Helen was watching from the open door. "What did he want?" She bit her lower lip.

Giraud grunted, saw the clouds roll across the sun. The shadow of the scarecrow stood long.

"He wanted me to sell the farm to him," Giraud told her. He stared at the shadow. Anger rose up in him momentarily. Giraud shook it off.

"What did you tell him?" Helen had her hand over her heart. She was worried what Jim's answer would be. She couldn't leave the farm now. Not right now. No matter how bad things got.

"I told him he was wasting his breath," Giraud said.

Helen's mind was at ease. She smiled. Giraud heard her sigh. He turned to her. Helen was off again, lost in her thoughts. Her face was radiant, a glow like a schoolgirl in love. "Get my lunch ready, woman." His voice broke her trance. Helen went back inside, slammed the front door hard.

It was sundown. Another dreaded sundown, Giraud was at the dinner table, trying to eat.

He heard Helen moaning, the sheets and bed springs making a melody. Jim's face was flushed with anger. But his mind would get lost in curiosity.

.   .   .

He sighed, pushed his chair back. Still listening closely, Giraud rose from the table. He trekked towards the bedroom. Stopping every few steps, Giraud would put a hand to his brow. I shouldn't----he told himself. Helen wouldn't----- Helen----she belongs to me. She belongs to me!

The door creaked open slightly. The setting sun shone on two bodies on the bed, covers and sheet on the floor.

A few months passed by. Nothing changed much, except Helen being pregnant again. Giraud resented the situation. It was not his child. He wished he had not visited Mrs. Ville. She was a self-described witch. Had a sign that said she sold charms and told fortunes. That was why Giraud went back to see her.

Inside her musty shop decorated with dead animals and masks from all over the world, the old woman smelled the air and looked in Jim's face for lies.

"You speak the truth," she mumbled.

Giraud made a face when Mrs. Ville fed a scaly creature in a glass bottle the eyeballs of a dead cat.

"I told you I was here to talk about the last business I had with you." Giraud said crossly.

"There's nothing more to discuss. What's done is done." The old woman stated firmly.

"You have to undo the spell. I'm going out of my mind---" Giraud caught himself. He inhaled, then exhaled a few times, trying to keep the anger down. "You have to help me..."

A few beats of silence passed. Mrs. Ville shook her head. "You knew the chances. You wanted a child so badly, I warned you."

"None of them lived more than a night!" Giraud sputtered.

. . .

"You know what must be done. A life for a life." Mrs. Ville pushed Giraud aside to retrieve a few bottles of green liquid.

"No, "Giraud shook his head. "I'm not giving up Helen's life."

"It's not specific," the old woman croaked. She coughed, spat out phlegm on the floor. "The spell only said a life for a life. Anyone would do."

Her back was to Jim. The thought, one the old woman placed in his head, ran amok.

Giraud picked up a poker that sat by the wood stove. He looked at the poker, touching the pointed end with his hand. His upper lip curled. He raised the poker over his head.

Then he stopped in mid-air. He put the poker down. He rushed out of the shop.

"I knew you wouldn't do it," Mrs. Ville said to no one in particular.

Giraud was on the hill, staring at the four tiny graves. Barnes appeared, huffing and puffing. Walking up a steep hill was too much for the older man. "What are we doing up here, Jim?"

Giraud looked up at Barnes. "You got those papers?"

Barnes nodded. "I didn't expect you to sell, Jim. You are a complicated man."

Giraud shrugged. "Suppose I am, Garret. Seemed I was always simple. The world is complicated." Giraud took the ten finely-typed pages and flipped to the areas that needed his initials and signature.

"Don't you want to read it?" Barnes was startled, then amused.

"Nope," Giraud said, went back to staring at the graves. "Look at them, Garret. They were once living beings."

"What are you talking about?" Barnes chuckled. "You drunk, boy?"

. . .

Giraud shook his head no. "People, Garret. Little babies."

Barnes' mouth opened and closed in silence. He didn't know what to say. "Who's babies...?"

"Each one born three months from each other. All this year, Garret. "

"Did Helen...? What in blazes-----no. You're pulling my leg-----you're dead serious." Barnes looked down at the house. He shook his head, backed away from Giraud before turning on his heel. "Well, thanks, friend. I'll be in touch. Tell Helen I said hello."

Giraud said nothing. He was lost in his thoughts. Barnes practically ran down the hill to his truck. Giraud heard the truck speed off, never once looking away from the graves.

He stood watching the graves for a few more minutes, when the sun setting stole his attention away. Giraud heard two crows cawing. The crows spoke to each other in their language, then one crawled inside the long gray trench-coat which the scarecrow wore.

The other one shook his wings free of any bad feathers or dirt, curled up in a ball, and formed the face of the scarecrow. Two more crows flew inside the trench-coat. One became the left arm, the other crow became the right arm. Giraud was in awe, mesmerized. Two more crows flew to the scarecrow, formed its legs.

The scarecrow left its podium that held him there in the daylight. But every evening, it was free to bring itself down from the two poles, fashioned together by rope, and forced into the barren ground a few yards from the graves. His face was black, feathery, mysterious black. Its eyes glowed yellow. Possibly the eyes of the crow. He walked as if its limbs were weighed down by weights on its feet.

. . .

The scarecrow walked past Giraud as if it didn't know he was there. Giraud knew what it was going to do and where it was headed.

It was headed toward the house, to Helen.

This angered Giraud. No more, he thought. He was sick of being sick to his stomach whenever he thought of Helen with this thing----this unnatural being.

Giraud felt for the .38 in his belt. He drew the pistol that was meant for Garret Barnes. Giraud fired, the bullet tore through the scarecrow's midsection with ferocity. The scarecrow fell to its knees. Hay tumbled from it to the ground in spurts. It looked down at its wound. In an instant the hay found its way back inside the scarecrow. The scarecrow stood in one clumsy act and continued on to the house.

Giraud screamed. He was on his knees. The gun now lay on the ground beside him. Blood poured out of Giraud's midsection, flowing like a river in his hands. His face showed confusion. The shadow of the empty podium where the scarecrow made his home enveloped Giraud in his last few moments of life.

One month later, Helen moved into a house on the edge of town, a house that had seen better days. She sat in the kitchen at the table, her baby drinking from her breast. She looked out the window and saw the sun setting. Helen smiled.

"Your father will be home soon," she told the child, pulling it gently from her erect nipple. The baby opened its yellow eyes and made a slight sound from its thin-lined lips. Helen touched the child's black feathery face with a hand. "I love it when the sun goes down."

———

A few years later, the farm was abandoned. Drusilla and Helena rode up in their carriage, the black horse clopping up slowly, tired from the inter-dimensional journey. They stopped the carriage and looked around. The Drake sisters liked what they saw. They found Giraud fastened to the podium, facing the sunset. Two crows flew over and sat on his shoulder.

Drusilla pointed the staff at Giraud. His eyes fluttered, his head jerked up. The crows flew off, complaining about being uprooted. Giraud fell from the podium, picked himself up. He stood in front of the Drake sisters, and accepted the staff.

THE DRAKE SISTERS were not happy with Giraud. The three of them sat at the kitchen table sipping that horrendous Cauliflower tea strained through cabbage leaves. Though they hadn't spoken yet, Giraud could see on their faces they were a little more than perturbed about recent situations. No one would be able to tell the sisters apart if they didn't wear different colored dresses that curled up to their necks, and usually covered every part of their body except their wrinkled hands. Drusilla always wore red or black, and Helena wore grey or white. Both had long, grey hair, tightly wound in a bun, except for one long black strand in the middle. They both were extremely pale, chiseled cheekbones, bright red lips and large black eyes with very long lashes that reminded Giraud of spider legs.

"You don't like the tea," Drusilla spoke first.

Giraud forced a brief smile, took a sip from his cup and swallowed. He fought off a bitter expression and smiled again. "No," he barely managed. "It's wonderful, Drusilla."

"I'm Drusilla," the one in white said in a monotone voice. "We're playing opposites today."

"We decided to have some fun," Helena said with a blank

expression. She smoothed out a wrinkle in the sleeve of her red dress.

"Since everyone else is playing around and we are trying to work hard, supporting the children," Drusilla said.

Outside the window, several children can be seen pulling weeds from the garden or gathering fruits and vegetables. Two girls about ten are talking, one girl is crying, showing the other girl her callused hands. Drusilla notices this. She rises from her chair and heads over to the cabinet, opens the doors angrily. She takes a microphone out from behind several wires connected to the wall.

Drusilla pressed a small, square button and spoke calmly into the microphone. "Get back to work, you worms...or you'll anger the monster!"

In the distance, the creature was making a meal out of a mound of raspberries. Drusilla bent down and switched on a lever that lit up red, began to hum and buzz. A force field surrounded the creature, giving him long electric shock treatment. The creature screamed and reared up on his tiny back legs, kicked its spiked legs.

The two little girls squealed. Holding hands, they ran off to the east end of the farm, past the fig trees.

Drusilla switched off the lever and the buzzing, humming went away. The electric shocks were gone as well, and the creature cooed as he lay on the dirt ground, trying recuperate. Drusilla smiled, closed the cabinet and returned to her chair.

"Now," Helena began.

"What are you going to do about those two runaways?" Drusilla finished.

"I have Goop and Gop looking for them..."

"Those idiots!" Drusilla and Helena said together. "You might as well sit here at the table and do nothing," Drusilla added.

"Where is your staff, Giraud?" Helena raised an eyebrow.

Giraud didn't want to answer. The staff came from the sisters, who had asked the creature to create it as well as bestow certain powers of wish and bring his worlds together so Giraud could walk the different worlds, collecting more children to work the farm.

Slowly, he spoke, clearing his throat several times. "Well," he sighed, before finally explaining. "The little boy who ran away first....he...tumbled into me...." He saw flames rise up in Drusilla and Helena's eyes. The fury twisting their lips as if they'd been eating lemons. "...and, well...."

"Get on with it, Giraud! I am tired of your hemming and hawing. Just spill it, will you!" Drusilla interjected.

"The runaways have my staff."

"What?!!" Both women slammed their fists on the table. Simultaneously, they extended their crooked fingers, two long fingernails outstretched in Giraud's mask like razor blades. "If you do not bring those children back to the farm, with the staff, I will unmask you! And you know what would happen if you are unmasked, don't you, Giraud?"

———

The creature always helped the children fall asleep with nice dreams. Dreams of their former homes, parents and friends. The creature would even sing them lullabies from its world. Beautiful, lilting hymnals about hope. Of course, all of this would happen while Giraud was asleep.

Giraud could feel and hear every thought the creature could feel. One time, when Giraud could not sleep, he heard the creature tell the children that one day, someone was going to free them. One day, he would go home. Giraud was so angry at the insolence of the creature's thoughts, he went to the shack where the creature was housed and beat him until the he passed out.

The creature felt it was his duty to keep the children's hopes alive. To tell them it was okay to dream of a better life and reassure them they would see their parents. Not in words, but in pictures, plant the idea that they could also take over the farm, free themselves. It seemed they responded better to the idea that a hero was coming to bring them their freedom. Humans were definitely strange beings to him. That worked to an extent, maybe a little too much. Johnny Fuhg decided he was going to bust everyone out. Johnny was caught trying steal Giraud's staff.

He was never heard from again.

Morale was low among the children. But rumor spread about two children that got away. Excitement got the children through the terrible weeks of the culling of bean sprouts and packaging the gold that the creature had created. The creature could somewhat communicate with those two runaways, but the message was often hazy and confusing. So he tried a different approach. The creature decided to manipulate the two runaways' path.

At the end of that month, the sisters would dress in their finest, hop in the carriage and their dark steed with red eyes would carry them to the different worlds to drop off the gold and crates of vegetables and fruits. On that day, Giraud was in charge. That day was coming, and Drusilla and Helena were not sure that leaving him in charge of the farm was such a good idea. It turned out, they were right.

JOLENE AWOKE SUDDENLY, a bright light shining in her face. The light came from a door hanging in midair. Jolene rose from her bed. Twenty other children who shared her quarters, a bunker house; or shack rather, also rose from their beds. The little blonde girl approached the door slowly. The door swung open and two children poked their heads out.

"Uggg!" Paul exclaimed. "We went in a complete circle! This is the Farm, Emma."

"We're here for a reason," Emma said. "We need to free everyone."

"Look," Paul climbed out of the door. "I hate to be a spoil sport, but I'm not going get into trouble with those mean old women!"

"We need to help," Emma said, climbing out of the door. As soon as her feet touched the floor, the door disappeared. "We were called here by the creature. He needs our help. He wants the kids here to escape. That's why we're here, Paul."

"I ain't going nowhere near him!" Paul folded his arms.

"Nobody said you had to!" Emma shot back.

"He's really nice," Jolene said. "He keeps our spirits up. He sings lullabies to us, tells us stories about two heroic kids saving us." Jolene looked down, fought back tears. "He's very good to us. They hurt him very badly. They work him just like they do us."

"So you are kids who's going to save us?" A little boy asked.

"It's them," another boy said, happily.

Whispers started from the back of the crowd and reached Jolene. Emma saw smiles on the children's dirty faces. Some of them actually started to jump up and down and become playful, cheering at the same time.

At that moment, another door appeared in a beam of light. The door swung open and Goop and Gop poked their heads out. "It's the Farm!" They cried out joyfully, and high-fived each other. A sinister smile crossed their faces. "There they are......"

Goop and Gop sprinted toward Emma and Paul. Paul squealed and dropped the staff. He hid behind Emma. "Don't let them get me!" He cried out.

Emma and Paul had no reason to be afraid. The other children had already grouped themselves in a mad riot. Screaming at the top of their lungs a war cry that could be heard throughout all of the known and unknown worlds, the children charged at Goop and Gop. At first, that mattered little to the twins. But a realizations dawned on the usually bullying overgrown brats. They just might get killed!

Goop and Gop turned on their heels and ran the other way as fast as they could, screeching and waving their hands. The children continued after them, even as they ran out of the bunker house. The footsteps of their heavy flat feet attached to those short fat legs, beat down the tall weeds outside the bunker house. The quick, piddle-paddle of the small feet belonging to the children raced onto Goop and Gop's heels. Jolene, who was in the lead, took hold of the back of Gop's shirt, turned him to the left slightly. This, in turn, pushed him into Goop. Both child-like men tumbled to ground, letting a loud squawk, a yelp that became an elongated scream.

The children seized them. Actually, they pounced upon Goop and Gop with such ferocity, beat them with such savagery, tore into the two fools with their bare hands; ripping clothing and tearing flesh.... witnesses would have thought that a mountain lion had been the attacker.

Goop and Gop screamed bloody murder and begged not only for penance from the children, but from anyone...anyone to help stop this travesty of humanity.

The back screen door swung open and flapped against the side of the house. Giraud stood in the doorway holding a machete. "What in the known is going **ON**?!" He bellowed angrily. Giraud saw the children terrorizing his assistants. At first, he wasn't sure what to do. He was actually a bit afraid. They were like little demons descending upon his moronic angels. What could have brought this on? Well, there was nothing else to do but chop those raving, murderous children into little pieces.

Giraud loomed over the angry mob cautiously. The children were too busy ripping Goop and Gop apart to notice Giraud. They were growling, screeching, screaming, even cursing at Goop and Gop! Giraud held the machete level with his boney shoulders, ready to strike the first child that bobbed its head up.

Then he heard a voice.

"NO!"

Giraud stopped. He heard the voice again.

"Please...don't hurt the children."

"Who said that?" Giraud swirled around in the dark night, looking in every direction.

"Children, stop hurting those poor men," said the voice.

All the children backed away from the Goop and Gop,

revealing a bruised, broken and bloody bodies covered in clothing that was nothing but shreds. Goop and Gop were in tears, their chests heaving to catch their breath as they whined about their horrible ordeal.

"Reveal yourself!" Giraud demanded, slicing the air with the machete. "I said show yourself!"

Emma appeared out of the darkness, gingerly leading the creature by a tentacle, Paul a step or two behind them. Giraud curled his top lip, antsy to use that machete. Emma and the creature shielded the children from him. Paul made sure he brought up the rear, and had enough room to run in case things got out of hand again.

"I see..." Giraud hissed, nearly spat out the words with calm, violent intentions. "...it's you."

This amount of violence is unnecessary, the creature said. It will lead to everyone's ruin. There are other ways to settle our differences. If...if only my brethren had come to that conclusion long before their demise, who knows what great things they could have achieved to help the rest of the societies they conquered after the discovery of the unknown worlds.

"Sounds like hogwash," Giraud said, still toying with the blade against his fingertips. Societies have to be ruled, and those societies' citizens have to be controlled. Either by force....or by trickery."

"He's right, you know," Emma concurred.

"You be quiet. You are just child. You have no sensible opinion."

Emma has something for you. A trade.

"A trade?" Giraud's interest was raised. The expression on his mask had changed from hateful hysterics to pleasant surprise. "What would you have that I would want....?" He let the words trail off when Emma presented the staff to him.

A soft glow materialized around the staff, and a stream of

light shot out a cross the ground. Giraud lowered the machete. Gradually, he sauntered toward Emma and the creature. When they finally met in the middle, the light from the staff cast severe shadows upon Giraud's face. Emma saw more evil in those eyes hidden behind that mask. She had doubts about offering the staff back to Giraud and tried to withdraw it when he took hold of her wrist, squeezed hard, then wrought it harshly.

"Oww!" Emma cried out, dropped the staff.

"No, Giraud, don't!" The creature screamed.

Giraud brought the machete level with his shoulders and came down swiftly, the blade buried deep into the creature's back. The noise that came from the creature was not necessarily a whelp or a screech, more like a combination of help and a wail. The creature scurried in a circle, pale yellow liquid ran from the wound. The children ran to its rescue, calmed it down. It became stationary, decided to lie on the ground, letting one child pull the machete blade from it. The scream was so loud and deafening, all the nocturnal creatures were quieted down.

Emma ran to the creature, bawling, tears welling up in her eyes. "Keep your dumb old staff! Nobody cares about it anyway!" Emma dropped to her knees and placed her head to the creature's, pursed her lips and distributed the kisses all over its rubbery skin.

"Ohhh," Giraud cooed as he retrieved his staff and showed it proudly to all who were present. "I assure you, my darling child, this all-powerful staff is not 'stupid' as you had stated." He noticed the shiny ball that sat on top of the staff was missing. Suddenly, pride had dissipated and anger had infiltrated Giraud. "You horrible children! What has happened to my beautiful staff?!" Giraud crooned.

The sky opened up and several tiny dots were dropping down in rapid speed. Giraud looked up, realized they were falling in his direction! A scream was lost in the back of his throat, but in the truest sense, it was too late to do that, and of course, Giraud had no time to run away. The tiny dots became larger, revealing it was Org and his newly acquired family of friends who had bestowed kingship upon him.

Org fell on Giraud, his hairy legs and butt cheeks landing on Giraud's neck and shoulders. The others fell around or near Giraud, recovering to warrior stances, ready for battle, clutching huge, fat tree trunks as weapons. Giraud was pushed to the ground, his mask shattering in multiple, minute pieces, spread as far as the bunk house. Org sat on Giraud's back smiling from sharp fang to sharp fang, caressing the shiny ball that once sat on top of the staff.

Giraud had lost the staff in the collision. He wailed, screamed, cursed, hands scraping the ground, bucked up and down, still he could not reach the staff, nor usurp Org from his perch. Giraud also felt several bones in his back become dislocated and disconnected from their usual routes. To boot, his ravaged, horrible, sagging, dried up face was finally revealed.

The world was still. No noise, no voices could be heard, no sound could be made. No movement by anyone, or anything, human, animal, or otherwise. The Earth had ceased to turn on its axle as did all of its inner and outer dimensions.

The night had become a bright day, if only for a few minutes. Witnesses would lay claim that this phenomenon went on for hours, but then again, Death operates on no one's time table.

The woman in black, whom Emma and Giraud had met earlier, floated down from a white void in the stillness. The only two who were not affected by the woman's appearance were Emma and Giraud. And Giraud...well, he was definitely not pleased with the old woman. But Emma was. She was a little lost for words. So the old woman helped her along.

"Just as I promised you, child, if you helped find the one I have lost, you shall get your wish," the woman black said.

Something occurred to Emma. "You....you did, you do all of this just to get Giraud," she cocked her head one side, thought a moment, and then added: "Didn't you?"

The woman in black let a smile cross her purple lips. "If that is what you think," an eyebrow on her powder-white face arched up. "Then it must be true."

Emma shrugged. "I don't really care one way or the other," she giggled. An influx of happiness took hold of Emma. She was glad to be going to her sister's house. She missed her terribly. "Do we all get to go home?"

"Alas," the woman in black said sorrowfully. "No, child. Not everyone."

"Wait...I don't want to be the only one..."

"Paul will be accompany you."

"What about Orgo?"

"Look at him," the woman in black said. "He's so happy he has found others like himself. He is home."

"The other children?" Emma asked incredulously. "The creature?"

"Emma, they are home. These children were far worse off than you or Paul. The creature, too. Only their conditions needed improving. You helped with that......as did the creature. Both you, the creature, and the promise of a hero...'

"Paul helped too!" Emma interjected.

"...or heroes...yes, Paul helped as well. My point, they will run this farm with the creature. Trust me, they will be happy for the rest of their lives."

"Okay," Emma nodded, smiled at the children and the creatures frozen in time.

Giraud could not move. But he found ways to throw tantrums and bawl his eyes out. He beat his fists on the ground and cried out, "Let me go! Please...Emma...you have to let me go! I helped you! I took you from a terrible place and brought you here...PLEASE! LET ME GO! DON'T LET THIS HORRIBLE WOMAN TAKE ME!"

The woman in black bent down to whisper to Emma. "Emma, may I have this soul?"

"I...don't know..." Emma thought of all the terrible things he did. Giraud lied to her about the farm and taking Emma to see her sister. He stole every one of those children. He sent the terrible twos---Goop and Gop after Paul and her. He hurt the creature with a machete. "Yes," Emma said. "You can take Giraud."

Giraud gasped. The woman in black became a swirl of black smoke that surrounded Giraud. He pleaded and begged as the smoke entered his open mouth and penetrated his boney nostrils. In one swoop, the woman in black and Giraud were both gone.

Everything returned to normal. The sounds of the nocturnal creatures saluted in the night, the humans and animals, or otherwise, moved about normally. Paul ran to Emma, asking what had happened. Just as the children did and the creature asked via telepathy. Emma quieted everyone down.

"Giraud is gone. Someone special took him."

"Oh, no, "Jolene said. "Those horrible old biddies are back!"

Just as she said that, a wagon rode up, carrying The Drake sisters.

Emma smiled. "Somehow," she said, thought of the irony of the situation. "I don't think they will be a problem." She laughed, shook her head.

"I don't get it," Paul said. "What's so funny?"

"That's okay, Paul," Emma told him. Orgo motioned for her to come to him. Orgo was still holding the shiny ball and a door just opened right in front of him. "When you're older you'll understand." She went to Orgo and hugged him. Orgo made loud cooing sounds and ran his oversized finger through Emma's hair.

"Wait," Paul rebutted. "We're the same age!" Paul followed a few seconds later.

"You go," Orgo said, handed the ball to Paul.

Emma looked past Orgo and saw that the children had

the Drake sisters surrounded. *Yes*, Emma thought. *They were going to be alright*.

"I'll miss you, Orgo." Emma sniffled, wiped tears from her tired eyes.

"Orgo miss you...Emma," he bent down and kissed her. With the swipe of a hand, Orgo ushered Paul and Emma through the door. But not before Emma ordered Paul to follow her.

Inside the corridor, crawling slowly, Emma said. "Come on Paul."

"Where are we going?" As if he had to ask.

"Home," Emma answered. "We're going home."

THE MORE EMMA and Paul crawled through the corridor, the narrower and tighter it became. The light became dimmer, until the darkness swallowed it up completely.

Emma felt a wall in front of her. She touched it with her other hand and the concrete moved. She pushed again with some force and it gave way. A burst of blinding light assaulted their eyes. She heard the concrete fall and explode on impact on the floor below. She crawled out of the corridor, tested the drop before trying to jump, and realizing that she was only a few inches from the carpeted floor.

Paul followed her down, only he had a little more trouble getting out of the square on account of his rotund figure. Emma helped him squirm out and he landed on one foot not so gracefully, but held his other leg in the air as if he were a ballerina that had just finished a performance of Swan Lake.

The block of concrete that Emma had pushed out of the corridor was gone. Disappeared, vanquished, just like...well, thin air, as the saying goes.

It looked like Paul and Emma had ended their adventure in someone's basement that had been turned into a study of some sort, and possibly a studio. The floor was carpeted except to the left where a bathroom was, which seemed to be where the studio began. There was an easel, several empty canvasses and every kind of tool an artist uses for painting. On the study side of the basement, there were rows and rows of books on a very tall and dusty bookshelf. There was TV, which played cartoons in the background. There were two EZ Boy chairs grouped with a leather couch and a clear glass coffee table. On the coffee table was a pack of cigarettes, an ashtray, and mug of coffee from the local coffee shop.

What intrigued Paul and Emma were the paintings hanging on the walls. There was a picture of Emma and Giraud, standing in the kitchen of her parents' house. They saw a painting of the dead man hanging from a tree. There was a painting of Org with Paul and Emma. To make a long story short, there was a painting of the children watching Giraud embed that machete into the creature's back and one of the woman in black taking Giraud away: someone had illustrated their adventures in the corridors.

Emma ran her fingers across the canvas of the last painting hanging, that of a hand placing a doorknob on a spot on the door where it had been missing.

"Don't touch that," she heard a voice say.

A woman in a grey dress materialized on the leather couch. She had dark hair carefully fashioned in a bun, and golden hoop earrings. Her skin was powder white, and that made her large brown eyes even larger. She was sitting perfectly still, her hands folded across her lap. She was calm, no expression on her long face. Her lips were blue—almost purple---- a wonderfully sculpted oval.

Emma knew her, she was almost certain, but...she didn't recognize her as a person she knew very well. There was a general, over-all feeling that she'd known the woman all her life, just well enough for names. "I didn't see you there," Emma said.

"No one does," the woman breathed.

"Is this your house?" Paul asked.

"Yes," the woman said bleakly. "I've lived here since I was ten."

Paul nodded. "That's a long time," he went back to watching cartoons for the most part. That's what got his attention anyway, until commercials interrupted.

"You did these paintings?" Emma asked.

"Yes. I've been painting and drawing since I was three. At least...that's how I remember how the story goes."

Another string of commercials broke the animation spell on Paul and he looked around, noticing the paintings. "These are pictures of us," Paul smiled and pointed. "Hey! Look, that's Org!"

"I have more in my room. There are more in the living room. And several that I have sold to dealers...given away to friends..."

"All of them....with us?" Emma asked. Paul was lured back to the cartoon after a commercial for a sitcom about twin boys dressed as Tweedledee and Tweedledum causing all kinds of mischief.

"Yeah," the woman smiled for a moment. "These scenes have haunted my dreams....and my nightmares, all of my life."

"Wow," Emma felt a little more than just weird about this meeting. She was on the verge of a major freak out. "I guess we should be going," Emma smacked Paul's arm and motioned for him to follow her. But Paul was too busy with the TV and never really paid her any mind.

"You can't go," the woman said. "This is your home now."

"Wait," Emma put her hands up cautiously. "You just said this was..."

"I know what I said," the woman became cross with Emma. "I know this is my house," she sighed. "This is your house, too, it has always been your house. I'm the one who needs to go. As soon as you hand me the doorknob in your pocket."

"What?" Emma fumbled with the shiny ball and it tumbled out of her pocket and rolled to the couch, stopped at the woman's bare feet.

The woman lowered her hand down and scooped up the shiny ball. She considered it over the now glowing ball of light, and nodded. "Yes," she sighed. "This is it." She stood, took a few steps toward the painting of the hand reaching for a missing doorknob. She turned to Emma and Paul, smiled. "Have a wonderful life......I know I did." She placed the glowing light where the doorknob was missing, turned her hand to the right. A gushing light paralyzed everyone. A moment frozen in time.

"Emma?" A voice called out. "Emma? Are you down there?"

Emma snapped out of the frozen moment and realized Lydia was calling her. She rubbed her aching eyes and called back. "Yes!"

"Well, come up and get your supper! You know I have to be at work by six and Tom will be home in an hour!"

"Alright! I'm coming! Give me a chance!" Emma replied, stomping her feet on the first step to make her sister not come down the basement.

"Oh, tell Paul his Mother wants him to come home too. She doesn't want him walking the neighborhood after dark."

Paul laughed. He walked past Emma on the tiny staircase. He was at the top, when he stopped, and turned to Emma. He had a huge grin on his face. "It's good to be home, huh Emma?"

She thought a moment, smiled back. "Yeah, Paul. It's really good to be home."

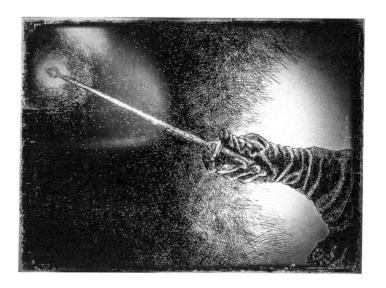

Dear reader,

We hope you enjoyed reading *Strange Corridors*. Please take a moment to leave a review, even if it's a short one. Your opinion is important to us.

Discover more books by Mark Slade at https://www.nextchapter.pub/authors/mark-slade

Want to know when one of our books is free or discounted? Join the newsletter at http://eepurl.com/bqqB3H

Best regards,

Mark Slade and the Next Chapter Team

Mark Slade is the author of A Six Gun and the Queen of Light, Book of Weird, Blackout City Confidential, Mr. Zero (Barry London series) and A Witch for Hire (Evelina Giles series) published by Horrified Press and Close to the Bone. He also writes, produces and directs the Audio drama Blood Noir, written by Daniel Dread (with Lothar Tuppan, directed by Daniel French.) and the weird western audio series, The Sundowners.

He lives in Williamsburg, Va with his wife, daughter, and a Chihuahua that does funny impressions of famous actors.

Cameron Hampton is a Masters Circle Member of the International Association of Pastel Societies, earning her Gold Medal in the Spring of 2007. She is a painter, photographer, sculptor, cinematographer, animator and illustrator. Hampton attended both Pratt Institute in Brooklyn, New York and The Atlanta College of Art (now The Savannah College of Art and Design) in Atlanta, Georgia. Also, she has studied independently in Austria, Belgium, The Netherlands, Slovakia, England and Hungary where she lived. Hampton has works in corporate and private collections throughout the world and has been represented by galleries in Amsterdam, The Netherlands, Atlanta, Georgia and Albuquerque, New Mexico to name a few.

She now works and spends time in Georgia, U.S.A., London, England and Utrecht, The Netherlands. Her work is currently represented by Carré d'Artistes in Mexico City, Mexico.

You might also like:
Ghost Song by Mark L'Estrange

To read the first chapter for free go to:
https://www.nextchapter.pub/books/ghost-song

Lightning Source UK Ltd.
Milton Keynes UK
UKHW021913121120
373303UK00003B/544